HELLO DARLING

KAYLEY LORING

HELLO
Darling

USA TODAY BESTSELLING AUTHOR
Kayley Loring

For Tom, Benedict, Colin, Jude, Luke, James, Michael,
Orlando, Henry, Daniel, Dan, Kit, Clive, Rupert, Max, Idris,
Taron,
and especially Hugh.
You're the dog's bollocks.
I could never get knackered from Googling you.

EVAN

*O*h Christ, the paparazzi.

Fuck me.

I was in such a hurry to get out of London, it didn't leave enough time for my assistant to book the Heathrow VIP service, and apparently my dark sunglasses and baseball hat aren't cutting it as a disguise today. I should have just worn a bloody mask since it's the day after Halloween.

"Evan! Morning, mate! Where you off to today?"

Just smile and keep walking, smile and keep walking. At least there are only two of them here today. This one's the nice photographer. I just have to stay calm and refrain from looking miserable. Because I'm not miserable. I'm on top of the fucking world.

"Taking a trip by yourself, then?" says the wanker photog who always tries to rile celebrities up. "You still in touch with Georgia, now that *Evangia* is no more? How you feel about Braden—you a fan?"

God, I want to punch this one in the face. My publicist would love it if I did. Anything to tarnish my squeaky-clean polite English gentleman image. She's literally begged me to go on an angry drunken rampage and snog Kylie Jenner in front of as many cameras as possible.

"International flight, then? You off for work? Where you off to, then?"

"Flying off to Hawaii to try to win Georgia back? Heard she's there with Braden. How's it feel to be dumped for a bloke who's nine years younger than you, eh?"

What a delightful question—so glad he asked! Maybe I should buy him a coffee and we can have a good long chat. And then I can punch him in the face.

Truth is, it doesn't feel good, but not for the reason people think. Thirty-one is starting to feel a bit old to be a bachelor. I honestly don't know how Hugh Grant managed it well into his fifties.

You know perfectly well how I managed it, you fool, says the voice of Hugh Grant in my head. *By not being a giant pussy. If you ever write your autobiography, it would be called The Subtle Art of Giving Too Many Fucks.*

You're right, Hugh. This time, you're right.

Smile and keep walking. Smile and walk. Almost there.

"Evan! Evan Hunter! Can I have your autograph, please?!"

Shit. A fan. A young one. I can't ignore her. I'll just stop to sign autographs for this sweet girl and the... crowd of twenty people who are following her...fuck

2

me…but at least they'll be between me and the paparazzi, and then I'll be at security in no time.

I do wish I weren't so well known for being a relentlessly happy and friendly fellow. It must be so liberating to be regarded far and wide as a moody shit who gives fuck-all about what other people think. What I wouldn't give to be "early career" Colin Farrell, just for three days. I'd even take 1995 Hugh Grant.

Nobody's stopping you from going cruising for a sex worker, you airy-fairy prat. I dare you to get arrested for lewd conduct—anything.

Shut up, Hugh. Nobody even remembers that little PR glitch, you lucky bastard. That all went down before everyone had camera phones and Twitter and YouTube accounts. Everything's so heavily documented now. Not that *that's* why I'm always on my best behavior. I'm going to spend so much time here signing autographs and posing for selfies with fans that the paparazzi will get bored and piss off to look for someone more famous to blind with their camera flashes…and because my fans are lovely and they mean the world to me.

And also because I give too many fucks.

I'll arrive Seattle in about ten hours, and it will be late in the morning of the same day. Couple of hours later I'll reach Port Gladstone. It will be fantastic to start this day over again on the other side of the world. Alone. Where no one gives a toss how I feel about the demise of *Evangia*. I can start this new month in a new town, where people won't care that I'm a movie star and I won't have to act like one. I'll have two weeks there before I officially begin work on the movie, so I'll have time to be me again, away from all the rubbish that comes with being Evan bloody Hunter.

There are many different reasons for taking a role in a film, limited TV series, or stage play. Occasionally it's because you really want the part. Sometimes it's purely financial. Sometimes there is so much pressure from your agents to be part of a package with other talents that it's difficult to refuse. Sometimes it's just a matter of timing. I took the part in this next film because of timing and location. I wanted to get as far away from London, New York, and LA as possible, as soon as possible. The small-town aspect of Port Gladstone, Washington seems perfect. No paparazzi to deal with, and it reminded me a bit of the coast of Cornwall when I looked it up online. The script is more than fine. I like that when my character comes to this town, he takes on a new identity and finds it very freeing, in the way that you can when you're in a new place, with new people. And the fact that I'll have to get back in shape for the part seems an ideal way to keep busy before production begins—not to mention it's a good way to keep my randy arse busy while I get my head sorted out.

The other great thing about this project is that it's unlikely I'll get involved with the female lead for a change, because the love interest role is quite small. Whoever the actress will be, she won't be around for very long. She hasn't been cast yet, but I'll only sign off on her if I'm definitely *not* attracted to her. Problem solved.

Now that I'm in the lounge, I can decompress and put all of that behind me. Wendy has sent me links to a few gyms in Port Gladstone so I can start getting back in shape soon as I get there. The first gym is open twenty-four hours, but it's one of those big chains with bright lights and loud music and too many machines packed in too close together. The second one just looks a bit too hippie-dippy for my tastes. Complimentary kombucha drinks and too much use of the words "energy" and "healing" on their website. The third gym looks promising.

Starkey Fitness. Not too large, not too small. Family run.

Hold up.

On the "About Us" page, there's a picture of one Stella Starkey, the gym's manager and yoga instructor, and she has—quite simply—one of the best faces I've ever seen. Fair skin, no sign of make-up, framed by dark hair. Her full lips are curled into a tiny smirk and a twinkle in her intelligent tea-brown eyes lets everyone know she can't quite take everything they're saying too seriously. Of all the stunning celebrated faces I've had the pleasure of gazing at in my life…how is it possible that this one is so enchanting to me?

Probably just the rebound-effect I've been so thoroughly warned about lately.

Ever since word got out that last year's Golden Globe winner for supporting actress Georgia March had "dumped her former co-star for someone her own age," concerned friends have been advising me that I will most likely have some sort of uncharacteristic emotional reaction in the wake of this. It's my first experience of being broken-up with. At the ripe old age of thirty-one. My agent has sent me a list of female clients he'd "like to discuss" with me before I find myself in another relationship, but the last thing I need is another relationship with another actress. Meanwhile, I've promised myself a monk-like existence for a while.

I need to take this opportunity to slow down and start to think about getting involved with the kind of woman I could actually get serious about for a change. It's time to look into buying that little house in Cornwall with a view and finding someone special to hide away with there when I'm not on set. I might be coming down with a case of whatever you call the opposite of wanderlust. Homehunger. I'm sure there's an untranslatable German term for it.

It's called being a giant pussy.

Sod off, Hugh.

Wish I could. You're the knob who's always wondering what I'd think about things.

It's just a picture.

A picture that I can't stop staring at.

I can't frequent that gym knowing there's a woman I'm this attracted to there—the whole point of taking this film was to throw myself into work... Oh, who the fuck am I kidding? Of course I'm going to choose that gym. Throwing myself into work has never stopped me from throwing myself into a pretty fanny at the end of a long day. I mean—it's a Hollywood thriller, not Shakespeare. I had all of my lines memorized after the second time I'd read the script.

Of course—she could be married. If not, she probably has a boyfriend. Even if she's single, she might not be into guys like me.

She might be the only woman I've ever met who isn't into handsome, charming, wealthy, world-famous British movie stars.

What do you think, Hugh?

Please refer to 1999 hit Notting Hill *for a completely realistic, not at all cheesy depiction of how easy it is for an impossibly likable mere mortal with floppy hair to date a glamorous movie star.*

And then please remind yourself that you are by no means a celebrity of Julia Roberts's stature.

So chances are fairly good she won't be into you.

But definitely try to shag Miss Stella Starkey once or twice because she's totally hot.

STELLA

I'm trying to remember the last time I *didn't* have a hangover the day after Halloween. When I was fifteen? Unless you count candy hangovers, then I guess it was when I was four. When was the last time I had a Halloween hangover that wasn't mixed with a hint of bewilderment, shame, and regret…? I know the answer to that, and I don't want to think about it. No need to feel hungover, bewildered, shameful, regretful, *and* sad. It's so unlike me to behave the way I do on Halloween.

I'm just never myself on October 31st. I suppose that's kind of the point of the holiday. I suppose that's the thing about living in a small town your entire life— Halloween is the only time people are open to seeing you in a different way. Or maybe it's the only time I feel comfortable being somebody other than who my family and community expects me to be. I guess that's why so many people eventually leave this beautiful place. But I won't.

It's the first day of November, and despite my own personal history, I still love this season here in the Pacific Northwest. It's all flannel and boots and pumpkin spice and the smell of burning cedar and pine logs escaping the chimneys. Some people feel weighed down by the overcast skies, but I prefer to think of the clouds as hugging the earth. And the beaches? Quiet and soul-crushingly beautiful. I can walk a mile along the shore and not cross paths with another human.

It's just me, the seagulls, the Lord Huron playlist that's infusing my brain through my earbuds, and the cool breeze caressing the beard burn on my chin courtesy of Jason "The Kwas" Kwasnicki and three too many pints of Guinness at last night's festivities. The one downside to this season is that there are fewer tourists to have dalliances with, so back to the local dating pool we go. It's sink or swim until Memorial Day. Good thing I don't care about dating. It's not usually an issue, since most of the local guys don't want to mess with me. Having a dad and three brothers who can kick most dude's asses without even trying will do that to your social life. I'm fine with it.

I had to get away from Main Street on my break. The talk of the town usually shifts seamlessly from Halloween costumes to Thanksgiving plans and recipes, but this year I've been hearing less about pumpkin pie and more about crumpets (what the fuck are crumpets?). There's going to be a major motion picture shooting on location here in a couple of weeks, and the star is from England. All the business owners of Port Gladstone have been Googling him to find out what he's into to try to lure him to their premises so they can take pictures. Mrs. Flauvich ordered a month's worth of Yorkshire Gold tea, crumpets, and marmalade for her deli. The window display of Clemmons Sporting Goods is now dressed to feature cricket and rugby. The Chef's Special of the month at the Golden Panda just changed from Egg Boo Young to Posh Spiced Rice with Diced Bangers, and the Wangs also printed up new To Go menus. They are now called "Takeaway Dish Menus." Fortunately, our finest tavern has always been well stocked with Guinness and Newcastle Brown Ale (unless we Starkeys have cleaned them out).

Who is this Evan Hunter guy, and why am I supposed to care? All I know is, he's not Loki and he's not on *Game of Thrones*. Supposedly he'll be in an upcoming JK Rowling series, so—three points for Gryffindor. But I'm not going to be waving the Union Jack until we know if it will be of *Harry Potter* or *Casual Vacancy* caliber. I haven't Googled him, even though I keep hearing: "Oh, he was so handsome in that one about the soldier who has amnesia." *Barf.* "I keep reading that he's going to be the next James Bond." *Oh really? If Sean Connery is still alive, then he should still be James Bond. End of discussion.* "Forget about the movies —have you seen those shirtless pictures of him in Barbados?" *Um. Have you seen those shirtless pictures of Jason Momoa in absolutely anywhere? Why do you ever need to look at anything else?*

The guy isn't even in town yet, and I'm already sick of him—although perhaps there will be someone else on the visiting film crew who I can have a fling with. A gaffer or a key grip (whatever they are). I may love this town with its Victorian-era houses and buildings, but fancy Englishmen have always made my eyes roll. So here I am, sitting on a log while eating a sandwich and staring out at the ocean, instead of shoveling a Cobb salad into my face at the deli while staring at a book like I usually do.

Also, I'm trying to avoid The Kwas.

I can still feel his tongue tickling my tonsils, and he sent me a text this morning that said: *Yeah!*

That's it. That's all it said. I don't even know how to respond to that, so I won't.

Twenty-six feels way too old to be drunk-kissing guys I went to high school with at parties. Even on Halloween. Not wearing my sexy sailor costume again next year might help with that. Or not going to a Halloween party at all would probably be even more helpful. Why do I do this to myself? Why can't I just be sad and stay home with my cat or hang out with my family like on every other holiday?

I pull my phone out from my pocket when I feel it vibrate. What a delight! It's another text from Jason Kwasnicki.

It says: *Hey hey!*

He is nothing if not succinct. I will have to pass on responding to this one as well.

Out of the corner of my eye, I catch sight of a man in black who's jogging along the path, heading back toward Main Street, his back to me. His tall frame is distinctly unfamiliar. He's wearing a baseball cap and running pants. He is fast. Good stride. Great form. Fairly lean but broad-shouldered. Fantastic male butt specimen.

Not my type.

Just as well.

I've consumed my sandwich down to the last bit of crusts, which I've saved for the birds. You're not supposed to feed seagulls bread, but they've been hovering. I have such fond memories of doing this with my mom when I was a little girl, so I always do it when there's no one else around. I toss bits of crust into the air for the fastest and the bravest of the flock, making sure to chuck a big piece directly at the nervous wonky-looking bird that's been waiting in the wings. *Hang in there, little guy.*

I take my time strolling back to work on the sand because it's wonderful out and I'll be inside for the next six hours. And I love this Lord Huron song that just started. I close my eyes for a moment, savoring the melody. When I open them again, I see the man in black, jogging in my direction. He's on the path, which is about thirty feet from where I'm walking, his pace slower than when I first saw him. I run my fingers through my wind-blown hair and get my smile ready.

He's wearing dark Ray-Ban Wayfarers, despite the mostly cloudy skies. Even from this distance I can tell he has the kind of jawline we don't see much of in these parts, because…beer and beards. He is staring intensely at the ground ahead of himself. Again, it's the kind of intensity one doesn't see very often around here, where people come to enjoy the laid-back artsy/seaport lifestyle. It's a kind of intensity that I can only describe as: HAWT. I can't see his eyes behind the shades, but judging by the way his shoulders and jaw are set, if he were looking at me the way he's looking at the pavement, I'd have to call it "panty-liquefying intensity."

But he's not looking at me like he's looking at the pavement. He doesn't look at me at all as he jogs past. Another thing I don't see much of around here is a human being who doesn't even glance my way—at the very least, we politely nod at each other to acknowledge one another's existence.

He must be from New York. Whatever. I've got other stuff to look at too, like the time. I should have been back at the gym five minutes ago. My younger brother hates being on phone duty because talking to faceless strangers who have questions is more painful to him than doing fifty weighted deadlifts and squats.

Starkey Fitness is not the largest gym in Port Gladstone, and it's not the one that's open 24 hours a day, but it is the one with the best membership renewal rate, the most consistent membership growth, and it's the only family-owned business in town where every member of the family can run a six-minute mile and hold a plank pose for a minimum of two minutes straight. I've been managing the business full-time for five years. I started helping my dad out with administration and expansion right out of high school. It wasn't the plan, but it became what I wanted. Living in this town, working with my guys and keeping them in line is a good life.

As soon as I step through the front door, Billy jumps up from the stool behind the front desk. I can tell by the way his wavy brown hair is standing up and out in front that he was pulling at it while he was on the phone with someone. His dark eyebrows are knitted as he stares at me, and I expect a reprimand or a "where's my sandwich?" but instead, he says, "Is it true you made out with The Kwas last night?"

I wince. "We didn't make out. He kissed me, and I paused before pulling away. Who told you?"

"Who *didn't* tell me? As soon as you left for lunch, people kept coming in here to dish."

"Great."

"You want me to give him a message from the Starkey Brothers?" He holds up his fists and makes his badass tough guy face.

"I think I can handle it." I pull a wrapped sandwich out from my jacket pocket, handing it to him.

"Thanks."

"Take your time eating it."

"Don't tell me how to eat a sandwich."

I muss up his already mussed-up hair. "I can't believe you never showed up last night."

"I got to see two women make out at Andy's. Five feet away from me. In person. I was in the right place at the right time, believe me."

"I'm so happy for you. Go talk to Mr. Hannam. He's looking at you like he wants to ask a question."

"Lookin' good, Mr. Hannam! What's up?" Billy

14

struts over to the cable crossover machine, where our newest sixty-seven-year-old member is looking a little confused about how to work the thing. Billy is the only person I know who can get a person stoked about using what looks like an old-school torture device. What Mr. Hannam doesn't know is, he's saving me from the *real* old-school torture device: being grilled by my brother about kissing boys.

I immediately get back to work, responding to emails, wiping down surfaces, working on our annual holiday season "Get Fit-Stay Fit" challenge. We have a letter board set up on the front desk with a phrase that changes daily, but I was barely conscious this morning when I assembled the letters to form: *Have a nice day. Get me a coffee.*

Not one person got me a coffee. I switch it to: ***Dear body: Maybe don't eat ALL the candy at once. Love, your pants***

I take a picture of it and post it on the gym's Instagram page.

I text my dad to ask if he came down with a cold. I could hear it in his voice yesterday, and I don't want him going for his usual morning hikes this time of year unless he's in top form. He immediately texts back: ***NO. STRONG LIKE BULL.***

I know this means he's getting sick, and I know that I will be bringing him soup later. But I don't push it, because we are both stubborn like bulls and it's no fun getting into a text argument with him. Because he just ignores my texts.

The business line rings. "Good afternoon, Starkey Fitness."

"Yes, hello," says a pert young female with an English accent. "I'm calling to ask if it's possible to pay cash in advance for your three-month membership?"

"Oh. Sure, I don't see why not. Payment in full, in cash, would be fine."

"Wonderful, thank you so much. One more quick question…"

"Yes?"

"Do you photocopy or scan your new members' identification cards when they sign up? For your records?"

"No. That isn't usually necessary."

"Fantastic, thank you!"

She hangs up. It's not the weirdest question I've ever gotten about memberships. Someone once called to ask if he could pay for his with a year's worth of fresh caught salmon. My dad said yes. We served it at our annual member appreciation dinner. When Mrs. Flauvich said the only way she'd join the gym was if she could eat on the treadmill, we said no but that she could pay for her membership with hugs. Her blood pressure has been lowered thanks to the exercise, and ours has been lowered thanks to her bountiful warm hugs. Win-win. That's how we do business, and we still manage to make a tidy profit. And that's why I love it here.

I don't even check the Caller ID when I answer the next call.

"Hey hey," says the voice on the line.

"Jason?"

"So you made it to work?"

"Why are you calling me on the gym phone?"

"I'm a member."

"Are you calling regarding your membership?"

"No, I'm calling regarding getting a drink with you later."

"I won't be drinking again for quite a while."

"Food, then."

My back is to the front door, but I hear the bells jingle as someone opens it.

"I won't be getting food with you. I don't go out with our clients. Company policy."

"I thought we had fun last night."

"Well, I had fun. And you had fun. We both had fun under the same roof, and for a brief period of time our faces were connected. But you are under no obligation to get either food or drink with me, nor am I under any obligation to do so with you."

"Why do you sound like a lawyer all of a sudden?"

"I've found it saves time. I'm sure there are plenty of girls who would love to have a drink with you, Kwas. Unfortunately, I'm just not one of them. Have a good day. Thanks for calling!" Hanging up the phone, I sigh, and turn to face the entrance.

It is startling to find a tall man standing in front of me on the other side of the desk. He's grinning as he hangs his Ray-Bans from the V-neck of his gray T-shirt. His black hoodie jacket looks more expensive than my entire wardrobe. His blue eyes are so sparkly, even in the diffused natural light of our reception area,

I think *I* might need to put on sunglasses to look at him. He's smirking as he watches me, waiting for me to collect myself, so I know he heard the end of that conversation. And I know that he's not only prettier but more polite than everyone who has ever walked through that door before him. Too bad I'm not into polite pretty men. *But hey there, pecs that are barely hidden beneath that hoodie and T-shirt—you have clearly spent a lot of time inside of gyms. What brings you here to ours?*

I have to clear my throat in order to speak. My mouth is suddenly dry for some reason. I straighten myself up and lick my lips. "Hi."

His eyes briefly drop from mine to my lips and back to my eyes again. That tiny subtle movement of his shiny eyeballs somehow sends a shiver through me, and I feel surprisingly sexy and caffeinated all of a sudden. He hasn't even spoken a word to me yet, but I already feel like he's told me I'm beautiful and presented me with an elegant box of tastefully provocative lingerie. It seems like an eternity passes before he finally opens his mouth, and when he does, all he says is "hello." And I swear it's as if no one has ever meant it quite so much as he does right now.

3

STELLA

"*T*hat's an excellent jack o' lantern." The tall blond man nods toward the small jack o' lantern that sits in front of the letter board on my desk. I carved our business logo into it—made a stencil first, but still. It *is* excellent, and not enough people have appreciated that.

"Thank you." *Nice jawline—it's so sharp you could carve a pumpkin with it.*

"Did you carve it?"

"Yes. I did."

Is that an English accent I'm detecting?

"Once, when I was young, I spent Halloween in Cornwall with my grandparents. It's traditional to use turnips for jack o' lanterns there, instead of pumpkins. When they're lit, they smell just unbearably awful. From then on I stuck to Easter visits." He shakes his head, like he's not sure why he just told me that. "True story," he says, smiling sheepishly.

Yup. English accent. Despite what he's saying, when he speaks it's like his voice is bringing me a cup of tea and drawing me a bath while composing a sonnet. Or is it calmly disrobing me while feeding me a butterscotch sundae and letting it melt onto my naked body? Something about that accent makes me stand a little straighter, raise my chin a little higher. And yet, something about it makes me want to chomp on chewing gum, blast Metallica from the speakers, and make fun of him.

"Sorry—are you talking to me about turnips right now?"

"Well, I was, but I think I'm done. I'm Evan. How do you do?" He holds out his large, manicured hand.

"Hi. Stella Starkey."

"Of Starkey Fitness." Polite, firm handshake, and yet he holds on just a second too long, holds my gaze three seconds longer than my stomach butterflies can stay still for.

I didn't even realize those butterflies were still alive in there. "One of them. I mean—I'm one of the Starkeys. I'm the manager. Welcome." Well, this is surprising… My stomach butterflies and my brain don't seem to share the same taste in men anymore.

"Thank you. I've just arrived in town today. I'll be here for a while for work. I think my associate called earlier to make sure you'll take cash in advance for the three-month membership?"

"Yes. She did. We do."

My brain is whirring. This is the jogger from the beach. Evan is the jogger from the beach. Evan is Evan

Hunter. Evan Hunter is the British movie star. Up close, it appears Evan Hunter the British movie star has a bit of a supernatural glow to him. Not like a *Twilight* vampire, but that healthy glow that beautiful rich people have in pictures and on film and you assume it's a filter.

I try to concentrate on what this strange vaguely glowing person is saying by focusing on his mouth, because it's pretty and it's moving.

What follows is a flood of thoughts and feelings that are so new to me, I immediately feel the need to catalog them so I can impose some semblance of control. The first thing I think is: That there is the most beautiful man I have ever seen. The second thing I think is: I don't like beautiful men. The third thing I think is: Don't I though? Fourth thing: Nope. Definitely not. Fifth thing: Wait, I have seen this guy in a movie. He was in the *Romeo & Juliet* video that Mrs. Greer showed us in English Lit. I was sulking the whole time because I had just had a fight with my boyfriend and thought the play was ridiculous. Sixth: That is a damn pretty mouth. He must exfoliate and moisturize those lips regularly, probably by kissing gorgeous actresses. Thing number seven: Shit, I've seen him in something else too. He was in the action thriller that was a modern adaptation of *Hamlet*. I walked out halfway through. He was good in it, but it was a weird combination of pretentious film school baloney and big-budget movie crap. I hated it. And I wasn't even in a bad mood that time.

I start shaking my head. "I'm sorry, I'm just going to

be honest and stop you right there and tell you that I haven't been listening to a word you've said."

He stops midsentence, sucks in his breath, and smiles. I'm sure it's quite common for people's heads to explode when they first start interacting with him. He smiles with his pretty mouth and his beautiful eyes. He has a kind smile, and it still just makes me want to mock him.

"I was babbling for the most part anyway. Is there some sort of form I should fill out, and is it all right if I use an alias? For confidentiality and all that." He shrugs modestly and searches my eyes to see if I actually realize who he is. There's no arrogance there. At all.

"Um. Yes. That should be fine. Rest assured, we will keep your membership here confidential, to the degree that we can. I mean. People will see you coming in and out of here. Some of them will recognize you, and some of them won't. Some will care and some won't. We have no control over that."

He laughs. "Understood."

"Promise you won't sue us if people find out you're working out here or, God forbid, if you sustain an injury on the premises?"

He grins. "You have my word."

I load up the three-month membership form on the iPad and hand it over to him, glad that I don't have to use a pen to write anything, because for some stupid reason my hand appears to be trembling.

"Make yourself comfortable." I wave toward the seating area to the side of the entrance. "Or...are you sure you don't want a tour of the gym first? You can have a complimentary first day—"

"Not necessary. I've checked things out, and everything here seems ideal." He says this while looking directly into my eyes instead of surveying the gym facilities.

My mouth goes dry again, so I nod and pretend to do some important typing on my laptop while he saunters over to the sofa and pats his jacket pockets, doesn't find what he's looking for, and then uses his fingers to expand the form on the screen. He probably needs reading glasses and forgot them. I like the idea of him in glasses, but I refuse to Google "Evan Hunter glasses" because I've Googled "Jason Momoa glasses" and I am all good, thanks.

When he returns to my desk, he places the iPad in front of me and waits for me to look over the completed form. I keep hearing his phone vibrate, but he hasn't checked it the entire time he's been here, which is yet another unusual thing for a modern human. He pulls out a wallet while he watches me read. "I put the number for the hotel where I'm staying and the name that I'm registered under. I'll be moving to a house soon, but—"

"Richard Diver… Wait… *Dick* Diver? Interesting choice of alias. You a fan of early twentieth century American literature?"

"Yes. Are you?"

"Why do you look so surprised?"

"I…I didn't mean to…"

"What, you think I'm all brawn and no brain?"

"I certainly didn't—"

"You think I just watch reality shows while I run on the treadmill?"

"Not at all, no."

"Yeah, well, I do. I read *Tender is the Night* back in high school. I re-read parts of it every now and then. For years I fantasized about going to a glamorous resort in the French Riviera because of that book. I read all of F. Scott Fitzgerald's work after devouring *The Great Gatsby* for English. So why do you identify with that character? Are you married to a wealthy woman with mental health issues?"

"Not married, no."

"Dating a wealthy woman with mental health issues?"

"Not currently."

"Beginning a descent into alcoholism?"

"Well, I have felt the need of a stiff drink ever since you and I began talking, to be honest."

"Ohhhh, I know. It's the pretty young starlet thing."

"Sorry, the what?"

"I bet you can relate to Dick Diver because of the pretty young starlet who adores him."

He furrows his brow, clears his throat, and stares down at the large bills he's pulling out of his wallet.

I do realize there's a fine line between sassy and assy and that I have just charged across it.

"And did you ever make it to a glamorous resort in the French Riviera?" he asks without making eye contact.

"What?... Oh. No. I did not. I resorted to a life of glamour in the Pacific Northwest instead. As you can see."

"I *can* see." The eye contact is back. The smirk is gone. In its place is a serious contemplation of me that makes me even more uncomfortable. Finally, he takes a deep breath and says, "Well, I should do some strength training. I'm trying to get a good workout in before I crash. Jet lag, you know."

"Right. The worst." I don't want to tell him how little I've experienced jet lag in my life, but I have a feeling he can tell. "My brother can give you a quick tour of the facilities." I try to get Billy's attention by waving. He's facing the back mirror, but he's looking at his phone. "Let me just—wait here. I'll get him. Oh, and we have Wi-Fi. If you want to check your emails. The guest password is 'glutes123'."

"Is it really?"

"It is *this* week. Be right back."

"I'm in no rush."

"Cool."

As I step out from behind the front desk, I try to walk like someone who isn't at all self-conscious about the fact that a movie star is checking out her backside, and I really think I'm nailing it until Billy looks over at me and says, "What is wrong with you?"

"What?"

"You're walking like you have hemorrhoids."

I lower my voice. "Shhh! Shut up. You need to give a new VIP client a quick tour. Be cool. That actor who's going to be starring in the movie they're shooting here just signed up for a three-month membership."

"No way!" He looks over my shoulder toward the reception area and then slaps my arm with the back of his hand. "Holy shit! I totally recognize him. What's his name again—Sherlock Austen?"

"Sir Monty Churchill the Third."

"Is it really?"

"No! It's Evan Hunter. But his alias is Richard Diver. We need to be discreet—don't yell out his name, and don't tell everyone he's here."

"Sis." He wipes his hands on the front of his T-shirt. "I got this. Watch and learn."

He nudges me out of the way and marches over to Evan Hunter with his hand outstretched, and I'm already embarrassed. The few other members who are working out on the machines don't even seem to have noticed him. "Hey, I'm Billy Starkey. Hi. It is such an honor to meet you. I'm a huge fan of your work."

"Hi, Billy. Thank you so much."

Firm handshake. Billy pats him on the back. Evan seems amused.

"It's so cool that you're here. The whole town's been talking about the movie and you—this is the most exciting thing to happen since the Bigfoot sighting."

"The big...foot?"

"Just a little local humor. Bigfoot actually sticks to the mountains. Hey, my boy Chet's an actor too! Maybe you can give him some tips sometime."

I just want to put a bag over my brother's head, but

the polite Englishman is nodding and smiling and going along with this.

"Oh, your son's an actor?"

"Yeah, no. Chet's my dog. He's been in a local commercial for a hardware store and a regional commercial for a pet supply store that shot over in Seattle. He's like the Tom Hanks of Labradoodles around here. He's so fucking cute and loveable—here's a picture." Billy whips out his phone and opens up his photo library. He literally has hundreds of pics of Chet, as well as an Instagram account, of course. "Sorry, you probably don't like swears."

He feigns a bit of a drawl. "Fuck yeah, I do. Let's see that cute little fucker."

"Hah! This guy's cool," my brother says to me. "You're cool, *Richard Diver*. I like you."

I cover my face with my hands while my brother holds his phone up to this poor guy. Some pet parents are so annoying. I never show strangers pictures of my cat Muffin Top. Unless they ask.

"Oh, he's very beautiful."

"Here, this is a better one."

"So adorable. I can see why he's a star."

"Right?"

I peek through my fingers and catch Evan Hunter smiling and winking at me while Billy swipes through his library to find the picture of Chet with a little cowboy hat on.

"Billy, I think Mr. Diver probably needs to get to his workout."

"Actually—is there a men's room I could visit first?"

"Yes! The *loo*—right? In the men's change room back there. Or if you want to use the employee restroom..."

I make a face at Billy. I don't want this fellow sharing a bathroom with me. I don't know why, but I feel very strongly about this.

"Change room will be fine, thanks." Evan Hunter heads off toward the change rooms, and I definitely don't stare at his butt as he goes, because that would be lame and also he's not my type.

"That's a nice guy right there. I like him. He's a real guy. Celebrities..." Billy muses. "They really are just like us."

I shrug and lower my voice. "Are they, though? I bet when he farts, it smells like roses and tiny angels blow trumpets out of his arse."

Oh my God, I'm ten. I'm a ten-year-old tomboy again, and I just want to beat that guy in a game of dodgeball. I want to hurl rubber balls and words at him, to eliminate him but also kiss him on the mouth maybe a little first.

My brother looks up from his phone and observes me in a way that he's only done a few times in my life.

I immediately feel uncomfortable and defensive. "What?"

He smirks. "Nothin'. He's good-looking, huh?"

"If you like that sort of thing."

"Good thing *you* don't."

"Good thing *I* don't. The whole package. With the blue eyes and pretty lips and the accent and being nice. It's too much. He's like those enormous chocolate chunk cookies they sell at the Costco bakery that are the size of your head. With the pecans? Remember I got a box of them once for all of us? We were so excited because they look amazing, but they were so thick and chewy we could only stomach like half of one. And anyway, it made me feel sick and I never bought them again. Too much."

"That is not a good analogy."

"Yes, it is. Your judgment is impaired by your man crush."

"Maybe so. I can't believe that girl dumped him."

"What girl?"

"Some young actress. Starlet. Whatever you wanna call her. I forget her name—Mrs. Flauvich was talking about it. Dumped him for one of those boy band guys. According to the Internet, he's heartbroken. That's probably why he's here early, I bet. To get away from the paparazzi. What, you didn't hear about that? Everyone's talking about it."

My eyes sting. "I am such an asshole."

"You just realizing this now?"

"Shut up. Here." I grab a bottle of water from the mini fridge under the reception desk. "Give him this."

Billy holds the bottle up with one hand, and with the other he gestures toward me like a game show hostess. "Ladies and gentlemen. She's not an asshole anymore!"

Evan Hunter must think I'm such a jerk! The whole starlet thing. I can't even believe I was so sassy with a new client. He was friendly and kind to me from the get-go, and I was a nonstop cheeky turd beast.

Honestly, this is not like me. I blame the Halloween hangover. Next time he speaks to me, I'll be super nice to him.

Probably.

I hope.

4

EVAN

I haven't felt the need to splash cold water on my face at a public sink since the time I met Dame Helen Mirren at the Old Vic when I was nineteen. And here I am, at a gym, in a town I'd never even heard of a week ago. Trying to pull it together. All because of a local girl I've only actually known for a few minutes. I feel like my armor has been pierced. I can't believe she figured out my alias so quickly. I've been using it for years, and no one has ever talked to me about it.

Stella Starkey. What a bold name for a bold young woman. She was completely right about why I'd originally identified with that character. There's always some shiny new starlet beaming up at me, and I've always been drawn in. But lately, I've identified with Dick Diver more because on some level, I've felt trapped by this life and persona I've chosen.

Who *is* this girl? She's even prettier than that picture.

I knew I shouldn't have chosen this gym. This is the last thing I need. And if I'm really serious about settling down—for one thing, she lives *here*, and for another, she's not old enough. She's probably not much older than twenty-five. Although, that would still make her older than the last five or ten girls I've dated. Dear God —is that true?

But I came here early so I could get away from everything, and I have to remember not to run directly into something (or someone) else so quickly.

I realize now that it was her at the beach. Her hair was different from the picture, so I didn't recognize her in passing. The first time I saw her was from a distance, but she was tossing bits of bread into the air for some enthusiastic birds. She threw a piece to one gimpy-looking seagull on the ground, same as I would have. Then as I was jogging closer, she was strolling on the sand with her eyes closed, ostensibly swaying to the music on her headphones, and she looked so sweet and at peace. I wondered what she was listening to. Like a tosser, I didn't meet her gaze as I ran past because I needed a few hours to myself. And now here she is, serving up a large helping of great American sass with a side of small-town charm and a stunning naked face that I find it difficult to tear my eyes away from.

Still, the last thing I need right now is to meet a hot young woman who can somehow see through me even though she doesn't seem to like what she sees on the surface. She doesn't even seem to like what she hears. This might be the first girl I've met in America who hasn't melted as soon as she heard my accent. She's immune to my superpower. If that's not a sign that I should keep my head down and my trousers on, I don't know what is.

Oh, who am I kidding? I need her to like what she sees. I need to ear-fuck her with my voice, and I want her to crave it.

I take one last look at myself in the mirror—at this face that can't seem to work its usual magic on the Port Gladstone lass... Probably for the best. I'll revert to Plan A—monk-like existence. I'll let the brother show me around, I'll exhaust my muscles and then go back to the hotel for a meal and a good long sleep. I'll feel differently about her tomorrow, I'm sure of it.

As with everything else in Port Gladstone so far, I'm pleasantly surprised by all that Starkey Fitness has to offer. Besides its manager, I'm referring to the sauna and steam room, pristine and tastefully decorated environment, well-cared-for state of the art exercise equipment, quality sound system, large studio for group classes, and a back room that's fitted with mats and boxing equipment.

"I wonder if it's possible to rent out this back room for stunt training?" I find myself saying out loud to my irrepressible guide, Billy. As if I won't be spending enough time here on my own as it is, trying not to ogle his sister.

"Yeah, sure yeah. We'll have to check the schedule because we use it for private training sessions, or maybe we can shift things around. My sister can work it out for you. You can talk to her about it. Or *your people* can…" He gives me a sly wink.

"Cool, thanks. I'll talk to my trainer first—he doesn't get in until next week. Until then I'll just be on my own here, getting back into shape."

"You don't look very out of shape, bro."

"Well, I'm just coming off three months of playing a lawyer, and I wasn't allowed to look too fit."

"Oh yeah? So you playing some kickass guy in this movie you're shooting here? Is it an action movie?"

"Not quite, no. It's a thriller about a guy who accidentally witnesses a murder in England, by a really high-profile powerful politician. He goes on the run, hides out in a small town in America until the bad guys inevitably find him. But there are a few low-key action scenes. Running chases, fight choreography, and the like. I'm looking forward to it."

"Awesome—that sounds awesome! You do your own stunts?"

"Whenever possible. Whatever the insurance underwriters will allow. I like a challenge."

"Oh yeah, yeah, insurance. I never thought about that. Well yeah, we got the mats and three kinds of punching bags—but I'm sure your guy will have all the gear you need. We keep everything very clean, and it's real private back here. Out there we have all the conditioning equipment, which you saw."

"Yes, very impressive. I definitely like what I've seen here." I feel the need to add, "Facilities-wise, I mean."

He gives me a look that I can't quite read and then asks, "You just get into town?"

"Yes, just today."

"You must have jet lag."

"I do indeed. The plan is to get in a good workout and then get back to the hotel to eat and sleep."

"What's the time difference? Here and London?"

"London's eight hours ahead."

He nods slowly. "So you'll probably wake up early tomorrow."

"There's a very good chance of that, yes."

"Well, we open at six. But if you want...I'd be happy to come in early for the next couple of days. Until you're all adjusted to our time zone."

"No... Really?"

"Yeah sure—what else am I gonna do? You want to come in at five?"

"I mean. That'd be great. If it's really no trouble."

"Not at all—it's my pleasure." I think I catch a mischievous glint in his eyes, but it disappears almost immediately. "My boy Chet gets me up that early every morning anyway."

"Right, well. Can't wait to meet Chet, and I'd really appreciate it."

After a good hour and a half of strength training, I feel right at home here. It's a really good setup. I like that the machines aren't all lined up too close together. I like the space. Everything is arranged very thoughtfully. The lighting is flattering—not too bright, not too dim. I look forward to spending more time here. A little too much, perhaps.

As I walk out of the men's change room, I see Miss Starkey emerge from the staff restroom. She has pulled her hair up into a ponytail and changed into a tight little sleeveless pink top and leggings that confirm my suspicions that she has the kind of body I want to lavish attention upon, with my hands and tongue, for hours and days. So lithe but soft and curvy.

Damn.

She looks up as she's walking toward the front area, scanning the room, and her eyes lock with mine. I've stopped to stare—so unlike me. Her pace slows, my pulse rises. She sighs, pushes loose strands of hair behind her ear. Looks down at her fantastically exposed milky white skin, and self-consciously crosses her arms in front of her breasts. But not quickly enough to hide the outline of those tell-tale nipples from me.

Well now, Miss Starkey.

Well now...

She looks away from me, nearly bumping into Billy. He stops her in her tracks and speaks to her quietly, forcing her to lean in. They both glance over at me. She reprimands him for something. He laughs it off, and she shakes her head, rolling her eyes. He pats her on top of her head. She punches his arm. Siblings. They're very cute together. Billy raises his chin at me, signaling that I should come talk to her.

I start to cross over to her, but she spots someone who's entering the front door. I follow her dismayed stare to the entrance and see a scruffy guy in a fleece jacket and jeans. Good-looking enough, I suppose. He salutes her and heads her way, but she speeds up and blocks him from coming farther into the gym. Billy has gone off to talk to a woman who's getting ready to use the rowing machine. Something about the way the guy up front is ogling Stella, and the way her body has gotten so rigid, makes me want to hover closer and listen to what's going on between them. I pull out my phone and pretend to read emails.

I definitely do not like the way this guy puts his hands on her bare arms, and neither does she. I can hear them talking about "last night" and how they'd just "had a lot to drink." This must be the chap she was talking to on the phone when I got here. Persistent bastard. Not that I blame him. Still, he doesn't get it. She's just not into him.

He says he's come to cancel his membership so she can go out with him.

Then she says in a voice that's suddenly so vulnerable, it embarrasses me to be overhearing it, "Come on, Jason. This is a hard time of year for me. I was just blowing off steam."

"Yeah, well, this time of year isn't the only thing that's *hard*, and there are other things you can *blow*."

And *that's* my cue.

"Excuse me, sorry. Could I have a word with you, Stella?"

"I'm having a word with her right now, man." His expression betrays no recognition of me whatsoever. Still, I don't want to get into a brawl with a local my first day here.

"Perhaps you should choose your words more carefully, then."

"Perhaps you should mind your own fucking business then, *Downton Abbey.*"

Oh, I desperately want to punch him in the face. "Perhaps you should leave the lady alone as she's requested."

"It's fine, thank you," she says to me and then turns back to the fine gentleman. "You need to leave now before I call *all* of my brothers over."

The look on this poor fellow's face tells me that little threat did the trick. He recovers slightly, puffs up his chest, and says, "Whatever. I gotta go anyway. Just don't call me all whiney asking for forgiveness, because you won't get it."

She throws her arms up in the air, exasperated. "In *what* world?"

"Cheerio, old chap," he says to me before making his exit.

Fuck. I should have punched him in the face.

Stella looks down at her chest again before turning to me. "Thanks. I'm teaching a yoga class in a few minutes, but my brother said you asked about using the back room for training?"

"Yes. Renting it, of course."

"Yeah." She goes round behind her reception desk to look something up on her computer. "How long would you need it for? Like, an hour or two?"

"More like blocks of four or five hours at least, for the first few days when I'm working with the trainer. If possible."

"Well, you're in luck. The guy who usually uses the back room for CrossFit clients is on vacation for a few weeks."

"What do you know. Meant to be."

She refuses to look up at me, types something. "So why don't you work things out with your trainer guy and then let me know. I'll figure out a price."

"I'll get back to you. See you tomorrow?"

"Mmhmm."

And now is the part where I leave, return to my hotel and around a hundred emails and messages that I'll have to respond to.

"Hey, um. *Richard?*"

I pause, wondering who she's speaking to in that hushed tone, and then I realize she's addressing me by my alias. I turn to find her looking at me with her head tilted, playing with her fingertips and wrapping one leg around the other. Awkward but graceful.

"Yes?"

"I just wanted to apologize."

"For?"

She smiles, looking down at her hands. I like her hands. Those hands like to keep busy. Those hands were trembling when she handed me the iPad. "I'm sorry for being an ass. Earlier. What I said about the starlet—I wasn't thinking."

"You *were* thinking," I say. "I like how you think...I *think*."

Her eyelashes flutter, and I believe, for one marvelous second, that I've cast my spell upon her at last. With three short sentences.

But in the next second, she snorts and rolls her eyes, turning away from me. "Okay, well. Definitely let me know when you figure it out."

Indeed. You'll be the first to know, you saucy little minx.

You can stop staring at her marvelous bottom now, you pervy git.

In a minute, Hugh. In a minute.

5

STELLA

*A*fter my yoga class is over, I am so relaxed and centered that I feel totally at peace with the world and have a new respect and admiration for our new British gym member. Just kidding—I feel exactly the same. Creating a relaxing environment, reminding people to breathe, correcting their poses while pretending not to hear students' queefs—this is not as relaxing as you'd think. Evan Hunter was gone by the time my students started arriving, which is probably a good thing, as they would have freaked the fuck out. No amount of Cow Face Pose can calm down Edna from Sunrise Coffee Roasters when she's worked up about something.

I head home once my older brother Kevin shows up. He and Billy will take turns looking after administrative duties this evening until Billy teaches his six o'clock core strengthening class and then Kevin leads a sculpting class. When Kevin walks in, I scan his bearded stoic face to see if he knows about Evan

Hunter, but it doesn't look like it. I'm impressed by Billy's restraint, until Kevin mutters, "I hear you're in love with a British guy."

I scoff. "More like Billy is." *As if.* "Does Dad know? God, he didn't tell everyone, did he?"

"Calm down. He texted Dad and me."

"Okay, but we have to be discreet about it."

"You're the one who's super obvious about being in love with a fancy actor, you star fucker."

"I meant about him being a member, not about— you know what? I'm not even. Don't forget to do the night deposit."

"I won't. Don't forget to *not* be a star fucker."

"I definitely won't, because I'm not one."

"That's what all star fuckers say."

I flip him the bird over my shoulder as I walk out the door. This is the joy of being the only girl in my family. I guess I'd rather have them tease me about a fictional crush on an actor than my all-too-real face-mash with The Kwas.

The sun has set, and as I drive home I scan the well-lit Main Street to see if anyone's running around screaming that they've spotted a movie star. So far, it seems he's still under the radar. He's pretty good at being incognito for a tall pretty man who glows. He certainly didn't cause a stir while he was working out today. He had the usual gym armor—wireless head-phones—plus that look of intense concentration that he had when he was jogging past me and ignoring me at the beach.

I did happen to catch sight of him when he was working his lats and delts and was somewhat impressed by his perfect form on the lat pull-down machine. But I keep an eye on all of our members when they're using the equipment. That's part of my job. It's also a part of my job to sometimes wear tight little spaghetti strap tank tops without sports bras, and this was the first time I had ever felt self-conscious when a member was looking at me. Although, I'd probably feel the same way if Queen Elizabeth saw me in a ballerina pink top that showed every tiny curve of my body, including the nipple curves.

Damn Brits. It's like I have an inborn fear of imperialism. I'm sure if I were around for Beatlemania, I would have just laughed at their accents and yelled at them to "go home!" Then gone home by myself to listen to *Rubber Soul* over and over again while crying. I don't know. *Does* the lady protest too much?

I mean.

Doth she?

I doth think not.

Sometimes a protest is just a protest.

As I pull into the driveway, past the main house, I wave to my landlord Whit and his husband. Whit is carrying a bucket and other cleaning supplies to his car, walking alongside Brett, who's holding a stepladder. Probably going to clean one of Whit's listings before an open house. If Monica from *Friends* were a middle-aged gay male Realtor, she'd be my landlord Whit. I love my landlord and his hubby.

I love my home. I live in the guesthouse on Whit and Brett's property. It's a pretty little one bedroom near the edge of their expansive backyard, which butts up against a small stretch of private beach. I have my own little enclosed garden, which my cat is allowed to enjoy on warm days as long as I'm watching over her. I never want to leave this place.

After feeding Muffin Top, I'm throwing together my version of my mother's recipe, the soup she'd make us all when we were feeling under the weather. I've got leftover roast chicken, a fridge drawer full of organic vegetables that have about a day left before they get ugly, and a pantry stocked with gluten-free pasta. I've got so much bone broth, if I actually consumed it all I'm sure I'd just become such a perfect physical specimen that no one would be able to handle it. Which is why I make a lot of soup for my family.

While my dad's soup is simmering, I receive a text from my oldest brother, Martin. He's at school in Bellingham, finishing up his sports psychology degree, and he sucks at responding to my texts. But then I get random ones like this: ***Hear I'm gonna have to punch Kwas in the balls next time I see him and now you're lusting after some pretty-boy Brit. S'up with that?***

S'up with that indeed. Not even going to dignify it with a response. I immediately write back that I miss him and ask when he's coming home. And he doesn't write back. Such a jerk.

I give Muffin Top thirty solid seconds of love and attention before leaving for my dad's. We had planned to go to a movie tonight, but I'm not going to let him leave the house. I'll go on my own. I'm dying to see this oldie but goodie on the big screen and can't think of anyone besides my dad who would want to see it with me.

My father still lives in the house we all grew up in. It's the house he bought with my mother, the one they were meant to live in together for their whole lives. It's less than a ten-minute drive from where I've been living for the past four years. I ring the doorbell and knock, even though I have a key and texted him that I was coming. I once walked in to find a pink-haired tattoo artist from San Francisco waiting for my dad on the living room sofa, buck-naked. After my initial reaction of wanting to stab my eyes with a fork and scream at my dad for being a dirty old man who obviously never really loved my mom, we decided that it would be best if I simply waited for him to answer the door when I come over. It's amazing how family conflicts can be worked through with a little time, a fair amount of dark ale, a promise to date age-appropriate women, and a new sofa to replace the one that was totally defiled by out-of-town ass.

I've seen what this man is like when he's devastated, and I'll do anything to keep him from being that vulnerable again. Even if that means giving him space to be a man and being completely (okay, mostly) nonjudgmental about the tourists he occasionally has discreet flings with. He's a good-looking fifty-eight-year-old widower with a hot bod. He's a catch. I get it. He made a family with the love of his life and built up a healthy family business. He's entitled to some out-of-town tail every now and then. We all are.

It doesn't change the fact that this house is still every bit my mother's. When my dad opens the door for me, he blows me an air kiss and then immediately cleans the doorknob with an antibacterial wipe. The skin around his nostrils is pink, and he's wearing baggy sweats and fuzzy slippers.

"Hey there, champ," I say as I carry the soup-filled glass container to the kitchen. In this natural light-filled kitchen, with its wood paneling, breakfast nook and garden-view, somehow the smell of my mom's perfume and oil paints and pies still linger. I know my father will never sell this house, and part of me is glad of that. Part of me feels like I should be encouraging him to move on, like my brothers do. But I also think they should just shut up, because why should he move on? This is the perfect home.

He slumps into the booth in the breakfast nook and stares out the window. He seems so invincible most of the time, I have a feeling it's a relief for him to be a big lazy boy on the rare occasion that he gets sick. Or maybe he does it to make me feel like I'm helping him —who knows.

"Ted show up to teach my class?"

"Of course. He's very reliable. I scheduled him for tomorrow too because you're not coming in."

He grumbles and mutters to himself and then has a coughing fit.

I bring a bowl of hot soup, place it in front of him with a spoon, and slide into the opposite booth. It's dumb how much I enjoy watching people eat my food.

"Mmmm. That smell. Smells like love and womanly care-giving."

I snort laugh. "It's not as good as when Mom made it."

"You give it your own special something. Something spicy but mellow. Like you."

"It's cumin. The leftovers will taste better. I didn't have enough time to let it simmer."

"It's warm and exotic but familiar, and I feel better already. Speaking of simmering… Anything interesting happen at work today?"

"Not really. The usual. Same ol', same ol'."

He arches an eyebrow.

My dad's eyebrows are sensational. When you first meet him, the first thing you notice is that he's ruggedly handsome, and the next thing you notice is that he could easily kick your butt. The next thing you notice is that his eyebrows rule the world. In an eyebrow fight, my dad's would beat Eugene Levy's with one eyebrow tied behind his back. But right now that eyebrow just wants me to know that he knows I'm full of crap.

"I hear your new boyfriend's a pretty Englishman. What's up with that?"

"Oh my God. I'm going to murder Billy."

"Sounds like *he's* the one who loves him."

"Exactly! You should have seen how he was falling all over him. It was embarrassing."

47

"And why weren't *you* falling all over him? He not scruffy enough for you?"

"Why are we even talking about this?"

"Because we don't want to talk about Jason Kwasnicki."

He is right about that.

I seriously need more girlfriends. Since my best friend Mona moved to Portland with her boyfriend last year, I have been up to my ears in testosterone. I went into Mother Hen-mode back in high school, got so much closer to my brothers after they encouraged me to start exercising several years ago, and now I'd say that Billy and my dad are the closest I have to best friends around here. But I will not do girl talk with them. I would rather endure their teasing than discuss boys. They love me and I love them, but they don't get me. I'll never be one of the boys for real, and I'm fine with that.

I clear my throat. Change the subject: "Have you heard from Martin? He's been pretty squirrelly with the texts lately."

"Have I? Let's see…" Something about his voice and the way my dad looks away makes me wonder if there's something he doesn't want me to know. "I talked to him a few days ago. He's good. Busy. Be here for Thanksgiving."

"He better be… I should start planning a menu for that. How many people are coming?"

"We've got a few weeks to figure that out, kiddo. Watched a couple of your boyfriend's movies on Netflix this afternoon."

"You did not."

"I did. One's a Cold War spy thriller, and the other was a quirky and delightful rom-com."

"Are you high on Nyquil?"

"Nope. I like him. He's very charming." He tries out some sort of cross between Crocodile Dundee and the Geico gecko: "Kinda made me wish I had some sort of an accent."

What is happening? My dad and my brothers are never fans of the good-looking men I've met in person.

"Well-defined rectus and transverse abs."

"Okay. Wow—is that the time?"

"You're sticking around, right? Wanna watch another one of your boyfriend's movies with me? It's an action movie based on *Hamlet.* Looks interesting. Could be. Or *not to be.* Get it?"

"Yes, I get it. And no, I've already seen it. I'm going to the theater."

"You're going to Butch and Sundance without me?" He is boyishly indignant. It's his favorite movie for many reasons, and we've seen it together many times, but I just can't sit here and watch an Evan Hunter film with my dad. Especially that one. "Who are you going with?"

"Whoever else happens to be in the theater."

"Aww. I don't like you going to a movie by yourself."

"I do it all the time."

"Why don't you go with Fireboy?"

"Who—Tanner? He was a man. A fireman. And he went back to Montana. And he didn't watch movies."

"He was an idiot."

"No argument. But he was only here for a week, so who cares."

"What about Biff the mountain man? He around?"

"Jace? He was hot. You liked him. And no, he lives in Spokane."

"I liked his boots. Isn't it time you had a real boyfriend again?

"Speaking of time—it's time for me to go!"

My dad wipes his mouth to cover his laugh, which quickly morphs into a coughing fit.

"Are you okay? Do you *want* me to stay?"

"Go," he says between coughs.

"Take a hot bath and go to bed, okay? Love you." I blow him a kiss.

"Thanks for the soup, honey."

I squirt antibacterial gel on my hands before opening the front door and again after I close it. I wish there were some kind of gel I could squirt into my ears that kills 99.9% of invasive thoughts about pretty boy British actors in fifteen seconds.

The Rose Theater is one of the jewels of Port Gladstone—a large brick Victorian-era building with plush red velvet bucket seats, high-end treats, and a state-of-the-art surround sound system. There aren't enough bodies here tonight for *Butch Cassidy and the Sundance Kid*, and it's a disgrace. Every Marvel movie is sold out here on their opening weekends, but one of the best American films of all time attracts about a dozen people, not including me and some guy who's sitting in my favorite seat—middle row center. I begrudgingly take a seat an aisle behind and farther to the left, pulling off my jacket and glaring at the back of the slouching interloper's head. He's wearing a black baseball cap, and…mildly glowing.

It's Evan Hunter, and he is asleep. The baseball cap is low on his forehead, but it's definitely him and he's definitely sleeping. His mouth is slightly parted, and his head is slowly starting to tilt to the side. An elderly couple takes a seat a few rows ahead of him. They notice him, but I don't think they recognize him. It seems like the right thing to do would be to wake him up before the movie starts. Sighing, I pick up my jacket and shoulder bag and walk over to the next row, stopping a couple of feet away from him.

He is slouched in his seat, his legs splayed out instead of up over the seat in front of him, because that would be inconsiderate. Even in the dim light, I can see the healthy bulge in his jeans, and I suppose I stare at it for one or two seconds longer than I should before clearing my throat. I tap his shoulder and say, "Hey. *Richard.* Wake up."

His eyes slowly open and his head tilts in my direction. He doesn't sit up or move his legs. He just licks his lips and says, "Hello, darling," grinning. He's barely even awake and he's flirting with me—practically a stranger. Who actually falls for this baloney?

"Hi there. I just thought I should wake you up so nobody sees you and, you know, takes pictures of you or something."

"That's very thoughtful of you. I had this insane idea I'd try to stay awake as long as I could to reset my body clock."

"So you decided to come to a dark room and slouch in a chair for a couple of hours?"

"I also love this movie and watch it whenever possible. Have you seen it?"

"Many times. Well, I'm sitting back there, so... Enjoy the show."

"Won't you join me?"

"Oh. Um." *Won't I?*

He removes his jacket from the seat next to him. "Please."

"Okay. If you promise not to talk during the movie."

"Talk over Robert Redford and Paul Newman? I would never."

I sit down next to him and feel strangely self-conscious. Again. The seats in this theater are wide and each have their own armrests, but his shoulders are wide and he seems to take up more space than a gentleman should. I place my jacket in my lap and fold my hands on top of it, like I'm in church or something. There are only a few inches between us, and this feels like a date for some reason now that I'm sitting next to him. I wish I had showered. I probably smell like soup. He smells clean and well-educated and worldly. He smells good. Fuck, he smells really good, and he hasn't stopped watching me since he opened his eyes. I turn to look at him and blink at him twice. *Yes?*

He is not at all intimidated by my body language. "Which do you prefer? Butch or Sundance?"

"Butch. No contest."

"No surprise there."

"You probably like Sundance."

"Why would you say that?"

"I don't know. Pretty Boy Club."

He blinks his eyes at me twice, mocking me. "You think I'm a pretty boy?"

I face forward again and cross my arms in front of my chest. "Don't let it go to your head or anything."

"I won't. Somehow I get the feeling it's not a compliment, coming from you."

I raise my shoulder to my chin and look at him coyly. "It's not *not* a compliment."

He laughs. "I'll take what I can get. And you're wrong. I'm a huge Paul Newman fan. Although I do think Redford is underrated, in a way. People only think of him as a movie star but he's a wonderful director."

"I agree."

"And for your information, there is no Pretty Boy Club. But if there were, the first rule of Pretty Boy Club would be to not talk about Pretty Boy Club. And Paul Newman was rather pretty too, don't you think?"

"Yeah, but he had an edge."

"You don't think I have an edge?"

I guffaw. "Chiseled jawlines don't count."

"Agree to disagree. But Katharine Ross. Now *she's* pretty."

"Understatement of the century." My mother looked almost exactly like the female star of this movie and *The Graduate*, but I'm not going to be talking about her with him. From the way he looks at me, I take it he sees a resemblance in me too. My dad has told me so. I don't really see it.

The Brit finally sits up and rearranges himself in his seat so that he's taller than me, and now his arm is touching mine. He looks down at me with his sleepy eyes. "So, Stella Starkey. You like twentieth century American literature, reality shows, *and* movies?"

"I don't really watch reality shows. I'm not sure why I said that. And I like *some* movies."

He watches me, amused. He's waiting for me to say something about *his* movies, and he also seems to know that I'm not going to. Fortunately, the lights dim to black and he finally turns his gaze toward the screen.

"This is a wonderful theater."

"Shhh."

He laughs quietly, slouching again.

When the silent film of the Hole in the Wall gang starts before the opening credits, it is so quiet I can hear him breathing next to me. I hold my breath, as if that will keep him from hearing the sound of my idiot heart hammering inside my chest, begging to protect its freedom. Gah! The beginning of this movie is so quiet! He can probably hear my thoughts too.

We both take a deep breath and nod at the brilliance of the moment when the film goes from sepia tone to color. We both laugh at the same great lines.

When Redford has his first scene with Katharine Ross, he leans over and whispers, "You really expect me to believe you don't like Sundance?"

"Shhh" is all I say. What I don't say is…of course I like him. He's just not my type.

He pulls something out of his jacket pocket. A baggie full of something. He brought his own healthy snack—what a rebel. He unzips the plastic bag and leans toward me a little, gently touches the back of my hand with his fingers to get my attention. That tiny touch sends shivers all through my body. It just makes me angry, which seems like a perfectly rational response.

I can see that he's silently offering me cashews with a polite smile.

"I'm not the kind of girl who touches a strange man's nuts in a dark theater," I whisper.

He laughs quietly. "Am I really that strange?" he whispers.

I shush him again and nod back toward the screen.

When the iconic adorable "Raindrops Keep Falling On My Head" sequence begins, we both smile at each other. I finally get comfortable, slouch down in my seat, and put my feet up against the empty seat in front of me to enjoy Paul Newman hamming it up on the bicycle.

Evan Hunter does the same.

There's something so intimate about watching a movie this close to someone who isn't a complete stranger. Especially when it isn't a big blockbuster that assaults your senses. Especially when you get so invested in the characters and start crying at the end.

Even though you've seen it seven times. It always sneaks up on me.

I can't hide it. I'm sniffling and wiping my eyes. He looks over at me.

It always gets me. Their choice to die. To live it up on their own terms together and then to go out in a blaze of glory together. It used to be how I saw myself living my life until several years ago.

"It's quite something, isn't it?" he says over the end credits. "The way they keep you laughing all the way until the end, even when they know they're about to go out in a blaze of glory."

I look over at him, wondering if it *was* so quiet he really could hear my thoughts.

6

STELLA

*M*ain Street looks strangely quiet and mostly empty when we emerge from the theater. Not that it's usually a hotbed of late-night activity. But it's not even ten p.m., and around here it's pretty much just us and the few others who've left the movie to return to their cars. I guess it's that day-after-Halloween vibe. People are at home recovering.

Evan Hunter holds the glass door open for me, smiling down at me as I walk past him, and I am so aware of how tall he is. I look down the street for my parked car. He shoves his hands in the front pockets of his jeans after zipping up his jacket, and before I have a chance to say "well good night," he asks me for a tour of Main Street.

"Unless you're in a hurry to go somewhere…"

"Oh. No. Not really. You aren't sufficiently tired out yet?"

"If only the company weren't so stimulating."

"Well then, maybe I should leave."

"I'll sleep soon enough. I feel like walking around a bit, don't you? It's a nice night. I can't remember the last time I went for a walk at night in a place this quiet, with such clean air."

"Okay. Yeah, it is a nice night. We're very proud of our clean air here. Let's go this way. We'll go past the hotel and then cross over and up."

"Lead the way."

I don't want to walk up in the direction of the gym. I don't want my brothers to see us together, even though I'm fully aware of how dumb that is. "So you've been to the Rose, obviously, but it's not just the theater we were in. There's also an event room upstairs and a screening room where they show cool little second-run movies. They probably should have screened Butch and Sundance in there. I don't know why they didn't."

"I think I know what my new alias will be," he says, grinning.

I look at him for a beat. "Harry Longbow?"

He looks completely surprised.

"It's the Sundance Kid's real name."

He furrows his brow. "*Tsk.* Know-it-all."

"Well, don't *not* use it because of me—I'll keep your secret."

"Nah, I'll have to come up with something better now. I don't want you calling my hotels all the time, trying to get through to my room." He can barely say it with a straight face.

"You're right," I laugh. "I wouldn't trust myself either." I point out the deli. "That's my favorite place to have lunch. FYI, Mrs. Flauvich is all stocked-up on your favorite tea and teatime snacks. As far as the Internet has told her, anyway."

"Is that true?" His eyes are all sparkly and wrinkly around the edges when he smiles. He really is a nice guy.

"Yeah. You should pop in there sometime and make her day."

"I will. That's so sweet."

"Billy and I are addicted to her sandwiches. She has gluten-free bread, and she uses all these amazing spreads."

"I like your brother Billy. He's very affable."

"Yeah. He's the Tom Hanks of brothers."

"How many do you have, exactly? Brothers, I mean."

This is starting to feel more like a walking date than a walking tour. "Three. Billy's the youngest. Kevin's two years older than me—he works at the gym too—and Martin's two years older than him. He's at Western Washington getting a degree in sports psychology."

"And you're their only sister?"

"Lucky me."

"How interesting. I'm an only child. Always been fascinated by siblings."

"Yeah, well. I'm glad I have them. Most of the time."

We come to the end of the block, and I press the button at the crosswalk. There are no moving cars for a mile, it seems, but...safety first. He stands next to me as we wait for the light to change. I feel ridiculous. I can feel him looking at me, smiling. I refuse to look at him, until I finally start laughing and say, "Oh fine," and look both ways before crossing the street. I can't take any more of this physical proximity. It's too much.

"So, what's the name of this movie you're going to film here?"

"Ah. Well, until a few days ago, the project was called *Untitled Alan Berner Thriller*, but I've been informed that the working title is now: *Cover-Up*."

"Oh, please tell me it's about you trying to frantically hide an enormous zit for two hours."

"Well, that *would* be a feat of acting because I've never had a spot on my face in my life."

"Really?"

"No, actually, I was riddled with them when I was thirteen. It was awful."

"This is our favorite tavern," I say, gesturing toward the pub to my left with my hand still in my coat pocket.

"McSmiley's?"

"Yup."

"Fancy a drink *now*?"

I laugh. "You really don't want to go to bed, do you?"

He grins.

"I mean go to sleep. No! I'm not having another drink for a long time. But don't let me stop you from having one."

"I was just being polite. I should head back; you're right."

We keep walking.

"Is it always this quiet at night?"

"No, it's just a day after the holiday thing, I think."

"Right, sure."

I step out into the empty road, feeling reckless and ready to jaywalk this time, since his hotel is right across the street.

He follows me but says, "I'll walk you back to your car."

"You don't have to. I'm just a block away."

"I insist."

"Okay. Thanks."

"Thank you for the walk. I feel right at home now."

"You'll have a nice time here, I'm sure. People here are really nice and content, and…well, to be honest, a lot of them were really excited that you're coming."

"Nice of you to say so."

"It's true."

"I like what I've seen so far," he says, smiling at me.

"Does that usually work?"

"Does what usually work?"

I wave my hand around him. "This. Whole. Thing."

He starts laughing and shaking his head again. He looks so tired. But still pretty. And confident. Which means it's okay for me to talk to him like this. Because pretty, confident British movie stars can handle this, and if they can't, then they don't deserve to be worshipped.

"I mean, I'll admit that I did feel the stomach butter-flies when I first met you. The voice. The eyes. The glow."

"The glow?"

"Yeah. Your famous rich person glow."

He runs his fingers through his hair, messing it up. "I didn't realize I did that."

"Well, I doubt that you *do* it. It's something you either have or you don't."

"Right. And what do you call this thing that you have?"

I wrinkle my nose. "Sass?"

"Definitely. If we're being polite. I meant your glow. Are you also famous and rich?"

"I don't have a glow."

"Oh, but you do."

"Okay. You're doing it again."

He arches an eyebrow. "Am I?"

"Seriously, you don't have to do this. With me, I mean. You can drop the act. The cameras are not rolling. There's no audience. Look around. We're the only ones on the sidewalk. Take a break."

"Why don't you give *me* a break?"

I sigh. "Sure."

"Really?"

"You want me to?"

He twists his lips to one side. "Not really."

I stop in front of my car. "Well, this is me."

I may be imagining this, but he looks a little disappointed. Not by my car but by the end of our walk. "You're heading home?"

"Yes."

"You live nearby?"

"Yes."

He nods. "So do I. For now." He does seem very, very tired.

"I know. I hope you don't fall asleep before you get to your room."

"That's the nicest thing you've ever said to me."

I giggle. I'm not a giggler, but he made me giggle. He looks pleased with himself.

"Sweet dreams, Stella Starkey. I hope you're able to fall asleep despite thinking about my glowing eyes."

"I think I'll manage."

He stands there, watching me open my car door.

"You're not going to stand there and watch until I drive away, are you?"

"It would be the polite thing to do."

"You really don't have to be polite with me."

I see something flash in his heavy-lidded eyes. Something dirty. "If you say so. I suppose I'll see you at the gym tomorrow. Your brother offered to open up early for me."

"I suppose I'll see you in the morning."

He nods, doesn't smile, turns, and slowly walks away toward the hotel. "Good night, stomach butterflies."

"Good night...Dick."

7

EVAN

*O*ccasionally, I'll read a script or a play and know immediately, with all my heart and soul, that I was born to inhabit a role. It seizes me, as if grabbing me by the shirt and saying: "YOU MUST BECOME THIS PERSON. YOU *ARE* THIS PERSON." Fortunately, more often than not, I do get the opportunity to take on those parts, but there have been times when they went to other actors. Rejection is a part of being an actor, and you do eventually learn to deal with it because you have to. But sometimes, God, sometimes it just hurts. I've always imagined it's how it would feel to be rejected by someone you're madly in love with.

As much as the media seems to want to paint me as heartbroken after Georgia left me for the boy, the truth is I was never in love with her. I liked her a lot; it was a delightful fling—fun while it lasted. She always wanted to attend events, parties, and clubs, and I rarely did. It never would have lasted forever, and I would have ended it in the classiest way possible eventually. She just beat me to the punch. Minus the classy part.

Was I surprised that she left me for Braden?

Let's just say that I was with her the first time "I Wish I Was in Georgia" came on the radio and could see the writing on the wall. I could see the excitement she was trying to hide. It didn't feel good at all—I went home alone in a foul mood and got pissed by myself for the first time in years. But it was more a "what the fuck am I doing with my life" kind of drunk, rather than a "why the fuck doesn't she love me the way I love her" sort of thing.

From the moment I started talking to Stella Starkey, though, I felt that pull. That soul-stirring, deep-down recognition that here is a character I need to know and that becoming this person—the man who falls for Stella Starkey—would somehow bring me closer to myself. It's exciting and unsettling. I want to get lost and found in the lush misty wilderness that is her personality.

Also, I just really want to shag her and get lost and found in her luscious fanny.

Ever since she opened that beautiful mouth of hers, I've been consumed with the desire to know what she can do with it besides surprise and arouse and crush me with words. When she told me last night that I could "drop the act" with her, it felt as though she had unlocked something inside me. Drop the act. With her. Yes, please.

I can't remember the last time I've been completely myself with a woman. I'm always the person they want me to be. I have a feeling she's got a bit of an act herself, this one. Beneath that crispy exterior is a center as sweet and soft as nougat, I'm willing to bet.

I realize I'm groaning out loud, and not in the sexy way. I feel that ache inside, that spectacularly awful combination of longing and excitement to see her again and the awareness that there will come a time when I'll have to say good-bye. It's too soon to be feeling this way. Why *do* I feel this way? And does it really matter why...if I like her this much?

It's four in the morning here, and I've been lying awake in the dark for an hour. Now would be a good time to make calls to the UK, and I woke up with the nagging feeling that I should be calling my girlfriend to check in. Then I remembered that I don't currently have a girlfriend. Then I remembered how good it felt to sit so close to Stella at the theater last night. And then I remembered her smooth exposed skin and round breasts in that tight little top. Those delicious curvy hips in those leggings. And let's just say my body is now convinced that she and I are a very happy couple. Still, it does feel a bit strange, not having someone who's waiting for me to check in with them.

I have been perfectly content being a serial monogamist. Hollywood insiders have made it entirely too easy to find appropriate girls to have flings with while on location when I wasn't in a relationship. When there's a production with a playboy director and-or producer at the helm, there is often a secret list that circulates amongst the chosen few men on set, of women who are "DTF." I loathe that term. In my mind,

I always tell myself it stands for Down To Frolic. The last time I was totally single while on location in Australia, I found out that the young lady I had been casually involved with for a couple of weeks was on one of those lists. I stopped seeing her immediately. I always used protection of course, but the issue was more that Hollywood was a small enough community as it was. I didn't need to be "Eskimo brothers" with half of the men listed in the opening credits.

It's still too early to leave for the gym. Thank God Billy offered to open up early, or I'd lose my mind. Or go blind from wanking to thoughts of his sister—best not to mention that when I see him. I sit up in bed, switch on the lamp, and pull my laptop from the bedside table. Time to check emails.

Not in the mood to peruse the long list of invitations that were passed along from my publicist's office to my assistant Wendy. Premieres in New York and LA, opening nights in London, fashion events in New York, Milan, and Paris. Happy to have a publicist's office and assistant to send my regrets for me and happier to have a good excuse to turn those down while I'm here.

When I see a message from Starkey Fitness, I am ridiculously pleased. It's forwarded from my secondary Gmail account—a generic email welcome packet from the gym. Nothing personalized, and yet I am smiling because I'm certain that it was written by Stella.

Welcome to Starkey Fitness! If you're a member— you're family. And our family likes to sweat. A lot.

God. I'm like a boy of twelve when it comes to this

woman. Before allowing my mind to wander, I catch sight of an email from my mate Liam asking if I'm available for a chat anytime soon and also where the fuck am I. I reply "yes" and "you'll never guess," tell him I'll ring him in a bit. Liam is the happiest sod I know. He was miserable when we were at the London Academy of Music and Dramatic Art together because he was always cast as the best friend to my handsome lead. Once we'd graduated, he decided to remain in London working on the West End and the BBC's finest productions, alongside the best actors and directors that England has to offer. He's never out of work, makes a perfectly good living, gets to see his friends and family all the time, and to top it off, he's been with the same wonderful woman since we were at school. If he weren't such a good friend, I'd want to kick him in the teeth.

"So," my friend says, with feigned gravity, as soon as he answers my call. "I hear that dear old *Evangia* is no more."

"Alas. *Evangia* is dead. Long live *Bragia*. Or whatever the media is calling it."

"*Georden*, actually. Which is unfortunate."

That makes me cringe. "That's awful. So you've been Googling her."

"Lord, no. I'm a card-carrying Hunterhoe."

I'm not sure who coined the term "Hunterhoes," but my beloved fans are surprisingly sophisticated and not as Dutch as they sound. There is, of course, some crossover with the Hiddlestoners and Cumberbitches.

My fans are just as well behaved and ladylike as Tom's and Benedict's. Except when they're not.

"You're the only one I ever Google," he continues. "So you're not miserable?"

"No more so than usual." I pause for Liam to snort-laugh. "I haven't even seen her in person for a month and a half, I think. We've been on different continents for work."

"Right. She was filming in New Zealand."

"Aha. So you *did* Google her."

"All right, just the once. We were looking forward to meeting dear Georgia. Well, *I* was, anyhow. Is it true she dumped you by text?"

"God no—where'd you read that? We'd always planned to meet up in Hawaii when she'd wrapped her film, but she called to tell me she's interested in someone else. It was all very simple and civil."

"Sounds boring as shit."

"Well, I guess that's why you'll never read the real story in the Mirror."

"Cate wants you to know that while she is a fan of OneLove, she will never listen to them again if you ask her not to."

"Please convey my appreciation to Cate and inform her that there are no hard feelings between myself and said boy band. She may proceed to enjoy their musical stylings."

"Dammit. I was really hoping to tell her they're banned from our home."

"Well, I'm not going to be the one to disappoint her. I'll leave that to you."

"Speaking of… The reason I wanted to speak to you. We've finally decided to make it official, Cate and I. I'm officially going to be the one disappointing her for the rest of my life. We're getting married."

"Liam! I'm so happy for you! Congratulations."

"Thanks."

"About time, I suppose. You've been engaged for what—five years now?"

"Bit more."

"Wow. I'm really, really happy for both of you."

"Good, because you're going to be a part of it. I want you to be in the wedding party. We're doing it in Sussex. Some lovely old barn or other. Upcoming weekend after Valentine's Day, so have your people ensure your availability and all that."

I laugh. "I shall alert the proper authorities. Thanks, I'd love to. I'll do whatever you need."

"Well, Cate would like you to bring a date who won't make her want to tear out her own hair on her wedding day."

"I'll see if my mum's available."

We both laugh at that, but my thoughts immediately turn to Stella—which is ridiculous because I haven't even known her for twenty-four hours. Although it really does feel like much longer. At the same time, I wonder if I can wait however many hours I'll have to before seeing her again…

So far I think I'm handling this not rushing into anything too soon after I've been dumped very well.

8

EVAN

With my baseball hat on, I carry two takeaway cups of coffee out of the hotel lobby and turn to walk up Main Street toward Starkey Fitness. It is still dark as night and the streetlamps are lit. The sidewalks are wide, and as I admire the well-kept brick buildings and charming storefronts—wondering why the hell there's a mannequin wearing Cricket whites in one window—I regret having asked my New York business manager to see about letting that secluded house sooner rather than later. Privacy is important, but this town is so charming, I might enjoy staying at the heart of it a while longer.

Speaking of hearts... Mine starts racing when I approach the gym and catch sight of the female Starkey inside it. Switching on the lights, she is suddenly illuminated behind sheer white curtains as if behind a scrim on stage, and I get a clear vision of how our dramedy will play out.

She is placing something on the floor behind her

welcome desk when I open the front door, the jingle of the bells causing her to freeze in position for a moment before turning to face me. Her face lights up as soon as she sees me. She takes in a deep breath, and then, just as quickly, she manages to assemble her facial muscles into a mask of polite professional welcome.

"Hello, darling. What a lovely surprise."

She purses her lips, blinks ever so slowly, and explains, "My brother bailed. He texted me late last night to tell me he didn't want to leave his place early because then his dog's digestive system would be off-schedule." She tilts her head to one side, squinting. "And aren't you the English actor who I told could drop the act with me?"

"I am that very fortunate English actor. And I have. You may drop your act with me as well."

Frown followed by a scoff. "I don't have an act."

"Oh no?" I watch her squirm adorably for another few seconds before offering a cup of coffee. "Regardless. I'm sorry to inconvenience you. I brought coffee from the hotel lobby. It's black—I don't know how you like it."

I expect her to say something like, "*I do like my coffee black—like my men.*" Instead, she smiles and says very genuinely, "Thank you. Mmmm."

I watch her inhale the bittersweet aroma and find myself catching my own breath as I watch her marvelous chest heave.

"You look very tired."

"I'm fine," she says, stifling a yawn.

"Liar."

She wrinkles her nose at me.

"I'm sorry to get you out of bed so early. It's quite the opposite of what I want."

I watch her gulp down her coffee. She stares at me, trying to decide if she heard me correctly, trying to decipher if I could possibly have meant it in the way that she thinks when I had said it so politely.

That's right. I want to get you *into* bed, not out of it, darling.

She shakes her head almost imperceptibly, trying to shake me off. But it's not going to be quite so easy now, is it? She clears her throat. "I will be fine. If this coffee doesn't wake me up, maybe you could tell me about those turnips in Cornwall again. That's sure to give me a jolt."

Well now...I think someone wants a spanking.

It's almost as if every time she opens her sassy mouth, that's what she's really asking for... A soft, undeniably sexual guttural sound escapes my throat as I picture it. I cover my mouth and cough politely. Incredibly, she doesn't seem to have noticed, because she lifts up a cupcake carrier from the floor, places it on top of her desk, uncovers it, and reveals it to be a bounty of mouthwatering goodness. Just like she is.

"Gluten-free carrot cake muffins? The cream cheese frosting is organic and lactose-free."

This time I don't even try to hide the loud groan. "You're killing me. Carrot cake is my favorite, and they look perfect. But I can't eat until after ten o'clock."

She looks a bit disappointed that I won't be

sampling her goods, and that pleases me. "You're inter-mittent fasting?"

"Indeed, I am."

She replaces the cover on the carrier after taking a muffin for herself. She takes a big bite out of the top of that muffin, savoring it and licking the cream cheese frosting from her upper lip. Then she wipes her mouth with the back of her hand and licks the bit of frosting like a cat licking her paw. She really is trying to kill me.

"Full-on workout schedule *and* intermittent fasting? That's like, the fitness model slash superhero regimen. Just how much of yourself will you be revealing to the audience in this film?"

"More than most women can handle." I grin as I lean forward to rest my forearms on top of the desk.

She laughs. And rightly so. I do too.

"I'll be shirtless in a couple of scenes. Just enough to earn those big bucks they're paying me."

"Really?"

"Not exactly. This isn't a big-budget film. We do the tent-pole films so we can afford to do whatever we want the rest of the time. Or *feel* like we could do what-ever we want, I suppose."

"Tent-pole films?"

"That's what they call the ridiculously massive budget event movies that essentially prop up the studio financially. So they can release one or two smaller films around awards season."

"Ah. Like the one you're shooting here?"

"Ideally. I mean…depending on how incredible I look with my shirt off. Might be good for an MTV

Movie Award. People's Choice Award for Best Pecs. As long as Hemsworth keeps his shirt on for the rest of the year, I'm a shoe-in."

"Well, I'll be sure to keep my healthy muffins and cookies away from you, then. For the sake of art and commerce."

"Don't you dare. Save me one or two of those, would you?" I plead, nodding toward the baked goods.

"I make no promises. They're very popular."

"I've no doubt, but I'll take my chances. I have a strong feeling I'll get to taste your delicious muffin one of these days."

Those brown eyes squint at me.

You have every reason to be suspicious of me, darling.

"Good coffee." I raise my cup and nod. That's enough talk of the lady's muffin for this morning.

She clears her throat. "Mrs. Dunbar makes the *third* best cup of coffee in town."

"She's quite a character, isn't she?"

"Oh sure. This town's just chock full of character."

"So it seems."

I watch as she places a new tea light candle inside the jack o'lantern.

"How long are you going to keep that on display?"

"Oh I don't know—how long do they traditionally keep them out in Cornwall?" She grins as she glances up at me, using a lighter on the wick.

Fuck me, I want to dip my wick in this one, something awful. I should probably ease off on the coffee or I'll be battling a monster erection until I begin my vigorous workout. Good thing I'm wearing a long coat for now. If I'd known I would be alone with her, I would have worn sweatpants in a heavier fabric. Or an athletic cup, because I wouldn't put it past this one to knee me in the groin if I continue flirting with her.

I clear my throat. "Did you go out on Halloween?"

"Yes. Did you?"

"I was getting ready to travel. Did you dress up?"

"I wore a costume."

"Do tell."

She looks down, pretends to read something very important on her computer. Oooh, she doesn't want to tell me. Must have been something naughty.

"Let me guess, then… Sexy witch?"

She raises one of her glorious dark eyebrows.

I stroke my jaw with my fingers. "No. Course not. Too on point."

She laughs at that.

"Wonder Woman?"

She smirks. "Also too on point."

"Sexy cowgirl?"

She rolls her eyes, but she also looks a bit nervous. Dear me, I must be getting warmer.

"Sexy…sailor? Sexy sailor."

Her eyes widen and she blushes. Nailed it. Dear God, how she blushes.

"Well now. Anchors away—were you a captain or first mate?"

"None of your business."

"I wholeheartedly disagree. Interesting choice of alias," I tease, mimicking her and her insightful probing from yesterday. "What—are you secretly dying to sail the seas? Or were you just hoping to meet some nice seamen?"

She nearly chokes on her coffee this time.

"You all right?"

She stares up at me and says, "Shouldn't you be focusing your curiosity about humanity on the character you're about to play in the movie?"

"Indeed I should, but he doesn't have quite as many interesting layers as you do."

"Well then, maybe you should be focusing on the very important workout that you had us open up early for."

"First of all—your brother *offered* to open up early for me. I would never have made that request. Secondly…yes. Why don't I get to it."

"Why don't you." She gestures for me to proceed, remaining behind the desk. It's almost as though she feels the need to blockade herself from me. And she should.

Perhaps I ought to take it down a notch. "Cheers." I take my coffee and start to walk away, toward the inner sanctum of the gym.

"Oh hold on," she mutters as I feel her rush past me. She jogs toward the men's change room, pushes the door open, and reaches in to switch on the lights. "There," she says. "Don't want you tripping around in the dark and then suing us."

"I promised not to sue you. I am a man of my word." I place my coffee in the cup holder of the treadmill and then unzip my coat. Watching her as I remove it, trying not to grin as I notice her eyelashes flutter as her attention swiftly passes from my bare biceps, down to my crotch in these dangerously thin sweatpants. And then she gazes round the room.

She shakes her head, powers up the treadmill and starts making the rounds, turning on all of the machines. "I assume you'll be listening to your own music with your headphones, but do you have a preference as to what you'd like me to put on?"

"Yes. Your Halloween costume."

She catches her breath before laughing it off. "I meant music-wise. On the house stereo system." I can see her blushing from here. God, how she blushes.

"Well, I think it would be rude if I used my headphones if it's just you and me here. I'll leave it to you to choose the soundtrack. Something to get me all jazzed up for my workout, preferably."

She smirks, turns, and skips over to the front desk.

Seconds later, Billie Holiday begins to drone from the speakers. "A Foggy Day." A fantastic song. Incredibly slow, until it picks up a bit. Funny. She is adorable.

"Not the right kind of jazz?"

"It's perfect, in fact." I start stretching.

"Oh good."

"Have you ever been?"

"To?"

"To foggy London town."

She shakes her head. "No. Never even considered it, actually."

"No interest?"

She raises her chin a bit defiantly. "Not in the least."

I don't pursue the conversation, and that seems to disappoint her. "Is that where you live?"

"It's where I grew up and it's where I own a home, yes."

"Ah. But all the world is your stage?"

I grin at that. "Hardly. But I have to go where the work is. Been a bit of a vagabond my whole life, really."

She nods.

I don't offer any more on the subject. I wait for her to bite. I don't have to wait long.

"You travel a lot?"

"Quite a lot, yes."

"Is this your first time in Washington?"

"Besides the airport in Seattle, I believe so, yes. I've been to Vancouver, Canada for a film. That's quite close."

"Yes. It's nice up there. If you like big expensive cities."

"I've nothing against them. You do, it seems."

She shrugs. She's removing the letters from the letter board. "I wouldn't say that. Just wouldn't want to live in one."

After I've done a suitable amount of warm-up stretching, I pull my iPad out from my messenger bag. I have to read a script that my agent sent me, and although it isn't the kind of thing I could pass along to my assistant, I don't think it warrants more than a cursory read-through on the treadmill. I reach into the side pocket for my reading glasses, and before I put them on, I notice Stella watching me and smiling.

"What?"

"Nothing. I just want to see what you look like with glasses on."

"Ah, well. Prepare thyself. It's pretty great. You ready?"

She nods enthusiastically, like a little girl.

I place my black-rimmed glasses on and turn my head to both sides. "Pretty incredible, right?"

"It's everything I'd hoped it would be."

She does make me laugh, this one. When the Billie Holiday song is over, she pokes around on a phone, and suddenly one of my favorite Clash songs comes on. I wonder if I've ever mentioned liking this band in an interview and if she's Googled me. And then I immediately despise myself for thinking it. Everyone likes "Should I Stay or Should I Go." It's a classic.

"If you don't mind," she says, disappearing into what looks like the back office, "Since I'm here, I think I'll get my sweat on while I can."

"By all means."

I look up and see her in the reflection of the mirror in front of me when she returns from the staff restroom, hair pulled up and back in a ponytail. I have picked up my pace on the treadmill, and she is wearing sweatpants that fit snugly around her marvelous hips and a tank top with a sports bra under it. I do like her body. Rounded but fit. In good shape but not too thin or too muscular. Womanly. Not unlike Katharine Ross.

I love that she appreciates that film. I once asked a young actress if she preferred Butch or Sundance, and she said, "Sundance is the most fun. And then the

Toronto Film Festival and then Cannes. Where's the Butch Festival?"

I look back to the screenplay on my iPad. I don't want to, but I also don't want to contemplate Stella's body any further in her presence. I did that enough in my hotel room earlier this morning.

I manage to ignore her while she stretches. She herself is placing earbuds in her ears. I can only assume it's because she's going to listen to music that's even more up tempo than what The Clash has to offer. She mounts a stationary bicycle in a spot of the room that I can't see her in if I just look in the mirror. I wish I hadn't turned my head slightly and seen how she mounted that seat with such grace and ease, because now I can only picture her swinging her leg over and straddling me.

I should be reading this awful script that I loathe but will probably end up doing anyway. My agent also represents the writer and director and told me that they are guaranteed a green light if I attach myself to the project. He said he can get me a five million dollar "pay or play" deal, so I'd get paid even if they don't end up making the movie. Problem is, if they do end up making the movie, I'll be committing myself to at least three of them because it's set up to be a franchise.

Maybe if I can convince them to shoot this crap here in Port Gladstone... Sign me up.

I very subtly turn my head so I can see Stella going to town on that bike. She has a lot of stamina. Good thing, because she will be spending hours riding me once I've made my move.

One of the themes of *Cover-Up* is hiding—from the world, hiding your identity, your true feelings. I suspect that Stella is somehow hiding who she really is, despite being a loud-mouthed queen of sass. She's hiding a romantic, wanderlustful dreamer who lives quietly inside her, and I intend to find out why and then coax her out into the world with me.

But then I might be ruining her. Maybe the thing that I find so attractive about her is how happy she is with where she is—the quality of satisfaction and the apparent total lack of longing. It's such a rare quality in the world I inhabit. How obnoxious of me to presume she would want to leave her world for mine.

Forty minutes later, I take a seat next to her on the bench as I rehydrate and catch my breath before moving on to strength training.

Her skin is damp from head to toe, glistening with perspiration, her chest heaving. She pauses to gulp down about a liter of water, giving me a chance to admire her long bare neckline. I am dying to lick the entire length of that salty wet neck.

She replaces the cap on her water bottle and looks up at the clock. "Damn. I have to get changed and open up. I'm a mess."

"I disagree. You were never lovelier."

"Pssh. You should see me after I've showered."

"I'd rather see you while you're showering," I mumble into my water bottle. Not my finest work, perhaps, but I couldn't stop myself.

She turns her head and looks at me, wondering if I just said what she thinks I said. "What did you say?" She sounds as if she's afraid to know for sure.

"What do you think I said?" I look at her straight on, not teasing.

Her cheeks turn the prettiest shade of pink as she presses her lips together and shakes her head. Is she demure? Is that what's really going on here?

"Glad you got your sweat on, anyway. You have a class today?"

"No, I teach every other day. Someone else teaches yoga today. Candace. She's much more advanced than I am. You ever do yoga?"

"I indulged a former girlfriend by going to a few classes back in London, but it's not for me."

"Really? But it's great for your muscles and joints. It's a good way to keep from getting stiff after all the training you'll be doing." She says the word "stiff" in such a coy way, I am almost certain she's trying to beat me at my own game.

"I'm completely resigned to being stiff after leaving here." I take another sip of water and then turn to face her.

She is speechless. Studying my face, trying to read me. I feel like an open book, but I understand how confused she must be. I myself am not confused. I know precisely what I mean and what I'm feeling right now and what I want.

I glance at her lips and lean in, almost imperceptibly, toward her. My lips are inches from hers, and if she tilts her head up the tiniest bit, I will give her the kiss of her life right here right now on this bench.

But she doesn't. She is frozen. Staring up at me, a gorgeous doe-eyed perspiring deer in headlights.

I am not who she thought I was, not who people think I am, not who I let people believe I am. I have accepted her invitation to *not* do my "whole thing" with her, so she will get a whole new thing from me. All she has to do is take it.

But she doesn't.

Not yet.

She frowns at me. Pulls back, stands up, and walks into the staff restroom, shutting the door and locking it behind her.

Fuckity fuck fuck says Hugh Grant in my head. *They're writing songs of love, but not for you.*

Fuck you, Hugh.

9

STELLA

I might have to stay in this bathroom forever. Or at least until my panties dry out. What the hell is happening? I pace around the tiny bathroom like a caged tiger, and then I start cleaning. The janitor cleaned overnight, of course, but he always misses a few spots, and it's not like my brothers or dad will ever tend to this stuff.

Why is Evan Hunter toying with me?

Am I secretly dying to sail the seas? Um. No. Let's not read too much into my sexy sailor costume.

Sail the seas.

Who does he think he is, and why is he bothering with me?

Sometimes a Halloween costume is just a Halloween costume.

Sometimes yoga instructors actually mean stiff muscles when they talk about being stiff.

Actors and their obsession with subtext.

I want to run back out there, punch the air, and yell out, *"You don't know me!"*

I definitely don't need him to know that I was up all night baking an obscene amount of goodies just to keep my hands off my own goodies. To keep my mind busy with measurements and temperatures and times, so I wouldn't fondle myself while thinking of him. I just couldn't get his voice out of my head. It's like he's cast some sort of Disney prince spell on me, the kind that never had any effect on me growing up. I used to tease my friends mercilessly for crushing on Prince Eric, and now Prince Phillip has waltzed right into my life, slayed the dragon that is my love for Jason Momoa-types, and is about to wake me from my slumber with a kiss.

I don't think I'm ready to wake up yet.

I am definitely not about to kiss him at the gym.

Or maybe I'm imagining everything due to a total lack of sleep.

He sure doesn't act like a brokenhearted guy who's been dumped. Or maybe this is just him rebounding. Maybe he really is sad and he's just been focusing his attention on me to get through this difficult period in his otherwise picture-perfect life.

Or maybe I just need to get out of this building. Take an early lunch break as soon as my brother gets here. Put a few blocks of distance between me and that thin tank top that accentuates every damn muscle beneath it. Big guys are definitely still my thing, but there's something very beautiful about the lines and smooth molded curves of his arms. Like a statue. Like a really friendly, charming, confusing statue with a fancy accent.

Now that I smell like Windex and flop sweat, I open the door and walk straight to the front desk without looking around for Evan. When I reach the desk, I realize the front door is unlocked and I hear Billy's voice. He's talking it up with his buddy Evan over by the shoulder press machine. I need to get out of here before he starts his strength training, because if I see him breathing out, veins in his neck bulging while his muscles flex, my ovaries might explode.

I leave a note for Billy at the desk telling him I'm running to the deli for breakfast and then I literally run out the door.

The mouthwatering thoughts of an egg sandwich fill my head for thirty whole seconds before I overhear talk of Evan Hunter, as always. I swear, Mrs. Flauvich is obsessed. She's been happily married for like forty years, but I haven't seen her this excited about anything since her daughter's wedding. And even then she was complaining about how the humidity made her daughter's hair frizzy.

She's at the register, talking to a woman that I recognize from the library, someone I've never actually spoken to, showing her something on her iPad.

"She's pretty, I guess," says the library lady, wrinkling her nose. "I don't recognize her. I just hope the movie people aren't noisy or messy." She nods at me as she leaves with her takeout bag.

"She's on a TV show that Missy watches, and it says here she got rave reviews for an independent film that was at the Sundance Film Festival last year."

I feel my stomach drop, and not in the good way. "Who's that?" My voice sounds suitably half-interested, I think.

"They've cast the actress to play the love interest in the Evan Hunter movie. Surely they will have a love affair on the set," she says.

"Can I get an egg sandwich," I say, grabbing the iPad to inspect this "love interest." Funny he never mentioned a love interest. Also typical. Also weird that it never occurred to me that there would be one. "What are you reading, Mrs. Flauvich?"

"Oh, I don't know. I just Google his name and see what comes up. A lot comes up. You're here early."

"Uh-huh."

She's got raven-black hair and bright white teeth and big blue eyes that look shrewd and don't match her broad smile. She is very pretty, but I might hate her. She looks like a fakey-fake. She doesn't look like anyone I'd want to get to know, and I can't imagine she'd be capable of the same conversations with Evan that I've had—but if that's what he's into...good for him.

"Just the egg sandwich for you, dear?"

"What makes you think he'll have a love affair with this actress?" I ask in a totally convincing nonchalant voice.

"Oh, you know. That's kind of his thing, it seems. All of his past girlfriends were actresses he worked with, I think. I mean. Just from what I've read—what do I know."

"Yeah, sure. Just how many past girlfriends are we talking about here?" *Don't tell me don't tell me I don't want to know.*

"Oh, I don't know. Let's see, shall we?"

She wipes her hands on a tea towel and waits for me to pass her the iPad. I want to run, but where would I run to? Back to the gym where that damn sexy Englishman is waiting to toy with the local girl's heart?

She pokes at the iPad screen with her index finger and then gives the thing back to me. My hands are trembling. I actually feel like I might throw up and get diarrhea. It's all humiliating and so darn confusing, because why would *I* feel like *this* about *him*?

And then it becomes clear, as I scan the many, many photos of this same man who's been making friendly conversation with me. There he is, with truly beautiful, young, glowing, constantly smiling actresses. His arm around them at premieres and black-tie New York fashion gala events and award shows. Yeah. That's his real life. He's just passing time here. He's just a nice guy, chatting with the local normal people, probably as research for his next role.

That's all it is.

I feel better now.

The cold sweaty palms are now dry and warm and ready to swat away all confusing thoughts.

"Thank you," I say, passing the iPad back to Mrs. Flauvich.

Thank you, Google.

And you're welcome, brain.

By the time I've returned to the gym, there are a few more members here working out, blocking my view of the actor, and a note from Billy that says: **WTF weirdo?!?!?!**

I respond to some emails, make some calls to suppliers, and when I hear the front door bells jingling, I look up to find a guy around my age. He's shaggy in all the ways that I'm used to, swiping a wet hood from his head and giving me a quick once-over and the "s'up" nod that guys usually greet me with when they walk in here. Not that shiny smile and handshake baloney that a certain someone tried to fool me with.

"Hey. Didn't realize it started raining."

"Just a bit. How are ya? I'm Donovan."

"Hey there, Donovan."

He smirks. "Nice place you got here."

"Glad you like it."

He pulls a flyer out from a plastic folder and places it in front of me on the desk. "So, I'm the assistant location manager for the film that's going to be shooting here in a couple of weeks—I don't know if you've heard about this?"

I clear my throat. "Yes, I've heard."

"Cool, well, I'm just going around to all the businesses on Main Street, giving you our information. We're in the process of applying for all the permits, but we just wanted you all to know that we will be disrupting things around here a bit, some days."

"Oh yeah?" *More?*

"You'll always be notified days beforehand, but there will be street closures on and off and parking for cast and crew around here."

"Oh."

"Yeah. It's not gonna get too crazy or anything—most of the scenes that are shot around here are pretty quiet ones. But we're going to be setting up a video village not far from your entrance here."

He points out to the sidewalk.

"What's a video village?"

"Like a covered area for the playback monitors and the sound equipment. You know, where the director and producers and actors will have their chairs set up."

"Actors too, huh?"

He rolls his eyes. "Yeah, you heard about the star, I guess?"

I glance to the side. I can't see Evan, but he's in there somewhere. "Yeah, people have been talking. This sounds like it might be bad for business."

"Well, the sidewalks aren't going to be blocked off. But whenever they're shooting, some asshole assistant director will yell out to everyone to be quiet while cameras are rolling, that kind of thing. If you have any complaints...I'm the assistant location manager, like I said—and you are...?"

"Stella. I'm the manager here."

"Oh cool. This is a cute town. I always meant to come by for a day trip."

"Oh yeah? Where do you live?"

"Seattle. But I'll be here for the next couple of months. What's fun around here?"

Me. I am. "Depends what you're into, Donovan." See, now this guy's more my speed.

He kinda laughs and then checks his phone. "Well, I gotta keep making the rounds, Stella, but here is my card. If you have any complaints or suggestions, call this number. It's my cell phone."

I take his card and tap the edge of it on the desktop. "Don't you mess up my town, Donovan."

"I'll do my best. See you around. I hope."

I wave at him with his business card in my hand and watch him put his hood back on as he heads out the door.

"Who was that—assistant location manager?"

I jump, startled. "Where did you come from?"

Evan Hunter appears out of nowhere, guzzling a bottle of water, wearing his coat and shoulder bag again.

"Have you been sufficiently informed as to the chaos our little production will be causing your quaint village?"

"I knew you were trouble as soon as you walked in."

"Right back at you," he says, screwing the cap back on his water bottle. "I'm sure he told you to call him if you have any complaints about the production, but..." He taps his chest. "I'm the guy to talk to." He cracks himself up.

"Oh well, I wouldn't want to bother you while you're busy taking your shirt off and making women swoon. You heading out?"

"For a bit. I've got a few conference calls scheduled, but I'll be back."

He's staring at the letter board. He's the only one who has so far. It says: **That's going to be your trouble—judgment about yourself.** It's totally appropriate for a gym and also happens to be a quote from *Tender is the Night,* about Dick Diver. I can't tell if he's offended. I didn't mean for it to be a message to him... I don't think.

"I know that quote," he says quietly.

He's pondering it too much. Change the subject. "Oh hey! It's after ten. I saved you a carrot cake muffin." I reach into my secret cupboard and then come out from behind the desk to give him his treat.

He smiles, a white-toothed, sparkly, crinkly-eyed smile as he accepts the muffin and a paper napkin. "Bless your heart."

"Well, I didn't want you fantasizing about how they'd taste and then feel let down." It's easier to flirt with him, now that I know that he can't possibly be interested in me. I lean my elbows behind me, on the desktop. My boobs just happen to be more pronounced and available for viewing now—that's not my fault; that's just how boobs work.

He glances down at them and then settles his gaze upon my baked good and takes a generous bite from the muffin top—not at all suggestively—and then closes his eyes, savoring it. The groan is deep and genuine and makes my heart flutter so much more than it should.

"Stella."

I love how he says my name, dammit.

"It's perfect. Thank you." Another bite. He really seems to like it.

"You're welcome." I watch his Adam's apple bob up and down, stare at my frosting on his lips, his long strong manicured fingers as they hold my muffin in front of his mouth.

I shake my head, clearing my throat. "So…what were you reading over there on the treadmill earlier? A script? You looked miserable."

He wipes a bit of frosting from the corner of his mouth and then sucks it off his fingertip. "For someone who's so uninterested in me, you're asking an awful lot of questions."

"I'm just making friendly conversation, but if you'd like to just stand there eating your muffin, go right ahead."

He swallows a laugh. "It was a script, yes. One that I hated and will most likely agree to commit to."

I wrinkle my brow. "Wait—you *will* agree to commit to? Even though you hated it? Why?"

"Because I have the same agent as the writer and director, and my involvement, believe it or not, means a lot of money for everyone else involved."

"But you don't want to get involved with it?"

"Not really, no. Especially after seeing the movie last night. I'd much rather hold out for a project I'm really excited about."

I shrug. "So don't do it."

He sighs. "It's not that simple."

"Why not? Because you don't want them to be mad

at you? My dad always says 'if you aren't pissing a few people off, you aren't doing it right.'"

His eyes suddenly get just a little bit shinier than usual and he smiles like I've just said the most brilliant thing anyone's ever said to him. "Well, *you* must be doing it right, then."

I smirk. "I like to think so."

"I have no doubt that you do."

He has demolished the muffin and looks around for a trash bin for the napkin and paper liner.

"I mean. Seriously, though. I know your decision affects a lot of other people and their careers and finances…"

"Exactly."

"But it's your career. It's your life. Why should you do something you don't want to do? Especially if you know you don't want to do it. The world doesn't need another crappy movie or another person who feels stuck doing things for other people."

At first, he seems stunned and speechless.

"Sorry. It's not my place. You're a big movie star, and I don't know what I'm talking about."

"No, it's not that at all. It's just that I usually get this sort of advice from people who are at least sixty. And when they give it, it doesn't usually make me want to…"

He blinks, shakes his head.

"Punch me in the face?"

"Again, quite the opposite. Point taken, Stella Starkey. You give me much to consider."

The gym phone rings, and I reach over the desk to

grab the receiver. "Starkey Fitness." Somebody wants to know about my brother's core-strengthening class.

Evan's still standing behind me. It feels like Mr. Hunter might be eye shagging me doggy-style. I quickly glance over my shoulder, and what do you know…he *is*. Only he doesn't blush when I catch him having his way with me with his eyes. Instead, he meets my gaze and confirms, wordlessly and unapologetically, that he was indeed having dirty thoughts about me.

I finish up the call and hang up the phone.

I really shouldn't look back at him again, because that would be some kind of continuation of a silent conversation that I have no intention of responding to.

He must be on the rebound.

He's probably just trying to mend his wounded ego after being dumped by that beautiful actress. I just happen to be the girl who's here at the moment. Like, literally the only single girl who's been here at the gym since he's been around.

Fuck it—I can't *not* look. I slowly turn to face him, and he has not looked away.

His expression is one hundred percent focused on me and filled with sexy sexiness, but still somehow appropriate for a gym setting. How can anyone look so clean while conveying such dirty thoughts?

He takes a breath and opens his pretty mouth, and just when I'm certain that he is about to whisper something so filthy it might make my knees give out, I hear a voice that is designed to keep my knees glued together: my dad's.

"Hey, honey! Ahhh, good to be back. Feels like I've been gone forever."

I clear my throat, and Evan's body language suddenly shifts from wordless dirty talk to proper English gentleman in the blink of an eye.

"Daddy, what are you doing here?"

"I feel great. Your magical soup cured me. Call Ted and tell him I'll lead my class today."

"Absolutely not, young man."

Evan turns to face my father, and I know that my dad recognized him even before he turned around.

"You must be the famous Richard Diver I keep hearing about. I'm Joe Starkey. We're happy to have you here."

"Oh, Mr. Starkey, what a pleasure."

My dad's hand reaches out toward Evan Hunter as Evan's reaches out for his, and everything slows down as I launch myself between them, yelling, "Don't touch him—he's contagious!"

Of course, I'm facing Evan, so as he lifts his hand away, it grazes the side of my boob. That is less mortifying to me than the realization that it was so important to me to protect this man from getting a cold—like the world would end if he got sick and couldn't train as hard as he needs to for the movie. He is not a world leader, and I am not his wife. What the hell?

Evan clears his throat, and my dad says "whoa!" and I can hear Billy laughing somewhere, of course.

I straighten up, step aside, and say, "He has a cold. Dad, our guest is preparing for a film. He doesn't need to get sick now."

"That's very thoughtful of you, honey."

"Yes, thank you. That's very considerate of you."

Silence.

"Okay. Let's all just acknowledge the fact that you accidentally touched my boob and get on with our lives, okay?"

"Good plan," says my dad.

"Obviously my life has been changed forever," Evan deadpans.

"All right all right."

"So has her boob's."

"Dad!"

Evan gives my dad a little salute and says, "Good to meet you, sir."

"The pleasure was all hers."

"Okay, just stop."

My dad and Evan are both grinning, and my brother is dying laughing over by the free weights like an ass. I go back behind the desk. I will never be a part of any boy's club or bromance, and it pisses me off more than it should, but I'm happy I was able to break the ice for them and now they'll have an inside joke that they can refer to forever.

Meanwhile, I'll keep standing here, frantically willing my nipples to stand down.

"I don't know if anyone's told you this," says my dad, who is thankfully unaware of everything that passed between his daughter and this man before he walked in, "but you're very charming."

"Thank you, sir. I don't know if anyone's told you this, but you have fantastic eyebrows."

"It has been said. Usually by my daughter."

And then my dad asks him how he works his transverse abs, and then they discuss intermittent fasting, and then I finally manage to get my dad to go home and back to bed.

Evan turns to face me, feet planted on the floor.

"Don't you have conference calls to get to?" I remind him.

He looks at me and smiles and doesn't say anything. Doesn't say something to make me feel dumb for being a spaz, doesn't say anything lecherous about touching my boob. Doesn't say one single thing that I'd expect from any other guy I've ever met.

And then he says something that I *really* don't expect from him: "I like you."

He continues to look me straight in the eyes and smile, until he's sure that I've heard what he's said, before turning and walking out the front door.

I have no idea what he's really going to do for the rest of the day, but I know that mine will be spent slowly realizing that he probably means it and that I like him too.

10

STELLA

*T*here's a kind of day in the Pacific Northwest—I don't know what meteorologists call it, and I'm sure the Native Indians have some beautiful term for it—where it's completely overcast and you can just feel the moisture in the air, and all this pressure is building but it doesn't rain. Part of you is like, "OH MY GOD JUST START RAINING ALREADY!" Part of you doesn't want it to start raining, because this time of year, once it starts it may never stop, and soon you won't even remember what it was like before everything came crashing down. That's how it feels between Evan and me now. The swelling pressure. The engorged tension. That's also how it feels in my lady bits. All. The. Time.

Evan Hunter has been here for one week, and I have spent one week trying mightily to deny my attraction to him. For the past six days, I've been coyly waving at Donovan the assistant location manager when I see him pass by outside the gym. And I've felt exactly zero flutters in my stomach when he grins back.

I have to admit I do enjoy this flirtation with Evan, if that's what it is. The super masculine guys I usually go for don't exactly flirt with me, and they definitely don't converse to such an extent with me. It's more like they stare me down until I'm ready to go back to their motel or Airbnb room, and then we have sex, and then we watch TV, and then I go home to my cat and a good book. I'm not complaining. My family and the gym and this town are all I need. But it's nice to have this kind of attention.

Word has gotten out around town that a movie star has been spotted on Main Street, but so far it seems people are keeping a polite distance. I haven't seen him quite as much the past few days. He has moved from the hotel to some secluded rental house, so he doesn't pop round as much.

Every minute spent in Evan's presence has become excruciating as I fight the exhilaration of feeling his gaze and hearing his voice and wondering if he makes every person he talks to feel like the center of his universe or if it's just me. I know the answer to that, of course. He's an actor. It's an act. But I get it now. I get why people like it. Every minute spent away from him, I see nothing but his bright blue eyes burning through me no matter where I look and hear his deep velvety voice echoing through my addled brain.

Evan Hunter has no idea that after I leave the gym, where I still play the part of a woman who is immune to his charms—the woman I used to be—I go home by myself to watch him on TV so I can stare at his face and listen to his voice without him realizing what it does to me. After Day Three, I totally caved and binge-watched every Evan Hunter film and limited BBC TV series that's available to stream on Netflix and Amazon.

I've never watched anything on screen where I knew one of the actors before. Unless you count the commercials that my brother's dog starred in. I've felt nervous and excited every time he was on screen. I've had a ridiculous smile on my face the whole time, and my whole body was vibrating. A rush. It's a rush! I don't know what it is about seeing someone on screen that makes them seem so much more crush-worthy. I even enjoyed watching the action *Hamlet* movie that I used to hate.

He wore so many beautiful suits in that movie. So not my thing, but he looks good in suits. Really good. Even better than he looks in fitness apparel.

I may also have watched approximately one hundred clips of his interviews on YouTube and video footage of hordes of young women losing their flipping minds at premieres of his films in Tokyo. Hunterhoes, his fans call themselves.

I mean.

I would never.

He's so charming and likable with everyone, it kind of makes me angry. I don't know if it's because I just don't have that switch that turns on the charm or the instinct to be charming with people. Or if it's because I hate that he makes me feel special when he's talking to me and now I know for sure that he does that with everyone and everyone—I mean *everyone*—falls for it. Billy is not the only guy with a man crush on him. Every late-night talk show host and interviewer seems to be positively smitten with this guy. Although...he's always a perfect gentleman with everyone on camera. Everyone says so in the written interviews.

While he's always polite and kind, with me—in private—he's sort of a naughty gentleman. I've never seen any hint of that in him with other people. It used to confuse me, but now it just makes me feel good.

Oh, did I mention I also read about fifty interviews? Not one of them mentioned hearing muttered dirty side comments that left them confused and wondering if they heard him properly or if they misread his intense gaze. But maybe it's a well-kept Hollywood secret?

Whatever it is, I'm convinced he's a warlock.

But that didn't stop me from seeking out my former English teacher Mrs. Greer—well, I didn't seek her out, but when I saw her at the grocery store, I asked her if I could borrow her copy of the *Romeo and Juliet* that he was in. Oh shit, 'twas that ever that a mistake. He was an impossibly beautiful teenager and so good at playing one who's ridiculously in love. That shameless show of eternal romantic love that had seemed so outrageous and unreal to me when I was a teenager who thought she was in love now seems so achingly real. But fleeting.

It's so much easier to fall in love with someone on screen. Even when that same person has been standing right in front of you. Maybe it's because on some level you know that what you're feeling for the person on screen isn't real, and if it isn't real then it can't hurt you.

And now, Billy has invited Evan Hunter along on a little family outing on our day off. It's the least sexy or romantic outdoor adventure imaginable, unless you're into watching Brad Pitt do it in *A River Runs Through It*: fishing.

While my dad takes my place as manager at the gym today and some excellent non-Starkey trainers teach our classes. Evan has enthusiastically agreed to join Billy, Kevin, Chet, and me on our last fishing trip of the year, because there will be a fishing boat scene in his movie. So it's research. He is a dedicated actor on location, and we are the locals who just happen to be helping him to get ripped and understand his character.

Billy, Kevin and Chet picked me up in Billy's SUV long before the butt crack of dawn, and now we're on our way to pick up Evan Hunter at the house he's renting. Billy is being all secretive about the address, which Evan wrote down on a piece of paper for him. Because Billy and Evan are bros, and Billy must protect his famous bro's privacy at all costs. *Puh-lease.* Like I'm going to post the address on Twitter or something. He's ridiculous. I'm just annoyed that Prince Fancysweatpants didn't give *me* the address so I can update our files.

That's my story and I'm stickin' to it.

We are only a few minutes' drive from downtown but in a sparsely populated residential area with large private properties that are surrounded by evergreens and nearby beach access. When Billy turns into a long, crushed-gravel driveway toward a two-level mid-century modern house, I realize that I know this property. This is one of my landlord's listings. He showed me the website for it when it first went on the market months ago, but due to its high asking price, it hasn't had many viewings. He leases it out for the owner on a week-to-week basis. I wonder if this is the house that I saw Whit and Brett leaving to clean that first day that Evan was here.

It's still dark out, and the small but exquisitely designed landscape in front is lit by accent spotlights and path lights. The front entrance light is on, and when Billy brings the SUV to a stop, we sit in silence for a moment.

"Well?" says Kevin, tilting his head back toward me from the passenger seat.

"Go get him," Billy says.

"Did you tell him we were on our way?"

"Yeah, he's ready. Go get him."

I shake my head as I unbuckle my seat belt.

I comb my fingers through my hair when I shut the car door, so my brothers can't see me primping, and walk up the curved stone path steps that lead up to the large front door. I can't see my brother's SUV from here. Most of the house seems to be geared toward views of the ocean and garden area. I hesitate, trying to decide whether I should knock or ring the doorbell, unzip my coat to expose just a little more of my sweater. Before I can make a decision, the door opens. And there he is.

He is far too handsome and pleasant at this godforsaken hour.

"Good morning, darling. Let me grab my things. Come in. Come see this house. It's fantastic."

"Oh, um…" Before I get the chance to protest, he takes me by the hand, leading me inside.

Half the house is floor-to-ceiling windows. Open-concept floor plan, polished stone and hardwood floors, exposed beam ceilings. But it's still somehow rustic and warmly inviting.

I could live here.

It's a surprising thought, since nobody's invited me to live here. I feel strangely at home anyway.

The house is sparsely furnished, but there are books and blankets and sweaters lying about. I can tell he's been using the fireplace, and for some reason this makes me happy. Glad that he knows how to use a wood fireplace. He may not look like a lumberjack, but I bet he'd go outside and chop wood for his lady to keep her hearth warm…

He gestures toward the windows at the rear of the house, the ones that would overlook the beach. "I wish it were lighter out so you could see the view of the water. It's really stunning."

I point down to the twinkling lights of the marina. "That's where our boat's docked." I point out toward a channel in Puget Sound that's just offshore. "That's where we'll be heading...for the winter Blackmouth." I'll leave the sexy talk of tidal flows and "mooching" to my brothers.

He is standing so close to me. His arm brushes against my shoulder. I can barely feel anything through my puffy waist-length coat, and yet it sends a shiver of delight all through me.

"I was half hoping you'd wear your sexy sailor outfit today." He continues to look out the window. "We *are* going out on a boat, after all."

"Yeah. With two of my brothers. Who have threatened to destroy many boys' lives just for saying 'hi' to me, so you should probably take it down a notch or twenty."

"I vow to be on my best behavior all day."

"Well, I guess now we're both a little disappointed," says some quiet husky voice that sounds an awful lot like mine.

Suddenly, his hand is in my hair, one hand on my waist, and he's turning me to face him.

"Can't have *that* now..." he whispers as he leans down, pulling me to him. It seems to take forever for his lips to reach mine, but once our mouths touch, it's like remembering a dream kiss—familiar and comforting.

"I do think about you an awful lot, you know." I feel his breath on my cheek, and hearing his deep, soothing voice so close to my ears just might be the death of me.

"Hmmm."

"If you don't think about me that way, I'll never touch you again. Just say the word."

I don't say the word. I can't say any words. What are words again?

After three seconds of me staring up at him with fluttering eyelashes and the sound of my heartbeat echoing around the room, he takes my face in his formidable hands and kisses me again. His mouth is hungrier this time, his tongue parting my lips and teasing mine until I respond by grabbing his jacket and sucking on his tongue. He groans, and in one second he has lifted me up by my ass, my legs wrap around his waist, and he's pressing me up against the window.

I gasp for air as he kisses my neck. "You call this your best behavior?"

"*You* tell *me*..."

My back instinctively arches and my head falls back because apparently I no longer have bones in my neck. They have melted beneath his hot tongue. The combination of his voice and lips against my skin is more than I can handle. But I want to handle him. My hands want to reach down into his jeans and handle that firm bulge that has haunted me ever since the movie theater. But now is not the time for that. Now is the time for me to know what it feels like to run my fingers through his floppy blond hair and kiss that mouth that has kissed fair Juliet Capulet, and now for some strange wonderful reason, it's kissing a sassy small-town girl named—Me.

"I have no complaints so far..."

He squeezes my ass, and my legs tighten around him. Every single part of me just wants him inside of me. Except for my brain and my heart.

He gently bites my lower lip and then he pulls away. "I love everything that comes out of your mouth, darling, but I really am dying to fuck you so long and hard you're too exhausted to speak."

"Oh shit," I whisper. "I want that too."

Our lips smash together again, and my hands have found their way under his coat.

"We have to go."

"That is very inconvenient," he breathes.

"We have to."

I kiss him one last time. He kisses me back with less fervor, trying to calm down, but my mouth can't seem to stay away from his mouth now.

"*You* are very inconvenient."

I pull my head back. "Sorry." He slowly lets me down, and I put my hands on his chest to push him away. "I didn't mean to be."

"Well, I did."

"That was—we can't—we need to go."

"Have dinner with me," he says. His voice is so sexy, I should probably wear some form of birth control on my ears.

"I haven't even had breakfast yet."

"Tonight."

"I don't think so."

He looks as though he was expecting me to decline the invitation.

I straighten myself up and head for the front door.

"Wrong way, unless you're headed for the bedroom."

I stop in my tracks and turn to my right. His hands

are on his hips as he controls his breathing, shaking his head. He runs one hand through his hair. "Stella Starkey" is all he says, and part of me very much wants to tear off my clothes and run to that bedroom. The other part of me wants to run out the front door and yell at my brother to drive away as fast as he can—head for the border; we gotta lose this guy! He just kissed me after telling me he'd behave himself! Who does that Brit think he is?

But I do neither of those things. I smooth down my hair with one hand while calmly walking toward the front door, zipping up my coat, and I say in my most polite voice possible, "Should be a nice day, but we have to get out on the water before sunrise."

"Right behind you," he says in a way that might be totally innocent and might mean he's going to take me from behind.

I just can't tell with this fellow.

When I'm outside, I see Billy fussing around with things in the back seat. He looks back at me like I've caught him red-handed, but I have no idea what he's up to. Kevin has Chet on the leash and starts pulling him away from a tree trunk that must smell amazing.

I just climbed Evan Hunter like a tree, and he smells amazing too.

I am walking a little too fast and keeping my face a little too expressionless. Both my brothers are studying my face.

"Shut up," I hiss.

They both laugh.

"Good morning, gents," Evan says, from behind me.

"There he is!" Billy is so happy to see him, it's embarrassing.

Evan one arm bro-hugs with both of my brothers and nods at me as if he's greeting me for the first time today.

"So, if it's okay with you, Ev, Chet's gonna be up front with Kevin, and the fishing gear's in the trunk, but the back seat's kind of full with rain gear and the cooler, so would you mind if my sister sits on your lap? It's a short drive."

"Oh, I think we'll manage if it's a short drive, sure," he says.

My brother has rearranged things in the back seat since I went into the house. What. A. Dork.

"Don't crush the cookies," he says to me pointedly.

I look down and see the box of giant Costco chocolate chunk cookies. Billy is watching me through the rearview mirror, his body trembling from holding in laughter. *Idiot.*

After a lifetime of cockblocking every local boy who's come near me, my brothers are all of a sudden trying to pimp me out—to a British movie star, no less. I've always known they were crazy, but this makes no sense on any level. The only thing crazier than their belief that I should be spending time with this fellow is *his*. If that kiss was any indication, he genuinely seems to want to shag me.

Evan wraps his arms around me after buckling the seat belt around himself, since it won't fit around both of our puffy coats. Evan's Union Jack is currently at half-staff and my All-American undies are half-soaked, and this little family fishing show is going from PG-13 to rated R pretty fast.

Billy drives around the circular driveway, back out to the road.

"So this is my dog Chet—the actor!"

"Hello, Chet."

"You can shake hands with him! Shake a paw, Chet! G'boy!"

Evan shakes paws with Chet across the front seat and leans in so Chet can lick his face.

Evan's face is getting a lot of action this morning and the sun hasn't even risen yet.

"Don't forget to give him acting tips."

"How could I? Well, Chet," he says, very seriously, to the Labradoodle in the front seat, "when acting for the camera, it's quite simple really: always hit your marks and tell the truth. Be punctual. Know your lines...and don't bite the hand that feeds you."

Chet barks in agreement, and now my brother Martin is the only Starkey left for this Brit to conquer.

I may have to amend my statement about fishing not being a sexy or romantic activity. The sun is rising over Puget Sound, the waves gently lap against the side of our boat. We have a view of the lighthouse. My mellow Pearl Jam playlist quietly plays from my Bluetooth speaker, and as Evan Hunter glances back at me while reeling in a fighter, I fear *I* may be the one who's on the hook.

It turns out watching a beautiful, well-groomed man work a banana weight, herring bait, and tandem hook while muttering "Come on, you fucker, you're mine now," with an English accent is actually quite arousing.

If I had a salmon for every time he and I have exchanged hot looks while my brothers weren't paying attention, we'd have a full icebox.

Evan seems genuinely impressed by our boat, and it is a source of family pride. It's a forty-foot convertible sport fishing boat that comfortably sleeps six, uncomfortably sleeps seven, and has a full galley and salon. It's called Cora's Delight, and it did delight my mother. Every time we come out on it, I bring a little bouquet of whatever's in season in her honor. She and my dad used to have date nights on this boat when we were younger. For the past few years, my dad has spent nights alone at the marina. We all feel as close to her on this boat as we do at the house. But I'm not going to mention this to Evan. When he asked about the name, I just said it's named for my mom and that was that. He didn't push it.

We aren't too far offshore, where the water's about ninety feet deep. I myself am not fishing, as I very hypocritically enjoy eating fish but refuse to catch and kill them because it's mean and gross. My duties include DJ-ing and making sure Chet doesn't jump into the water or make too much noise. Meanwhile, Billy and Kevin and Evan Hunter are drinking beer for breakfast and quietly bro-ing out while holding their rods.

I guess it's a cheat meal for Evan. He seems to be throwing all caution to the wind this morning. I wish I didn't like it so much.

My stoic brother Kevin, whom I have seen smile perhaps ten times in my entire life and goof around maybe twice, stands behind Evan Hunter, grinning at me. He's pointing at Evan, and mouthing, *He likes you!* And then he winks. And then he mouths the words, *He wants to nail you so hard*, while thrusting his hips back and forth and miming spanks.

This continues while I remain expressionless and notice that Evan is staring at something behind me. I turn my head to confirm that he is watching Kevin's reflection in a window. I look back at him. Evan gazes down at me. He doesn't give my brother shit, and he doesn't waggle his eyebrows at me. He just watches me until I cannot take it anymore.

That's when I bring Chet with me inside.

I'm in the short narrow hallway, coming out of the head, when Evan steps into the hallway, blocking me. Wordlessly, he stares down at me, takes one more step closer so there is no space between us. I shift to the side so he can pass, and as he does, his whole body brushes against mine. This tiny little dance is enough to make me gasp, and my knees actually give out. His hands brace me immediately.

"You all right?"

"Yeah… Waves."

"Yes. Waves."

11

EVAN

*W*ell, this is the life. I haven't felt as relaxed as I have this past week for... more than two decades? Is that possible? Since before I graduated from acting academy. Always working, always meeting people. Always on my best behavior with the people I meet, even when it's like talking to a cardboard cutout of a human being. It's exhausting. I've been sleeping so soundly and waking up excited each morning, knowing I'll have the chance to see Stella. Except *this* morning, actually—it's that feeling of the day before the school year starts.

My stunt trainer is getting into town today. Beginning tomorrow, for five days, I'll be spending five hours a day with him at the gym. Soon there will be wardrobe fittings and makeup and lighting tests. The director will want to hang out when he's here next week. The other actors will be here. I'll have to start doing press again. My publicist keeps nudging me to Tweet or Instagram so people know that I'm happily getting on with my life, but I don't want the world to intrude upon my happiness yet.

The echoes of Chet's barking keep me from slipping into the state of mild anxiety that usually precedes a film shoot. Stella has re-emerged with the dog and is trying to dampen his excitement just as she tries to dampen mine. I hope she has more luck with the Labradoodle. I have no intention of giving up on her.

As for her wonderful brothers, we get on so well, it's only a matter of time and a few more beers before we start humping each other's legs. They've been very understanding about not posting pictures of me with the fish I've caught, but the photo that Stella took of the three of us guys holding up our fresh catch is now the home screen image on my phone.

While Stella crouches on deck, holding Chet's leash and trying to keep him from noticing the sea otters that are swimming by, Kevin and Billy start asking me first date questions.

"You got brothers or sisters?"

"Neither, unfortunately. Only child. Fair number of cousins, though. I've always loved being around other people's families."

"Yeah, we're awesome to be around." Billy laughs at his dumb joke.

"You are, in fact."

"Enh. Some days are better than others. Your parents back in Jolly Old England?"

"Yes. Well, they've always been based in London. But they both travel quite a lot. Since before they had me. I think they're both in different parts of the world right now, actually."

"Oh, they aren't together?"

"No they are, very much so, but their work often keeps them apart. My father's a cultural anthropologist, and my mum's an art historian. They're always off to foreign lands for research projects when they're on sabbatical. It used to be a lot of fieldwork, or giving presentations at conferences, when I was growing up."

"Like where?" asks Kevin, the quiet one.

I don't need to tell them how many times I was the new boy in school. They don't need to know that's why I have this annoying need and facility for being liked by everyone. I don't need to explain this to Stella because I have a feeling she can figure all that out for herself. "Well, my mother's all over Europe, but my dad's interested in coastal societies all over the world."

"He should study us!" Billy laughs.

"I think he'd love it here, actually." I glance over at Stella, who is doing a very good job of looking like she isn't listening to this conversation at all. But I see how her body shifts when I mention my dad liking it here. I see how her head tilts, like she's sifting through the information she's just received, categorizing and analyzing it. It doesn't even make me uncomfortable. She finally turns to face me, slow blinking like a cat who's giving me her blessing.

"Sounds like a fancy family," says Billy.

I won't mention that the reason they could afford a life in academia is because my father's family is filthy rich. "Not necessarily. I mean, my parents are academics. But from my grandparents' generation on back, on my mother's side, it's mostly the blue-collar sort, as you'd call it here. Fishermen in Cornwall, for example."

"So that's how you know how to fish like a boss?"

"It is. My grandad used to take me angling. Sadly, his arthritis prevents it now."

"That and the fact that you're a big-time movie star."

"I don't think being a big-time movie star necessarily prevents me from doing anything." I make sure Stella hears this. "It just prevents a lot of people from expecting me to be interested in certain things, like fishing. Which is why I really appreciate you inviting me along."

Right on cue, Chet starts barking at the otters and Stella takes him inside to the salon.

"You get to see your parents much?" Kevin asks.

"Not as much as I'd like. We're all busy, but we Skype regularly and I bring my mum as my date to premieres whenever she's available."

"That's cool. That's nice." Billy stares out at the water for a bit before continuing. "Our mom died back when I was in high school. Stella had just graduated."

"I am so sorry. I had no idea."

"Yeah, well. Stella wouldn't have told you. She barely talks about it with people. It was a car accident. Right around this time of year. She went instantly, or so we were told, so…"

"That must have been very hard on the family."

"It wasn't easy," Kevin says. "But we got through it. Thanks to Stella, mostly. I mean, it was probably hardest on her and my dad, but she took care of him in a way that we never could. All of us, really."

"She's a nice lady, at the end of the day. Believe it or not." Billy gives me a side-glance before taking a swig of his beer.

"I believe it."

"Hey, you want a cookie? They're really good. A little *too* good, according to some people."

I stare at the box of enormous biscuits. Everything's so much bigger in America, including my appetite when I'm here. My appetite for all things, including sex and cookies. "I do want one, thanks."

I don't want to jump the gun or anything, but it seems I have the blessing of the Starkey men when it comes to their sister. The ones I've met, anyway. Between myself and The Kwas, I'm the better option for now, I suppose.

Returning from the head again, I take a seat in the salon to say hello to Chet. Stella is reading a book and eating an apple. I sit here, nuzzling the dog's neck and staring over at her until she's ready to acknowledge my presence.

"Have dinner with me."

"Where?"

"Wherever you'd like to. It's my last night before I start training with my stunt coordinator, and I want to spend it with you."

"I'm sure you can find something better to do. Or *someone* better to do."

"Are you? Because I'm sure I haven't. And I'm quite sure I won't."

When she's chewed that apple down to the core, she stands up, still holding the book, and she glances down at me as she walks past to toss the core into the bin.

"I keep forgetting to tell you," I say, changing the subject and keeping my attention on Chet, "that I did end up passing on that project that I hated."

"Really? Good for you. And look at that—the world hasn't ended." She comes back round and takes a seat next to me. "Was your agent mad?"

"Actually, he apologized for sending me that crap. He knew it was shit. It was fine. Then two days later I saw in the trades that the same project got a green light with James McAvoy attached instead of me."

She scrunches up her face. "Who?"

"Bless you for that." At least I'm not the only UK actor she doesn't give a shit about. "Do you already have plans for tonight?"

She fixes me with one of her analytical stares and finally asks, "Are you rebounding from being dumped? Because if that's what this is—"

"I don't know. I've never rebounded from being dumped before. And I've never felt so drawn to a woman the way I'm drawn to you."

"Is that a line?"

"No. Somehow the God's honest truth about how I feel about you always sounds like a line. I don't know what that means. I don't know if I'm attracted to you because I'm not dealing with something else. I just know that I'm really fucking attracted to you. Georgia and I were only a superficial couple. I mean, we did have an on-set romance; we had great onscreen chemistry. We worked well together as actors, and the rush of the initial romance lingered for about five minutes after the wrap party. But you never want to admit that it was just a set flirtation, so you keep going. You try to make it work. She was my girlfriend for about six months, but we barely saw each other in the last month or so. I don't know what else to tell you other than to reiterate that I'm really fucking attracted to you."

She blows out a breath, and I feel I've inched toward my goal.

"Come to dinner with me."

"You mean at the house you're staying in?"

"If you so desire."

"I do not desire so."

"A local restaurant of your choice, then."

"You don't really want to go to a restaurant with me, do you?"

"Well, no, if I'm being honest."

"Because you don't want to be seen and photographed alone in public with me."

"Because I'd like to wine and dine you as close to a bed as possible. To save time."

She laughs. Thank goodness. But she still shakes her head.

I remember the phone conversation I overheard that first time I walked into the gym. "Oh that's right—you don't eat with gym members, do you? Company policy? Well, my membership is limited anyway, and I don't know if you've heard, but life is short. When a pretty boy English film star invites you to dinner, you should take him up on his offer because it might be the last."

"Okay. I'll be sure to let Jude Law know that I changed my mind."

"Psshh. I've had dinner with Jude Law. There's nothing pretty about the way he eats."

"Well good. I'm not into pretty."

I lean in and whisper in her ear, "I think you're getting into it."

"I don't think either of us really wants to get into it in a restaurant." She bites her lip and runs her fingers through her hair while letting her eyes trail down my body—God help me. "However," she says, voice barely above a whisper, "I will see you tonight."

"The great American cut-to-the-chase. Thank you. I'll order in." I type something into my phone before handing it to her. "Here's my current disposable mobile phone. Add your number."

The contact name I've set for her is **Sassy AmericanGirl**.

"It makes me sound like a doll or some Korean romantic comedy movie on Netflix, but I'll take it." She adds some numbers, returns my phone to me.

I immediately send a text to that number, but I don't write what I really want to say, until I can confirm that she did in fact give me her real number.

Her phone vibrates in her pocket, which pleases me.

She rolls her eyes when she sees my text, which simply says: **Hello, darling.**

I watch as she adds my number to her contacts and

types in words that are clearly not "Evan Hunter" or "Richard Diver."

She tilts her phone so I can see the screen, and I burst out laughing when I read: **Randy BritishActor**.

"That's me," I say. "But only when it comes to you."

"Sure."

"It's true. More than ever when it comes to you, it seems."

We both check to make sure her brothers aren't listening or in some way concerned by the fact that she and I are alone together in here. They certainly don't appear to be. In fact, I'd be willing to bet that they're both rooting for us to get together. If they only knew what filthy thoughts I've had of their only sister... Sometimes it really does come in handy, being English. There is currently only one person in America who has even the faintest idea of what a "horndog" I am, but it's all thanks to her.

"We should be heading back to the marina soon," she says. We are speaking in hushed tones, and it only adds to the sexual tension. "When would you like me to arrive at your house?"

"Well, I'm intermittent fasting, so I have to finish eating by seven—food, that is." I try to stifle a laugh, but even I can't pull off a line like that.

She nudges me and bursts out laughing.

"I'm so sorry about your mother" is what I really want to say. What I've wanted to say for a while. But something tells me she doesn't want to hear it unless she's told me about it herself, and something tells me she

won't be open to having that conversation with me for quite some time. I'll wait.

I can't wait much longer to part those shapely legs and shag the living daylights out of her, but I'll wait patiently for her to open up to me in other ways.

12

STELLA

$\mathcal{O}$kay, so Pretty Boy can charm my socks off *and* dirty talk my panties off. Big deal. Obviously, the only way for me to prove to him that I'm immune to this British actor nonsense is by sleeping with him.

I'm going to prove it to him so hard.

Just one time, and then we're out of each other's systems. He'll move on. I'll move on. But this is probably the only time in my life that I'm going to have dinner and sex with a movie star...so why not enjoy it? I'll have an exciting and totally inappropriate story to tell my grandkids one day when I'm drunk on schnapps.

Surprisingly, I am not even nervous. Even more surprisingly, I am excited. I can't wait to get this over with. Let it rain!

I will eat that enormous chocolate chunk cookie. I will eat one whole impossibly charming cookie until I'm sick of it. And then I won't want another bite, and then that box of overwhelming cookies will go back to

England or wherever, and it won't matter if I start to crave it or not. It will be gone. Because that's how the cookie crumbles. Even the unbearably moist and chewy ones.

I have a feeling I will be dealing with a level of manscaping heretofore unknown, so I've spent an unprecedented hour getting ready for this...*whatever*... and I have brought my A game. I will also be bringing the food. He offered to cook salmon, but I'd rather he didn't handle any more fish today prior to handling me. I insisted on picking up dinner on my way to his house so he wouldn't have to give out his credit card info and address. He put up a good fight and insisted on repaying me immediately "in every way possible."

Puh-lease.

But also, yes please and he'd better.

"You look pretty tonight!" says Mrs. Wang at the Golden Panda. "Order for two—you got a date, huh? Lemme guess. Kwas?"

"No!" Oh my God, how does Mrs. Wang know about the Kwas incident? "Definitely not Kwas."

"Out of town man? The usual for you, right?"

"Out of town, yes. Usual? Not exactly." I am trying so hard not to smile, my face is sore. I am dying to tell her that Evan Hunter will be eating Golden Panda's Chef Special tonight, but I can't. Or I won't. He and I haven't discussed it, but if he wanted to be incognito at the gym, surely he prefers to be discreet in matters of the bedroom too. I always do.

As I pull up and park in the driveway behind his rental car, somehow bringing "takeaway" Chinese food to share with him feels so domestic and cozy, and I get this weird vision of me doing this on a regular basis.

I carry my coat over one arm and the plastic bags in the other. It's not very cold yet, and I want his first impression tonight to be of me in this outfit instead of a puffy coat. I'm wearing a tight-fitting sweater dress that hits midthigh, bare legs, and black knee-high boots with over-the-knee socks.

"This is just one night," I tell myself as I walk up the steps to his front door, and—fuck me—the door is open and he's gripping the doorframe with one hand; the other is casually rubbing his abs under his charcoal gray t-shirt. He's barefoot, wearing black jeans without a belt, and he looks recently showered and hungry and hot. He looks so fucking hot I almost turn and run away because I may have underestimated just how big and delicious a cookie he is.

"Hi," he says, so serious I wonder for a second if he's in a bad mood.

"Hi."

He looks at me with that panty-melting intensity that I had imagined possible the first time I saw him running at the beach. I just hadn't imagined that he would ever actually make *my* panties melt. I just didn't see myself standing at the entrance of his rental home while holding bags of Chinese food in my hands and a life-threatening amount of tension in my lady parts.

"Bloody hell," he mutters to himself. "Gorgeous. You're a proper dish, Stella Starkey. Get in here, will you?" He takes the coat from me and gracefully hangs it up, somehow managing to never take his eyes off me.

I've been undressed by a man's eyes before, but they usually seem to just rip my clothes off. Evan Hunter's eyes are slowly unwrapping me, layer by layer, until I am so far beyond naked, all that's left is the sad lonely soul who lives deep inside those layers. The one who will never admit that she needs a mate. The one who knew as soon as she saw him that he threatened to do just this—peel away the layers. The one who will stop fighting the good fight for one night.

I'm starting to regret the decision to wear a tight sweater dress, because—warmth. My entire being just got warmer. The way he's looking at me is making me perspire. It's not like when we're at the gym— that's my turf. It's not like this morning, when I knew my brothers were outside and we had to get going. I'm alone with him in his space right now, but I feel like he is all up in mine, even though he's standing five feet away from me. He studies the length of my legs, as if he's trying to decide what he wants to do with them first. When he notices me squeezing my thighs together, he smirks and magically becomes the polite gentlemanly host anyone would expect him to be.

"Sorry. Let me take those bags from you." He steps forward, letting his fingers tangle with mine as he takes the plastic bag handles from me. "Smells good. What are we having? I hope you kept the receipt so I can pay you back." He carries our dinner to the kitchen counter. "Actually," he continues, "I don't have small bills, so I'll just give you this fifty and we'll call it even. Delivery charge and all that."

He pulls a folded-up fifty-dollar bill from his pocket and holds it out to me.

I take it and shove it into my purse without arguing. He won't have to struggle with me tonight. I place my purse on the dining table and walk over to the window that looks out toward the water, while he starts to unpack dinner. The fact that he hasn't kissed me upon arrival leads me to believe that he needs to restrain himself in this situation, and I'm glad. I like that.

Every room is dimly lit and amber-hued. I can hear music from another room—classical. Of course. I don't know why it hadn't occurred to me before—Evan Hunter is obviously a vampire and he has invited me here to feast upon me. And I am fine with that. What a way to go!

"I wish I could have gotten you here a bit earlier," he says, almost cheerily, "before the sun went down. I really want you to see that view."

"I've seen it online, to be honest."

"Oh?"

I touch the window, right about where he had me held up against it this morning, right about where I somehow managed to not grab his perfectly sculpted ass.

"Yeah, my landlord Whit is the realtor who listed this place. I saw the listing online when it first went up."

"Is that so? What a coincidence."

"Not really. He's got all the best listings in town."

"Oh really? I am very fond of this one. Red wine?"

"Please." I startle at the small sound of the cork popping out of the bottle. I am so jealous of that wine bottle because I can't wait much longer for the pressure that's been building inside me to be released.

"My agent had a few bottles delivered—pinot noir from Sonoma. Hope it's good. And to your liking."

God, I love how he says "pinot noir." I love how he says "good" and "your." I can't believe it used to make me laugh, the way he says things, because now it just turns me right on.

"We'll let it breathe a bit."

That voice.

That accent.

I. Get. It.

Boy, do I get why his fans like it now.

Soothing, like a cup of chamomile tea, but dirty like someone spiked it with whiskey. He could read the lyrics to Lil Wayne's "Pussy Monster" on NPR on a Sunday morning, make it sound like he's doing a Jane Austen reading, and there wouldn't be a dry pair of panties in America. Maybe every actor from the UK has that superpower, but I bet not that many can back it up with the kind of lip and tongue action that Evan Hunter can.

I had every intention of letting him wine and dine me, but there is no way I will be able to eat dinner right now.

I turn around, leaning back against the window.

He places two wineglasses on the counter and regards me, tilting his head, knowing exactly what I'm thinking. He rests his hands against the counter, leaning forward, watching my hands as they pull down the hem of my sweater dress and then slowly graze my outer thighs and hips on their way behind my back to press against the windowpane. I don't know how I'm able to hold his gaze as he walks toward me, but as soon as he reaches me and places his hands on my hips, I exhale and go slightly limp because his touch makes me feel so weak. My body has absolutely no more desire to resist him.

He pulls my hips up toward his as he kisses me gently and excruciatingly slowly. One hand reaches for my face, his thumb tracing my lower lip. My eyelids flutter open to find him staring down at my mouth, contemplating it. To prevent myself from whimpering, I turn my head to kiss the palm of his hand. He caresses my hip and ass while the other hand makes its way from my jaw, down my neck, my collarbone, opening up over my breast and continuing down to the hem of the dress. All the while he's studying my face, as I tremble from head to toe. Even as his fingers slip between my legs to find that my underthings are drenched.

"Fucking hell," he exhales, and with one swift motion he lifts the sweater dress up over my head and stares down at me in my white lace bra and panties and my over-the-knee socks and boots.

I reach for his T-shirt, and he lets me lift it up over his head. I drag my fingertips down his pecs and abs, and just as I am about to take hold of that tantalizing bulge in his jeans, he lifts me up in his arms and carries me over to the sofa that faces the window, depositing me so that I'm seated. He says, "Spread your legs," and I do. He lowers himself between them, kneeling on the rug, staring at the strips of lace around my hips and the little triangle of cotton—-a mere suggestion of underwear, really. He rips the lace on either side of my hips and, before I can protest, states that he'll buy me a new pair. Pulls my hips forward, hooks his arms under my thighs, grabbing hold of my ass, and just buries his face between my legs like he's moving in.

I grab on to the back of the sofa behind myself, nearly passing out because the warmth of his tongue between my folds feels better than pretty much anything I've ever felt...until he flicks at my clit with the tip of his tongue and then sucks on it.

"You taste even sweeter than I imagined you would, Stella." His hot breath on my vulva is what will surely kill me.

My back keeps arching and I keep pulling away from him, because...the swirling and the thrusting and the sucking—"It's too much!" I find myself gasping out loud.

He yanks me in closer.

"We can do other stuff now if you want," I whimper as I try to wriggle away again. This feels like the first time, all of a sudden, maybe because this *is* the first time someone has put this much effort into pleasuring me.

"I'm not stopping until you come all over my face and scream my name, and then, I assure you, we will do the 'other stuff,' my dear."

He licks my inner thigh, all the way back up to the most girl part of me, as he lifts my legs to rest over his shoulders. The heels of my boots dig into his back, and he seems to like it. I relax into the sofa, grab fistfuls of his hair, and let the orgasm shudder and wave and then rip through me until I do just as he said I would. I scream and whisper his name until I am nothing but a spineless mass of post-orgasmic skin and bones.

He wipes his mouth with the back of his hand, lifts himself up to kiss me. And then he lifts up one of my legs, then the other, as he unzips and removes my boots. He carefully pulls down my socks. Oh shit, he's going to undress the rest of me slowly now, and we've only just begun.

His usually shiny blue eyes are so hooded, so bleary and clouded over with lust. Now *this* is something you never see on screen. Nostrils flared, every muscle of his body tense. I suddenly have just enough energy to reach for his jeans, unbutton and unzip them, and pull them down along with his boxers to release a monumental, jaunty erection. It is just as tall, handsome, and surprisingly naughty as he is. I wrap one hand around the shaft of it and lick the tip just once. He groans so beautifully and then drops down on the sofa beside me. Lifting me up and around to straddle him, he unhooks my bra.

"At long last," he mutters, massaging one breast and then taking the nipple in his mouth.

The fingernails of his other hand drag down the skin of my back, lightly enough not to hurt, surprising enough to send a shockwave through my center. I place my hands on his knees, lean back and let him feast.

What a way to go.

Hot damn.

Evan Hunter isn't just a movie star.

He's a sex god.

And I am in so much trouble.

13

EVAN

"*I*t's not after seven yet," she teases. "Still time to eat *food* before you enter the fasting phase."

I'm still catching my breath, collapsed on the bed, on my back and covered in sweat. "I think we've already burned about a thousand calories between the two of us."

"Well, I do consider myself a part of the team that's whipping you into shape."

"You'd better not do this for all your gym members."

She pauses for a moment before sitting up and replying. "You are the first. Don't let it go to your head."

I tug at the sheet she's holding loosely around her chest.

She lets it fall, revealing her swollen breasts, skin all pink from so much sucking and friction. And, ahem, perhaps one or two playful bite marks for good measure.

"Very little has been going to my head since you began mauling me, I assure you."

I reach out to brush my thumb back and forth across her left nipple. It hardens so quickly, despite her meek protest.

"I did not maul you." She trembles at my touch, smirking nonetheless. "Get over yourself."

"Get under myself."

And…cue exaggerated eye roll.

She is so ready for more, and I am right there with her.

She is so responsive, and it is such a turn-on.

"Get over here, gorgeous." She complies so readily to my whispered command. After all that resistance, she seems to have made a decision to give herself to me completely tonight. Her body, at least. And I couldn't have directed the scenes better, the way she both wanted me and hesitated so deliciously at the same time when she first came over and then opened up in a way that surpassed my expectations.

I squeeze that gorgeous breast, and all I know is…I do want to be a good host, but dinner will have to wait because the only thing I want in my mouth right now is that nipple. I pull her to me, and she sighs as she strad-dles my waist, offering herself to me and my hungry hands and tongue. I need to make her moan and call out my name again. Absolutely everything else will have to wait.

It's been just over an hour, and I've already had her riding my cock on the sofa, her tits bouncing glori-ously before and against me. I've bent her over the back of the sofa and taken her from behind, holding on to her beautiful round hips while drilling her. In bed, she brought my Dick Diver back to life with some epic licking and sucking, and then I spun her around on top of me so we could pleasure each other at the same time. It was obviously the first time *that* had ever happened to her, but she proceeded like a damn courtesan until we both came noisily and relentlessly in each other's mouths.

She has made it clear to me that I could have her any way I want her, and I will take her every which way eventually... But now I just want to be on top of her, to press myself inside her and stay there for as long as I can. Because this feels good and right and sweet and hot.

She tears open a condom and rolls it onto me, like she's carefully wrapping a gift for both of us. I've never been with a woman who seems to enjoy doing that quite so much. She squeezes the base of my shaft with her confident fingers, slides her other soft hand down to cup my balls, as if she's just checking in with them, and fuck yeah, this is by far the best first date I've ever had.

She makes herself comfortable against the pillows as I position myself above her. We're already so at ease with each other; it's difficult to believe there was ever a time when we weren't naked together like this. I prop myself up on one hand, drag the fingers of the other down my tongue—the taste of her on my skin—to wet them before placing them between her legs. Her eyes squeeze shut and then open again as she gives me a look, like: *"Yeah, that wasn't necessary, but thanks."* She is always wet for me, it seems.

I do like this view. Staring down at those big brown eyes. Her expression's somehow vulnerable and lusty, and God help me, it makes me want to take care of her and do dirty, filthy things with her.

I hold my breath so I can hear the satisfying gasp she makes as I enter her and keep pressing until I can go no farther. When I rest my forearms on either side of her, she grabs on to my shoulders, slowly rocking her hips to let me know that she's ready for me to proceed.

She is so tight and warm and wet and willing; it takes everything I've got not to explode five seconds after I'm inside her. But I don't. I lower myself down to kiss her. She sucks on my tongue and bites my lower lip, and I pull away so I can angle myself deeper into her and make her cry out in surprise, "Oh shit!" There is no pretense with this one. She isn't worrying about how she looks from certain angles. She's just a gorgeous woman who likes sex, it seems.

"You like how I'm fucking you," I growl.

"Yes, I like it," she hisses. She curls her legs tighter around mine, and her arms snake through mine, clinging to my upper back so she can bear down on me while I thrust harder and harder. "You fuck those pretty starlets like this?"

Well now, isn't she just full of surprises... "Only you, darling. Only you get fucked like this."

"Why?" she sighs. "Why me?"

"Because..." My throat is so tight. It's hard to talk,

but all those voice lessons really pay off at times like this. "Because you turn me on, Stella Starkey. Because you want *me* to fuck you, not some idea of me."

"Yeah," she says, her voice soft and girlish. "I do." She wriggles around beneath me and performs the most brilliant close-up magic trick I've ever experienced, because suddenly her legs are straight up in the air and resting against my shoulders.

Fuck yeah, yoga.

"I want you to fuck me harder."

I grab on to the bed frame for support so I can do just that.

"At your service, madam," I grunt, plowing into her, delighting in the little sounds of pain and pleasure that escape her lips.

"Say it," she says, clawing at my skin.

"What?"

She shakes her head, sounding a little bit delirious. "Anything. Everything. Don't hold back."

Christ.

Welp. Better represent England as best I can… Here goes… "Your pussy is so hot and wet and tight around my cock."

"Yes."

"That's just for me?"

"Only you."

"You like it when I fuck you hard and fast?"

"Yeah."

"Yeah you do. This what you meant when you said to 'drop the act'?"

"Oh yes!"

"How'd you like my fancy accent now?"

She cries out, jolts and shudders and bucks around, unable to respond with words, and I have my answer.

"That's what I thought. You want me to fuck you with my voice or my cock?"

"Both," she whimpers. "I want to hear you come inside me again."

"That's what you want?"

"Yeah."

"That's what you wanted all along, isn't it?"

"Yes. Evan. Yes."

Somehow, I manage to delay my orgasm until after she screams my name one more time, holding me so tight. It's so fucking hot, and I let loose a deep, animal sound, releasing so much of myself that it's difficult to believe there will be anything left of me when I'm done.

But there is.

More than ever.

And I'm all hers.

So much so that it should scare me, but it doesn't.

And I think I know how much it scares her, but I will help her get over it like it's my second job.

It's after nine o'clock when we finally consume the reheated Chinese takeaway straight from the containers, naked under the covers, famished and fully satisfied at the same time. In the morning, my sheets will smell of sex and Stella Starkey and Posh Spiced Rice with Diced Bangers.

She's enthusiastically and messily sucking noodles up through her puffy lips while staring at me rather thoughtfully. I'm expecting her to say something very profound or possibly to give me shit about asking whether she wanted me to fuck her with my voice or my cock.

Instead, she says, "What are some British terms for naughty body parts? Like, fanny doesn't mean ass to you, does it? It's in the front, not the back."

"Indeed. *Your* fanny means the world to me."

She nudges me with her knee. "Come on. I like *arse*. What else?"

"I'm quite fond of *bum*, myself. *Bollocks* for balls, of course."

"Bollocks," she repeats. "I love it!"

"I love how you handle my knob. You have quite a way with the dangly bits."

Her face lights up. "Dangly bits!"

"And your jubblies are divine."

"Oh well..." She blushes. "Cheers. I'm a big fan of your knob, and you did fantastic work with my fanny."

"Ta!"

"I wish I could see your bum and dangly bits all the time. It's a shame you ever have to wear clothes," she says, her mouth full of rice and braised green beans and adorable filth.

"Right back at you. Although, I have been told I look rather fine in a suit."

"You do!" she blurts out and then covers her mouth

like *that* of all things is something she should be embarrassed about.

I squint at her. "Have you seen me in a suit, other than my birthday suit?"

She seems impossibly shy all of a sudden. "I've seen the *Hamlet* movie."

"So you *have* seen my films."

"Not all of them. Just the ones I can currently watch for free at home."

This pleases me more than it should. "And did you enjoy watching them?"

"I did enjoy watching them. I mean, I didn't love all of the movies or shows, but I do enjoy watching you on film." She does an imitation of a cheesy vaudeville producer. "You really got something, kid—you got what it takes to be a star!"

I laugh. "You really think so?" It's humiliating how much I want her to like my work.

"Uh-huh," she says before sucking one lucky noodle into her mouth. "Your eyes contain all the sadness and joys and mysteries of the world. Your chiseled jawline and abs convey a deep understanding of human nature."

She does enjoy teasing me, this one. "Piss off."

"I probably should..." She looks around for the time.

"No, stay."

"Okay... I'm sorry I'm such a jerk to you. I don't know—I think I'm...intimidated by you."

I drop my chopsticks into the container and stare at her.

Her head jerks back. "What?"

"I'm just wondering if that word means the same thing here as it does in the UK. Are you sure you meant to say *intimidated*?"

"Yes! I'm not an idiot."

"No, you're not. You also don't strike me as someone who's the least bit intimidated by me."

"Well, maybe *I'm* the accomplished actor, then. Because I am. I mean, I don't care about the movie star stuff. Or I do, but not in the way that most people do. I've never been with a guy who's older than me before."

"I'm not that much older than you."

"Worldlier, then."

"Ah, well. That I can understand. I am exceedingly worldly. Pretty fucking classy too, wouldn't you say?"

"You really are. I mean... You are an accomplished actor. Obviously. I was impressed. I *am* impressed. By your talent." She can't say it while looking at me, and she's blushing. It's so cute.

"Well, thank you, that means a lot to me, really. You're the Sandra Bullock of gym managers, yourself."

She laughs so hard she snorts.

"See what I mean?"

She slaps at my arm.

I've never had this much fun in bed with a woman. I wish this night didn't have to end.

Half an hour later, it does, somewhat abruptly. She suddenly looks around with a sad expression on her face, gathers up the containers and dishes and chopsticks, and searches for her clothes.

"You're more than welcome to stay," I say earnestly, "but I'll be getting up at five for a few conference calls."

"No, thank you. I don't like to leave my cat alone all night."

"What's your cat called?"

"Muffin Top."

"I hope to meet him or her one day."

She nods and smiles politely but doesn't seem to believe me.

"Why are you getting dressed?" she asks.

"Because I'm about to walk you to your car."

"That's not necessary. It's cold out. Stay in bed."

I exhale slowly as I continue putting on warm sweats and socks. Not a great look, but it probably is cold out. We are both stubbornly silent as she waits for me, and I take her hand after pulling on my heavy coat, leading her out the front door to the driveway.

"So I'll see you at the gym tomorrow?"

"I'll be there. You'll be in the back room mostly, though, right?"

"I'll be there to warm up for half an hour, and then my stunt trainer Jim will be working with me in the back room all day. Should be exhausting."

"Right."

"My entire schedule changes starting tomorrow."

"I get it, Richard Diver. You don't have to explain. Tourists have been coming through here my whole life. You get to know them. It can be nice. But they always leave. And I always stay. And life goes on. So don't flatter yourself and worry about breaking my heart. Somebody already beat you to it."

144

She holds my surprised gaze, unwavering, until she can tell that her words have sunk in, and then she unlocks her car door with the key fob.

This woman.

"What I was going to say is, I'd like to see you again tomorrow night, if you'd like to come by again."

And now it's her turn to look surprised.

"Oh."

"I'd like to see you again the next night as well and whenever possible while I'm here."

"Oh...so...you want to...have a fling? While you're here?"

"For starters. Sure, you can call it that."

She shifts her weight from one foot to the other, straightens her posture. "What about that actress who's coming?"

I'm enjoying watching the rapidly changing expressions on her face so much it's difficult to follow the conversation. "Which actress?"

"The one who's going to play the love interest. In your movie. Don't you want to meet her first? I mean. Don't you always...you know. Fall for your leading ladies?"

"Oh. Jess. Right. I've already met her, once or twice, at events. She's...good on screen. I signed off on her because the director likes her and it's not a very large role. She was fine in a couple of things I've seen her in, but we're represented by the same agency in America and I was encouraged to support her as a fellow client."

She wrinkles her nose. "Wow. Again with the agency. Don't you make any decisions on your own?"

"I've just made one. I like you, Stella Starkey. I enjoy talking to you. I enjoy your body with my body. I want to do more things to your body, on a regular basis, in different positions, from every possible angle. Fast and slow and rough and so gentle it will probably make you angry. If you're up for that, and I think you are, come back tomorrow night. I don't want to do those things with anyone else. A fling. Sure. Call it that."

"Um…okay."

"Good." I notice her shivering as she leans back against her car, so I wrap my arms around her.

"But I have rules for flings with out-of-towners," she informs me.

"Oh, *do* you? Hit me."

She clears her throat. "What do you mean?"

"I want to hear the rules."

"Well, I don't usually *tell* the guy. They're just rules that I have."

"Well, I don't usually agree to things without knowing what I'm agreeing to. Even when I'm making weak decisions to appease the world's largest talent agency."

She considers this. "Okay, but now I feel really self-conscious."

"Interesting. I've had my head between your legs for half an hour, but you feel uncomfortable letting me inside your head."

Her eyelashes flutter, and I can feel her body melt just a little as she remembers just what I did to her down there, but she recovers quickly. "I'm not letting you inside my head. And I don't think it was a full half an hour, so once again, please get over yourself."

"Never. Do go on."

"No telling personal stories."

"Not even about Cornish jack o'lanterns?"

"Especially not that story."

"Well, that's my best one. I'm glad I got it out of the way early. Look at you—telling me your rules. You're already breaking one of them for me. I like that."

"I'm breaking precedent."

"Semantics."

"No sleepovers. No coming to my home. No I love yous, not even as a joke. And no fraternizing with my family. But...too late."

I scoff at that. "I refuse to let you come between my bromance with your brothers."

"But I still don't want to let them know about us. Not yet, anyway."

"Understood. We both appreciate discretion. What else?"

"That's it."

"Interesting."

"What?"

"I was expecting you to say 'no butt stuff,' but since you didn't..."

"Good night." She tries to wriggle free from my grasp, but I'm not letting her go just yet.

I release one hand from her back so I can tilt her chin up and kiss her softly, parting her lips with my tongue until she relents and kisses me back hungrily, makes little sighing noises. I would love to wake up to this in the morning, but I will play by her rules for now. I pull away from her, and it takes her a moment to open her eyes.

"Sweet dreams," I say, grinning. "Drive safe. Text me when you're home. I mean it. I won't sleep until you do."

She nods. "See you tomorrow."

And tomorrow, and tomorrow, and tomorrow.

I stay right where I am in the driveway, watching until her car is no longer in view.

Hand on my heart, that was among the Top Ten First Dates I have ever witnessed. That was the first date equivalent of the comedic masterpiece I made with Sarah Jessica Parker.

Fuck you, Hugh.

Honestly, though. It was top notch. Well done, you. Don't cock it up.

14

STELLA

*P*roduction has begun on *Cover-Up*, or as it's more commonly referred to: "that Evan Hunter movie." He refers to the very long list of things he has to do for this film simply as: "work." I think of it as: "that thing that Evan does when he's not doing me."

Much of the population of Main Street has gotten wind of Evan spending time at our gym with his trainer, and suddenly we're getting so many new members and sign-ups for the Get Fit Stay Fit holiday challenge. Still, people are polite and cool when they do see him, and true to form for this wonderful town, things haven't gotten too crowded or crazy. So far, it's a win for the Starkey family, although I'm well aware that I'm secretly the big winner in this scenario.

People have started coming in from out of town, just to get a glimpse of Evan Hunter and take pictures of him, sometimes with him. When he's on set, there is always at least one policeman standing guard on one side of the barricades, keeping the peace. Seems a bit much to me, since there's something about Port Gladstone that mellows people out, but apparently there is a rather large production assistant stationed outside his trailer whenever he's in it, because one or two feverish young ladies have attempted to sneak inside and throw themselves at him.

Poor girls. I get it. I didn't, but boy do I ever get it now. And they have no idea just how yummy he really is.

The one time I dared to leave the gym with him one morning before he left for the set, a group of middle-aged women who were walking out of the bookstore across the street saw him, almost got run over when they jaywalked without checking for traffic, handed their phones to me to take pictures of them with him, and literally didn't even see my face. One of them used to be friends with my mother, but I didn't say anything. I want to keep this fling a secret and stay inside the bubble for as long as possible.

Every day, I go home to Amazon deliveries from him—that way he doesn't have to give out his information to the local florist or have his assistant handle anything. He sends bouquets of flowers, he's sent a cat bed, toy mice, and catnip for Muffin Top, as well as seven very nice pairs of panties to replace the ones he's so shamelessly and magnificently destroyed. Whenever companies send him gifts care of the production office, he attempts to re-gift them to me and my brothers. Billy is the ecstatic recipient of several types of men's grooming products, designer clothing, and canisters of whey protein. Kevin has graciously accepted a cashmere scarf and one pork pie hat that wouldn't look good on anyone. I agreed to take the scented candles, which I plan to re-re-gift to Mona, and jars of local honey and a crate of Evian water, which I donated to the food bank. Being a beloved movie star certainly has its privileges, and it doesn't hurt to be friends with one either.

Today, the Starkey Fitness letter board says: *"Actually that's my secret—I can't even talk about you to anybody because I don't want any more people to know how wonderful you are."*

The one person I know who'd recognize the quote from *Tender is the Night* hasn't been in today, and even though I saw him for a wildly entertaining hour last night, I find myself missing him.

When Kevin gets back from his break, I walk the long way to the deli for lunch so I can pass by the "video village" that is set up on a side street today.

I spy several groups of women, mostly younger than I am, squealing and holding their fingers up in heart shapes at someone, and that's how I know Evan Hunter is near. Seriously, though, don't those girls have jobs or classes or something? I catch sight of Evan smiling and making a hand heart gesture back at them, but when he sees me from about thirty feet away, his smile gets even bigger. He pulls out his phone, takes a seat in his folding chair under the canopy, answers someone's question, and three seconds later I feel my phone vibrate in my pocket.

Randy BritishActor sent me a heart emoji.

It's not raining, so I decide to lean against a store-front and text him back.

ME: How's your day?
RANDY: Appalling. So far not one second of it has been spent with you on my face.
ME: Sad. Hope that's a concern that the Screen Actors Guild can tackle on your behalf.
RANDY: Funny. Concerned you'll lose all sense of humor when i'm tackling your bottom half later.
ME: Please don't worry. Not much can stop my wise cracks. Not even your tongue in my crack.
RANDY: Hold that dirty thought, you saucy vixen. Time for me to do a very serious scene with a brilliant Emmy winner who's playing a retired cop.
RANDY: Some tech nerd can just erase my massive erection in post-production.
RANDY: I know this because I had one all through the BBC series I did with Sir Ken Branagh. Guy made me harder than an Oscar statue. I look forward to filling you in about such movie magic later.
ME: I look forward to being filled in by you...

"I saw him at Safeway buying organic kale at night." Mrs. Flauvich is practically levitating as she passes me my sandwich. "It's a good thing I've already had kids, because my ovaries exploded."

I can't stop myself. "Did you talk to him?"

"Oh God, no. I just stood there, squeezing avocados and looking at him out of the corner of my eye, and then he got a phone call and walked away. He was all smiles, all of a sudden. It was probably that actress."

It was me.

"I don't think she's in town yet," I say, pretending to be totally clueless and vaguely uninterested. "Is she?"

"Well. Whoever it was, he was very happy."

It was me!

He was buying food to cook a late dinner for us. I reminded him to buy condoms because I just wanted to hear him say the word "condoms," because I love how he says "condoms," like con-domes. He makes them sound so respectable and important. And he quietly told me that he can't just buy the sort of colossal con-domes he uses from a supermarket because he has them custom-made by dirty randy craftsmen in Great Cockland so they can withstand long, vigorous sessions of fanny-pounding.

For some reason, I really dig keeping this a secret. In a small community like mine, being able to keep a relationship secret is a rare and wonderful thing. Wait— did I just use the word *relationship*? I meant fling. Fling-thing. Fling-a-ling-a-ding-dong.

We're really good at flinging together.

People at the gym are starting to notice that we stand just a little too close and stare at each other just a little too long. People assume I have a crush on him. Billy and Kevin and my dad keep asking me what I've been doing with myself lately—why do I seem so happy, they wonder. I tell them I've been practicing a lot of yoga at home, drinking more green tea than usual, and that they should mind their own business. They know exactly what I've been up to, of course, and they know I'll never tell. Evan seems to be keeping up his end of the bargain too, so far…

God. I get so little sleep and I'm in a sex haze all the time. Just thinking phrases like "keeping up his end of the bargain" immediately makes me think of the tip of his cock and the way he's groaned when I've slid it into my mouth. The way he's made me groan when he presses it between my legs, teasing and torturing me before finally penetrating so deep inside me. That dull pain that morphs and quickly fills me with a kind of pleasure that erases everything else.

That's what I'm thinking about when I'm at the deli again after a couple of days, when Mrs. Flauvich is talking to the lady from the library about how her daughter told her that there are pictures all over the Internet this morning of Evan Hunter and Jess King, the actress playing his love interest. They're hugging on Main Street and you can see part of the deli's awning in the background. They're on set, acting out a scene of course, but someone took pictures with their phone and the celebrity gossip sites and Twitter are supposedly flipping out about how Evan has moved on from Georgia and wondering if "JessEvan" will be the next It Couple.

I remember a time when all Mrs. Flauvich talked about was pie, Port Gladstone city council meetings, and how to remove sun-baked seagull poop from her awning.

"What did I say? I wish I had bet money on it—look at this! He's already PDAing with the actress." She holds up her iPad to show me and Library Lady.

"What's 'PDAing'?" I ask.

"Public displays of affection...ing"

"It's just a rebound," says Library Lady with a shrug.

"You don't even know about Evan Hunter," shushes Mrs. Flauvich.

"I don't have to. I know men, and if it's only been a few weeks since he was dumped, then he's not in a real relationship with this next girl. His penis is. Doesn't matter if he's a movie star or a fisherman. That's men. That's *penises*."

Yup. That's right. I'm in a secret, casual, nonpermanent relationship with movie star Evan Hunter's penis, and he is in a rebound relationship with my fanny. And every single part of me is fine with that.

Totally, completely fine with it.

On my way back to the gym, in the rain, I feel my phone vibrate and duck under an awning, hoping it's a text from Evan.

It's a text from my best girlfriend Mona, in Portland.

MONA: Hey stranger! Long time no talk! Also—have you seen Evan Hunter around town? Asking for my grandma.

MONA: Okay, that's a lie. Asking for me. Don't tell Rob I think he's HAWT.

Okay, maybe it would feel good to just tell one person. Just one out of town person so I'll have someone to talk to when it's over. Years from now when my boobs are starting to sag and I'm up to my wrinkled elbows in laundry and PTA meetings, I can call Mona up and be like, "Remember that time I was having sex with that British movie star? That was real, right? It wasn't all just some long weird Halloween hangover dream?"

I text her, asking if she can FaceTime in private, ie. the ladies' room in her office, and I go to my parked car behind the gym.

It is so good to see my friend's beautiful dorky face on my iPhone screen, my heart hurts. As soon as she sees my face, she pushes her long bangs out of the way, leans in closer to her phone, and gasps. "Oh my God. Are you in love?"

"What? No. Shut up. Why?"

"You're definitely fucking someone."

"A lady never tells."

"So I've heard. So tell me immediately."

"Uhhh, let's discuss the subject of your texts first, shall we? You actually *know* who Evan Hunter is?"

"You're joking, right? That's like asking if I know what water is. He's a combination of two of the most important male star elements—handsome and likable. Although I guess for you, those elements would be

Jason and Momoa… Is that why you made out with Jason Kwasnicki on Halloween?"

"How do you know about that?"

"Someone, I forget who, posted a picture from that party, and I could see you guys in the background. I didn't bring it up because I figured it was just your usual Halloween craziness."

"Yeah. Something like that."

"So have you seen him? Evan Hunter?"

I cover my mouth and make the dumbest giggly squeaky sound.

"You have? You've seen him?"

I somehow manage to get my shit together long enough to tell her that he's been a member at our gym for a few weeks but we had to keep it a secret.

"Shut. Up. I can't believe you didn't tell me!"

"I just told you it was a secret."

"Yeah. And you *told* me."

"Well, it's not really a secret anymore since filming has started. How did you find out he's here?"

"I follow some of his fan pages on Twitter and Instagram."

"What? Who *are* you?"

"Dude, I've been a Hunterhoe for years. I just stopped talking to you about it after you made us walk out of the *Hamlet* movie—which, by the way, I went back and saw again by myself. Twice."

I grin. "I sat next to him at the Rose, the first night he was in town."

"No way."

"We took him fishing."

"*What?* Shut up. Are your brothers friends with him now?" She squeals. "Tell me everything! I can't believe a celebrity finally comes to PG a year after I move away! Remember that time we followed the guy I thought was the actor who played Frasier Crane for half an hour, but it was just some random pretentious bald guy?"

All of a sudden, I realize that the tip of my nose is tingly, there's moisture in my eyeballs, and my voice gets all croaky. "God, I miss you. I can't talk about this with anyone here."

"I miss you too. I wish you'd come visit."

"I can't."

"Why?" She frowns. "Is Muffin Top having another irritable bowel flare-up?"

I shake my head. That was my excuse for not visiting her in Portland the last two times, and it was a valid one. I can usually come up with ten good reasons for not leaving town, but I realize now that there's only one reason I don't want to for the next two months. Because I don't want to miss out on time with Evan while he's here.

"I'm seeing Evan," I whisper.

"What? I know you've seen him. I need details."

"I'm trying to tell you…because I can't tell anyone here…Evan and I are seeing each other." I don't know why I can't just say "we're fucking each other." Yes I do. It's because the truth is it's more than that. I just haven't allowed myself to think it yet. "We have been *shagging* each other. At his rental house. On a regular basis. For a week."

She stares at me. "That's not funny."

Finally—a sane reaction to the insane concept of Evan Hunter and me together. My dad and brothers are completely bananas about this. Evan is completely bananas about this. We don't make sense together.

"I know. It's not funny. It's tragic."

She looks so confused. "What are you…"

"I mean. If you don't believe me, it's fine, whatever. How's your job? I like your hair."

"Wait—Stella. Just…give me a minute to process this. It's like you're telling me a new planet's been discovered but you don't have a picture of it to back it up, so I'm like…*okay*…"

"I don't have a dick pic to show you. Mona."

"Dammit!"

She holds her phone up closer to her face to inspect me closer. "Holy shit. This is real, isn't it?"

I nod.

"Holy shit. HOLY shit!" After about three seconds, she bursts out laughing. I have to look away from the screen because her phone is shaking so much. "He is literally the opposite of your type!"

"No kidding." This is why I called Mona. She gets it. She'll talk some sense into me. "It's crazy, right?"

"I mean…I'm…I'm honestly so happy for you, but also my ears are burning up and I might hate you a little."

"Trust me, I hate me a lot right now."

"Shit. Stella. If you aren't enjoying this, I will murder you. I will slowly drown you with the tears of the millions of females on earth who would give their left tit just to kiss Evan Hunter and hear him say their name—and you're 'shagging' him on a regular basis at his rental home?"

"I know. I'm such an asshole. I have no idea why he's wasting his time with me."

"Oh my God, stop it right now. You're amazing. You're a fucking peach, and any guy would be lucky to have you. But I am so jealous right now. I mean, I love Rob, he totally gets me, the sex is still good, we'll probably get married next year, blah blah blah. But Christ, please just tell me Evan Hunter has a tiny pencil dick and he's pathetic in bed so I can go on living my life."

That's when I freely begin weeping. I am so glad I don't wear mascara.

"Oh fuck, Stella. You *are* in love."

"What?" I wipe my nose and my eyes. "No I'm not. It's not serious. It's just really fun. He's nice. And he's… really, really incredible in bed. Like, so incredible. Like, there are no words for how incredible he is in bed. He's just too good to be true, and it would honestly be a relief if he turns out to be some serial killer who harvests my organs while I'm still alive or something."

"Jesus. Stella."

"And his cock is so damn big and beautiful, I can't stop thinking about it—"

"Okay, that's enough. You got it so bad, girl. Now I'm glad I'm not you, so thanks. It sounds really terrible. I bet you can't wait for him to leave town."

A fresh bucket of hot tears gets dumped on my cheeks, and I can't wipe them away fast enough.

"I don't know why I'm crying. This is so weird."

"Oh, buddy." I hear her sigh, but I can't see her through this stupid eye waterfall.

"I just keep thinking about how much my mom would love him."

"Yeah. She would. And you know what else?"

I make a little croaking sound that's supposed to mean, "What?"

"She would hate that you're not enjoying this while you can."

"I am. I really am. It's fun. I swear I'm having fun. It's just that you're the first person I've talked to about it, and I haven't talked to you in so long. I'm just having a weird meltdown, that's all."

"Uh-huh. Let it out, babe. I got all day for this. Except I have to get back to my desk in five minutes."

"Shit. I do too. I'm sorry—let's talk about you, seriously. How's work? How's Rob."

"Yeah, you know. There are no words for how incredible it all is." She laughs.

"I miss you."

"I know. I'm sorry we suck at staying in touch."

"Why are we so bad at this?"

"I don't know. But we'll get better. Okay?"

I nod.

"Well, if you can find a moment in between orgasms, try to ask Evan Hunter for a signed headshot for Grandma Betty, will you? Although she might be so thrilled, she'd actually drop dead from the excitement."

"Okay."

"And Stel...I mean it. It won't kill you to really enjoy this, you know. You deserve it. You deserve him."

I nod, just to stop her from saying any more ridiculous things. Once we finally sign off, I manage to find a sad old unused piece of Kleenex in my glove compartment. It disintegrates between my fingers when I blow my nose, and I can't help but look around, expecting to see Evan outside my car, shaking his head and going: "Yeah. I'm out. Nice knowin' you."

Instead, I get a text from him asking if I can sneak out from work for half an hour or so this afternoon. I manage to take three deep breaths and let him know that I will do what I can. Part of me is actually hoping he wants to tell me in person that he's fallen madly in love with his co-star, to put me out of this misery. Most of me knows that she'll never be an issue; it will always be me.

The nightmare continues when I get back to the gym. Billy sees my bright red-rimmed eyes, tells me he needs to talk to me, and pulls me back to the office. I'm usually the one pulling him into this office, getting all Big Sister up in his face. This time, I just slide into the armchair and wait for him to ask me about Evan.

He stares at me for a bit before speaking.

"What?"

"You started making plans for Thanksgiving yet?"

"Yeah. Sort of. I already got the turkey. Why? Are you bringing someone?"

"Naw. But let's talk head count. Martin's bringing his girlfriend."

"Are we actually referring to her as his girlfriend already?"

He rolls his eyes. "Well, Martin refers to her as his

girlfriend, so yeah. All the grandparents are traveling, right?"

"Yeah. Cruises."

"Kevin and I aren't bringing anyone. How about you? You planning to bring anyone to dinner?"

"No. Whit and Brett are having their own party, and Mona's going to be with her boyfriend's family in Butte."

He lowers his voice, even though no one would be able to hear us in here. "What about Evan?"

"What about him?"

"He's gonna have four days off from shooting, and it's not enough time for him to go home."

I shake my head. "He's not going to want to come to Thanksgiving dinner."

"How do you know?"

"I don't, but I'm not inviting him."

"Then *I* will."

"No you won't."

"Then *you* invite him."

"Billy…"

"I mean, it's been five years, Stel."

"What? This has nothing to do with Cody."

"Course not. I know you think I'm the dumb one, but I do *see* things, and I know what I know."

"I don't think you're dumb. It's just…"

"Well, it must have something to do with him. I mean, you have these little flings with guys who are passing through, which is fine. But they're guys you'd never actually get serious about. You aren't looking to date anyone local, even though you don't ever want to leave. And then this fucking classy stud comes to town, and you act like he's all wrong for you."

"It's not like I don't…but he's not even…"

"Your type?"

"I wasn't going to say that. He's not even American. I mean, he lives in London, and he's always off being an actor all over the world, and I…"

"Have a cat? Too bad they don't make carriers that you can put small animals in that fit under the seat in front of you on a plane."

"That would be too stressful for her."

"For her or for you? You know Dad would love to look after Muffin Top. You have options. No one's got you or her under house arrest."

"Yeah." I sigh. "Whit and Brett could look after her too."

"Exactly."

"But I mean, what's the point? Our lives can't possibly mesh. I can't move to London. He'd never move here."

"You never thought Cody would leave here. People are full of surprises."

"Low blow."

"Wasn't meant to be. What I meant is: People are surprising. Just look at Martin with this girlfriend of his. No one ever thought he'd want to settle down."

"Well. They haven't settled down yet."

"Yeah, but he's—"

"What? Bringing her to Thanksgiving? We'll see how long they last."

He shakes his head at me. "I'm just saying. You get

along great with Evan. You share the same values. You both think I'm awesome."

I squeeze his shoulder. "True."

"Just invite him to Thanksgiving. If you don't, I will."

"I have rules."

"Yeah? I've got an ass—feel free to kiss it."

15

EVAN

I send a text to "Sassy AmericanGirl" requesting that in half an hour she come to base camp and meet me at my trailer, which bears the nameplate "Alan Winslow" after my character's name. I tell her that the security guard (a retired policeman) and my burly on-set production assistant (a dude who clearly doesn't give a shit if I bang someone in my trailer but seems a bit chatty) will be around outside the trailer and they have been advised to let her in. I told them that she is my "dialect consultant." She doesn't even have a clever response to text back to me, surprisingly. She must be busy.

Exactly half an hour later, I'm startled by two loud knocks on my trailer door. My PA's patented two-knock alert.

"How's it going?" I hear Stella ask.

"Not bad," he replies. "How's it going for you?"

"It's going very well."

I open the trailer door and reach down to help my lady up the steps. The first thing I notice is that her big brown eyes are pink-rimmed like she has allergies. The next thing I notice is that she's wearing a large formless coat and those black high-heeled boots that remind me of the first time I tasted her, and frankly, that's all I expect to be thinking about for a while. "Hello, darling," I say. "I'm ready for my lesson."

"I'm ready to give it to you," she says saucily.

I nod at the PA and shut the door. I'm wearing sweats, and I hug her over her big coat, even though it's damp. She coos softly.

This is her first time in my trailer. It's a big one. Fit for a king but cozy. I keep it neat, of course. The TV is on, the blinds are closed, and now the air smells of Stella—fresh-baked goods and a hint of a musky citrusy floral something or other. Whatever it is—one whiff and I'm a goner.

"It's good to see you," I say as I pull away from her. "Thanks for popping by. I have to be in the hair and makeup trailer in an hour."

"Okay. Do you usually put a sign on the door that says 'If this trailer's rockin', don't bother knockin'?"

"I'm usually far too professional to do the things we're about to do in a trailer. Best we stay as quiet and still as possible."

"That will be a challenge."

"You up for it?"

"I can see that *you* are…" She reaches for the unapologetic bulge in the front of my sweatpants and leans in to kiss me before removing her voluminous coat.

Because I am a gentleman, I reach for her coat to help her take it off and then hang it up on the hook behind the door. Because this woman makes me feel like a naughty gentleman. When I turn to see that she's wearing her sexy sailor Halloween costume, I grunt and mutter, "Well, fuck me... Ahoy, matey." It's not quite as revealing as it was in my filthy imagination ever since she first told me of it, but I don't know which is stronger—the urge to make her get down on all fours to scrub the deck so I can spank her or the urge to spank her, throw that coat back over her, and reprimand her for wearing that outfit to a party that I was not present at.

"Know where I can find any nice seamen?" She blinks at me innocently.

Her top is so low cut and her breasts are so pushed up in it, they're like two flesh-colored fishing buoys stuffed into a tube sock. Yeah—there are just too many urges to act on. In the end, I always just want to stare at her and touch her and kiss her all over.

I somehow manage to whistle. "Well, I can see why you were so popular on Halloween."

She covers her face, adorably embarrassed. "I can't believe I wore this in public."

"I can't believe I only have forty-five minutes to get off with you."

"In the dialect of these parts, we say 'make out with you.'"

"Fuck that. Get those parts over here now." I sit down on the padded bench and pat my lap, hold my arms outstretched.

She straddles me, careful not to rock the trailer, but it seems sturdy enough.

I bite my lower lip as I stare down at her sublime tits. "At least we know you'd never drown…"

She laughs quietly. "I told my friend Mona, who lives in Portland, about you today. She said she'd drown me in the tears of the millions of women who'd die just to kiss you and hear you say their name if I don't enjoy this fling."

"Sounds like you'd better enjoy it, then."

Last time we were together, Stella and I had the "I'm clean" / "I haven't had sex without a condom in years" / "Me neither" / "I'm on the pill" conversation, so we are no longer using those custom-made products from Great Cockland. It just felt so damned good, and I never expected to feel so close to her so soon.

She maneuvers my sweatpants out of the way and lowers herself down onto me. God bless America and God bless Stella Starkey—she's not wearing knickers. I groan and whisper, "You are a very bad sexy sailor, indeed."

"Anchors away," she sings.

I inhale sharply and then hold my breath as I grip that luscious bum and stare up at her. We maintain eye contact while she does all the moving—and she barely moves at all, just bearing down, swaying a bit from side to side, front to back, and squeezing—all part of the challenge of not rocking the trailer. But honestly, it's so hot I might never want to do it any other way.

Finally, I lower my head to kiss her breasts, and we cover each other's mouths when we come. We remain quiet and it is exquisite, and each time I have sex with her I know she fears it will be the last. While we catch our breaths, I put my arms around her, holding her so close, I wonder if she knows I fear the same thing. I have never felt this way about a fling before, that's for sure.

"We fit together," I say in her ear.

"Yes. Like this, we do."

In all ways, I think. I hate that she doesn't see that. I brush the hair out of her face and kiss her, softly at first and then more and more vigorously, as—impossibly—I feel myself slowly growing hard again inside her.

"Oh my God," she gasps as my hips begin to rise. "If your refractory periods are this short now, what were you like when you were eighteen?"

"There weren't nearly enough beautiful women in sailor costumes on my cock when I was eighteen." I grin. "It's you, I swear it."

I know she doesn't really believe it, but she takes it. She'll take what I give her while she can, and I am astonished by how much I'm willing to give her. I just need to her to know that I'm not acting.

Once I've changed and we're both cleaned up and she's put on the panties that she kept in her coat pocket, I insist that she put her coat back on and sit on the opposite side of the trailer from me while we chat. I need to get back into professional actor mode soon, and I don't trust my cock around this woman and her sailor costume. And her body and her mind and her long dark hair and fragrant smooth skin and the enchanting sweet little noises she makes when she kisses me.

"What's your schedule like for the next week?" I ask. "I've been invited to the mayor's house for dinner with some other actors and the director and producers. I wish I were allowed to bring a guest, but—"

"I wouldn't go to that guy's house even if I *were* invited, and he'd never invite me anyway."

I sit back and clasp my hands behind my head, elbows out. "And why would that be, do tell?"

"Let's just say I was a vocal supporter of the man who ran against him in the last election—my landlord Whit. I suspect our current mayor is a tad homophobic. Anyway…it's a nice big Victorian house. I'm sure it will be a nice event."

"Well. Hopefully we can meet up afterwards."

"How *is* your co-star Jess? I've heard the gossip blogs are excited about 'JessEvan.'" She doesn't sound jealous, exactly, but the fact that she's bringing this up at all does concern me.

"Shit," I say. "What'd you hear? I'm sorry, darling. My publicist's assistant sent me an email about it I think, but I haven't bothered to read it yet. Whatever it is, it's rubbish. You know that, right?"

"I do—calm down. There's pictures of you guys hugging, but you're obviously doing a scene."

I rub my face with both palms. "God." I lower my voice. "She's apparently pissed off because I haven't been 'hanging out with the cast and crew enough.' Whatever. It couldn't be any less important. She's fine in the scenes. That's all that matters."

Stella exhales, and I think I hear her mutter to herself, "Here goes..." before straightening up and saying "Well, speaking of dinners with other people..."

"Yes?"

"You guys have a break for Thanksgiving, right?"

"We do..." I am trying not to grin.

"Well, if you don't have anything more interesting planned..."

"I don't."

"You don't know what I'm—"

"Doesn't matter—I'll come." I lean forward eagerly.

"To Thanksgiving dinner? At my dad's house? With all my brothers. And Martin's new girlfriend, whom I haven't met yet."

"Yes."

"Really?"

"Of course. Should I bring anything?"

"A lot of alcohol. For me."

"Sounds like a recipe for disaster. Can't wait."

She gets up and moves toward me, and before I can stop her, she sits on my lap in her big long coat and wraps her arms around my neck. "You really want to come to our little family Thanksgiving dinner?"

"I do, very much. I've never been to a Thanksgiving dinner before—well, not at someone's home, anyway. At hotel restaurants. My father will be so jealous—it'll be like anthropological research. Course, I just want to be with you..."

She nuzzles my neck. "Me too."

She starts to pepper my face with kisses, but I lift her up and pat her on the bum through her coat. "All right, back to work we go—go on, you siren, you."

"Okay—well, I think we've accomplished a lot!" she says as she reaches for the door handle.

"Yeah, I'll call you later," I say, sounding exactly like a man from the Pacific Northwest, if I may say so myself.

It appears to freak her out a bit. "Wow. Is there anything you can't do?"

Yes. I can't stop thinking about you. I can't seem to get you to believe how much I want you. I can't stop thinking about all the places I want to take you, and wanting you by my side, and knowing that you won't always be there. I can't remember what my life was like before I met you and I don't want to.

"Well, I can't roast a turkey," is what I say. "So I look forward to seeing what you can do with one."

She beams. "I can't tell if that's supposed to be innuendo or not, but I make a damn fine roast turkey. So bring your appetite and don't forget the wine."

I open the door and hop out of the trailer first so I can hold her hand as she steps down to the ground. It's sprinkling rain, and in my peripheral vision, I can see people milling about, so I don't kiss her even though it's all I want to do.

I hold out my hand to shake hers. "Thank you for the insights, Ms. Starkey," I say loud enough for people to hear, and then I lower my voice. "And thank you for rocking my world while managing to not rock the trailer."

She blushes. God, how she blushes. "Anytime."

If that were true, I'd be the happiest man alive.

16

EVAN

I don't know why I'm so nervous—it's bizarre.

I've already circled the block twice before parking just across the street from the house that Stella grew up in. It's a lovely, large old house with a nice front yard and several cars crammed into the driveway. I can just imagine her running around the lawn with her brothers when she was little and probably sneaking out of a second-floor window, climbing down a tree to meet up with some lucky bloke at night when she was a teenager. For some reason, I just can't imagine what it will be like when I set foot inside that house now and sit down to a private family dinner with her.

Usually when I meet a girl's family, it turns into a media circus because it's always in a public place. Stella's been slaving away in the kitchen since this morning, so I suppose I'm the last to arrive. I've already met most of the Starkeys, but this is my first Thanksgiving dinner as a guest in someone's house, and I'm not entirely sure exactly what her family knows about my involvement with Stella. I suppose I'll have to keep my hands off her just as I do at the gym, which is no small feat. It's so unlike me to overthink this kind of thing, but pretty much everything about me when I'm with Stella is unlike me, really. Or *more* like me than ever, perhaps. Hard to say.

I don't spend enough time with my own family. My nan always invites me for Christmas in Cornwall because my parents are shit at celebrating holidays, but I'm usually either comatose at home in between jobs or shagging an actress and listening to her feelings, which used to be my part-time job. God. Being with Stella Starkey is fucking stellar.

I reach for the two bottles of wine, red and white, feeling as though I should have more to offer. They're such a friendly, casual family, and here I am fretting like I'm approaching Buckingham Palace. Actually, I didn't fret at all when I met the Queen because I knew exactly what to expect. I even changed my clothes three times before leaving the house today, finally settling on jeans and a sweater.

Oh, you got it bad, honey, and that ain't good.

Shut it, Hugh. Take a day off, will you?

As soon as I ring the doorbell, and hear Chet barking inside, and Billy's loud happy voice saying he'll get it, and Stella yelling at him to let *her* get it...I feel more at ease. I do like this family a lot. I want Stella to meet mine. I want Stella to meet my friends. I want Stella to see my flat. I want Stella.

The front door opens, and instead of Stella, her

father Joe greets me with his fantastic eyebrows at ease and his smile warm and genuine. "There he is—get in here." He pulls me in for a one-armed man hug. "Wow, you've bulked up since I last saw you. Did you up your protein intake?"

"A bit, yeah. And healthy fats. Been doing a lot of boxing in your back room with my trainer."

Also been having a lot of sex with your daughter wherever and whenever possible...

"Well, I hope you're ready to ingest a ton of carbs today, because Stella has been a maniac in the kitchen for hours."

"Is that right? She requested I bring a couple of bottles of wine. I hope these are good."

He doesn't even look at the labels when he takes a bottle in each hand. "They're great—we'll have these when we sit down to eat. We're drinking beer now. I'll get you one."

"I'll take one, thanks."

"I'll be right out, Evan. I just have to finish basting this bird!"

"Smells incredible," I call out. It really does—rosemary and lemons, I think. Very Mediterranean.

Billy and Chet come out to the foyer to greet me with equal amounts of enthusiasm as Joe disappears with the wine. I'm led into a large living room area by the open dining room, where Kevin gives me a nod and I'm introduced to the eldest brother Martin and his pretty girlfriend Lauren. Martin is fit, probably around my age. His glasses and stubble make him look like the intellectual of the family. He and Lauren never seem to stop holding hands, and I envy them. After hearing from Lauren that all of her friends would "freak out" if they knew she was meeting me and after I tell her and Martin a bit about the film, Stella emerges from the kitchen looking every bit the domestic goddess. I may be one bite of pumpkin pie away from dropping to one knee and begging her to marry me.

"Hey," she says, oddly shy and soft-spoken. Her family backs away, returning to the big screen TV, and she gives me a friendly hug. Her hair smells of so many comforting kitchen aromas. She feels so warm, I just want to sink into an overstuffed sofa with her in front of a fire and watch Netflix while drinking a hot toddy and fondling her. Why can't that be my life, even for a weekend?

She hands me a bottle of Newcastle. I really do like this family. "Hey," I say, giving her arm a squeeze. "Happy Thanksgiving."

"Thanks for coming." She curtsies. "Are you... having a good day so far?"

Bless her heart, she appears to be a bit nervous too.

"Did some reading and laundry at home mostly. Emails, nothing exciting. You need help in the kitchen?"

"Nope, I've got it all under control. It's all about timing. I've got like four timers going, but we're in the home stretch."

"Cheers," I say. "You're not drinking?"

"Not until I'm done cooking."

"I love this house."

"Do you? Good. I do too. I'll show you around in a minute, if you want."

The rest of the family yells at the television as I take in the room. That's when I notice the painting that hangs above the fireplace. I take a few steps closer to inspect it. It's a view of Port Gladstone. Stella watches me stare at it.

"I've seen this painting before. Online."

"It's one of my mother's."

"Your mother painted it?"

"Yes, she was a really wonderful painter. This one was sold to the former mayor, but after...after I graduated, she gave it back to us. That's why you would have seen it online. A picture of it's still on the former mayor's blog. So it comes up when you Google Port Gladstone."

"It was one of the reasons I wanted to come here. That view. Where is it?"

I see the rims of her eyes turning deep pink and watery. Her lower lip quivers. "It was right around where I first saw you running on the beach. But you didn't see me. You were just staring at the pavement." She looks so vulnerable all of a sudden.

I desperately want to take her in my arms and kiss her. "I saw you," I say quietly instead.

"You did? That first day?"

"I saw you before I ran past you. Feeding the birds. Closing your eyes, listening to something. What were you listening to?"

She smiles and pulls her phone out of the back

pocket of her jeans, opens up an app, and plays a dreamy ballad on low volume. "Lord Huron."

"I like it. Hey, there's something else I want to tell you."

"Gah!" says Billy from across the room. "Turn that feelsy music off. We're trying to watch football over here!"

"How can you hear it from all the way over there?" she says. "You have dog ears."

As if on cue, Chet barks and runs over to us, tail wagging. He really is a star. Which is why I managed to get him a day of work on the movie in a couple of weeks, playing my neighbor's dog. When I told Billy, he grabbed my head with both hands and kissed me on both cheeks. "You learned your lines yet, Chet?"

He barks. What a pro.

"Yep. Nailed it. Good boy."

Stella turns off the music and looks up at me, smiling, but her lower lip is quivering again.

"My darling," I whisper, pushing long dark strands of hair out of her beautiful face. She looks back toward her family and steps away from me.

"I should go check on the timers. Oh—you were going to tell me something."

"It can wait." I've waited this long. What's a few hours more?

Before we sit down to eat, we all gather for group photos in front of the fireplace. Before we start eating, as Joe says, so we still fit into our jeans in these pictures. Stella is the only one helping Joe set up the tripod and camera, as the guys still watch the game, but once we're all assembled, I stand behind Stella. She reaches back to hold my hand. Our fingers intertwine as the camera beeps and the flash goes off, three times.

"Don't worry—my family has been informed that if they post pictures of you on the Internet, there will be swift punishment of the knee to the balls variety," my very lady-like hostess whispers when we're done posing. "I told Martin to tell his...*girlfriend*, but I can't vouch for her." She frowns at the lovely Lauren, who seems eager to gain Stella's friendship as far as I can tell. Stella's used to being the only girl in the family. I get it. I understand the scene immediately. Stella has a lot of respect for her oldest brother, and Lauren is a worthy girlfriend for him. Stella fears she'll be displaced. It's sweet, I suppose. And how much of a self-centered actor am I that my tiny emotional reaction is to feel a twinge of jealousy because I'm not the only one she's concerned with here?

When Joe shows me the shots to get my approval afterwards, I don't think I've ever seen myself looking quite so happy and at peace, or Stella looking so hopeful. "Can you send me those?"

"Of course." He seems pleased by the request. "What are your folks up to this week—oh wait. They wouldn't be celebrating Thanksgiving." Joe Starkey may already be approximately one out of three sheets to the wind.

"Correct," I pat him on the back. "They're both back home in London for a short while, actually. I Skyped with them earlier." I told them about Stella, but I suppose he doesn't need to know that. "My mum made me promise I'd eat until I'm full today."

"Aww," says Joe. "Sounds like my wife." Before I can think of what to say to that, he says, "Speaking of eating—let's eat!"

Billy has muted the television and set up a Spotify holiday pop music playlist. The dining table is big and covered with huge platters of food, a big simple vase of flowers in the center (that I had sent to Stella yesterday), and lovely but casual dinnerware that invites you to relax and eat and feel at home. It all feels rather European, for such an American occasion. No one stands on ceremony. We appear to be sitting wherever we wish to, and I wish to sit next to Stella. Stella appears to wish to be next to the wine. She pours herself a full glass of white wine and gulps much of it down before holding up the bottle to me.

"White or red?"

"Is there any white left?"

"Give me a minute and there won't be."

She may be a tad more nervous than I thought.

Billy reaches across the table to grab a hot bun, and Stella smacks the back of his hand, making him drop it. Yes, she definitely sees herself as the mother figure here. I make like I'm reaching for a hot bun to see what she'll do, and with the reflexes of a vampire, she seizes my hand and pulls it under the table, squeezing it as she leans in to tell me that they have a little ritual before they eat. I don't even try to surreptitiously reach for her thigh, that's how much I love this hand holding. That and the fact that her father is seated next to me.

"Instead of saying grace," Joe addresses Lauren and me from the head of the table, "Cora liked us to go around the table and say what we're thankful for before we eat. So if you don't mind, we'll do that before digging in."

"Oh that's great. That's what we do too!" says Lauren.

"Kevin, why don't you start."

Kevin sighs. He doesn't like to talk, but I've poked my head in when he's teaching a class, and he seems to love yelling at people to engage their core. "Okay. I'm thankful for all this food that we'll supposedly get to eat eventually. I'm thankful for Dennis the new barber because he's upped my beard game this year."

His family hoots and applauds his beard.

"And I really like my job, so that's cool. Thanks, guys."

Billy barely even waits for Kevin to finish before launching into his soliloquy. "I'm thankful for my boy Chet. I'm so grateful to you, Evan, for getting him a job."

I nod and smile.

"I'm thankful for Mom, for bringing me into this awesome family, in this badass little town, and I'm super thankful that I finally got this deep V-cut here..." He lifts up his T-shirt to display his lower abs.

Martin whistles, and Lauren applauds. "I think I need some pictures of you two for my girlfriends," she says, pointing at Billy and Kevin.

I can tell that Stella is working hard to keep a smile on her face. She lets go of my hand and sits up straight in her chair. "I'm thankful for this wine. I'm thankful that Mom collected kitchen timers, because every dish turned out perfect today. I'm thankful for my family and this town and my cat's health and my home and the gym and my new friend..." She looks over at me coyly. It feels better than the time Anthony Hopkins thanked me in his Olivier Award acceptance speech.

I clear my throat—not because I'm choked-up by how much I like this girl sitting next to me but because I'm a pretentious actor and we do this to attract attention while pausing for effect... "I am very thankful that I've come to Port Gladstone and met this family. I'm thankful for my parents' health and the good fortune I've had in my career and my new friend..."

Joe waits approximately half a second before taking his turn. "I'm thankful for Cora and this beautiful family she gave me, and this house and this town and the gym, and my eyebrows, and Stella's and Martin's new friends, and I hope these other two dummies can make a nice new friend or two by *next* Thanksgiving."

"Or twelve," quips Billy.

Martin keeps his arm around his beaming girlfriend and says, "It's great to be home. I've loved being in Bellingham, but I can't wait to get back here for good next year."

Stella claps her hands together quietly, like a little girl. "Yay."

"I'm thankful that Stella didn't screw up this meal like she did last year..."

"Hey! That was *your* fault because you got me drunk while I was cooking!"

"And you don't need any help today, obviously." He smiles. "I'm thankful for all of you guys here at this table, but this year I'm especially thankful for this angel walking into my life and turning it upside-down and around and right-side up."

"Wow. I got dizzy just listening to that sentence," Lauren says. "I'm so thankful for this amazing meal you've made for us, Stella. And to Joe for inviting us to this wonderful house, and to Kevin for his beard and Billy for his abs, and Chet for being so cute, and Evan Hunter for being so dreamy and for being here—which is insane. Most of all, I'm thankful to Martin for being the best guy I've ever known and leading me to the opportunity to work with you all at the gym next year."

Everyone looks at Stella for three awkward seconds before Joe raises his glass and says, "Cheers—let's eat!"

Stella appears to be a bit gobsmacked as everyone passes around dishes and loads up their plates. Joe deftly changes the topic by asking me about the movie. I oblige, but all I want to do is take Stella's hand under the table again.

After polishing off another glass of wine and a turkey leg, Stella blurts out, "I'm sorry... Can somebody please tell me what Lauren was talking about? Are you going to be working at the gym next year?"

Lauren gives Martin and Joe a look.

"Umm, well, I guess it's not official yet..."

Martin pipes up. "We're planning to expand the business when I get back, you know that. But not just my sports psychology practice—Lauren is going to be our in-house health and wellness consultant, plus she can help you out with managing the expansion. We're taking over the lease next door. I thought Dad told you."

Well, I guess this is the awkward family stuff that always comes up at holiday dinners.

Stella looks at her dad, her eyes pink-rimmed and watery as they seem to be so often lately. Apparently it's not allergies after all. "You've all been planning this? And you didn't tell *me*? The manager?"

"Not *planning*, honey. It's early stages—it came up in one big conversation we had once when we were all Skyping."

She drops her fork. "You were all Skyping without me? When? I don't understand why you wouldn't mention it. It's one thing for you guys to have an ongoing text conversation that doesn't include me—I don't need to hear about athlete's foot and jock itch and how you make fun of me—"

"We do not text about athlete's foot," says Billy. "You're just so resistant to change." He's gripping his fork and knife so tightly his finger pads turn red and white. "We didn't want to stress you out and deal with you getting upset until it was necessary."

"Oh, well-played, guys. Now I'm totally not upset about the fact that you don't give a shit about me when it comes to the family business that I've helped run for years!"

"Everybody gives a shit about the work you do," her father assures her.

Lauren and I exchange a quick glance between nonfamily members before she says, "I didn't know you guys didn't tell her. I'm so sorry, Stella. I thought you knew about this. You guys should have told her. She's the manager."

I see Stella's body relax a little. She slow-blinks at Lauren and says, "Thank you. I don't mean to make a big deal about it. I think it sounds great. I just don't know why I had to be blindsided about this."

"We apologize, Stella," says Joe. Something he obviously doesn't say to anyone very often. "Can we get back to eating and talking about your friend's movie now?"

Before either of us can respond to that, the intro to that OneLove cover of "Rockin' Around the Christmas Tree" comes on over the speakers, and everyone stares at me wide-eyed. Like they expect me to burst into tears or flip the table. Billy jumps up and runs over to the old iPod that's hooked up to the sound system to skip the song.

"For the record," I say, "I prefer their cover of 'Jingle Bell Rock.'"

After dinner and dessert, when the Starkey sons are clearing the table and Stella and Lauren are cleaning up in the kitchen, seemingly bonding, Papa Joe leads me over to sit next to him by his old armchair. He is now, conservatively speaking, just under two sheets to the wind. Not maudlin but certainly more emotional than usual. Stella, meanwhile, is still drinking beer while doing the washing up.

"You're a good man, Mr. Hunter."

"Thank you, Mr. Starkey. You are an excellent one."

"I try. I was a good husband, I know that. I'm only a pretty good dad, but I try."

"Stella thinks the world of you."

"Yeah, well, she's very forgiving. After Cora died… You know about what happened to their mother?"

"I've been told, yes. I'm so sorry."

"Yeah. It's hardest around the holidays. And at dinner every night, really. But we get by. Life goes on. But it changed all of us. I was broken, and I never should have let my kids see me like that. But what can you do? At first I indulged Stella's caregiver instincts because it seemed to make her happier and more focused. Everyone likes to feel needed and important, right? But I was just fooling myself. I liked keeping her close. I don't think I clipped her wings, but I certainly didn't encourage her to spread them."

I say nothing because I've enjoyed more than one conversation with an inebriated older person in my day, and I'm never the one with something interesting to say in these situations.

"She's happy," he says, looking toward the kitchen. "I mean, she's usually content and fine and all, but lately she actually seems happy. Aside from that thing that just happened at dinner. Because we're idiots. We're just not good at dealing with her sometimes. No matter how much we love her." He looks over at me. "*You're* good at dealing with her."

"I enjoy her company." Classic English understatement.

He nods and looks disappointed.

Fuck it. "I really like her, Joe. A lot. If it's all right with you, I'd like to try to be less discreet about…the time we're spending together."

His phenomenal eyebrows reach skyward.

"I'm not asking for her hand in marriage—yet. I just meant to say that once it gets out that we're seeing each other, it could change things."

"Ah. Sure. Sure sure."

"I'm not worried for *me*. It's more for her and your family business."

His hands grip the arms of the armchair like he's bracing himself for something. "You aren't expecting, like, media chaos or anything, are you? This place is pretty mellow."

"God no, nothing like that. And please know that I've always been mum about the girls I date, but it always gets out somehow. I'm making too big a deal of this already—forget I said anything."

He's staring up at the painting of the beach and the ocean. Something tells me it won't be difficult for him to forget what I said. He really is melancholy about his wife.

Two hours later, after indulging in the enormous cookies that Billy brought, after a very loud and competitive game of Charades, wherein Stella, Lauren, and I totally crushed the Starkey men, it's now time for me to head home. I have to respond to dozens of emails from people about the play I'll be doing next in London and give that play another read-through.

Stella stands on the front porch with me, swaying a bit as she holds both my hands. It's started to rain rather hard. The air smells of pine-scented chimney smoke, and the neighborhood is so very still and quiet aside from the rain.

"I'm sorry we didn't get to spend more time alone together today. I never got to show you the rest of the house. Do you want to see my old room?"

"Not unless you're prepared to explain to everyone why a famous movie star is unabashedly fucking you in it. I don't think I could control myself."

"I just might be fine with that, you know. I'm super tipsy." She leans forward, resting her forehead against my chest.

"You're colorful."

"I'm drunkity drunk, and I'm embarrassed."

"You shouldn't be."

"What are *you* like when you're drunk?"

"Unbearably dazzling."

"I bet you are. Do you wish you hadn't come?"

"I wish you were in my bed with me right now."

"Why are you so wonderful? I'm an idiot. I overreacted at dinner, didn't I?"

This is a trap. I know a conversational trap when I hear one, and this one has been casually laid out for me, but it's a minefield. Fortunately, my answer is an honest one. "I think they should have discussed it with you, but I also think they weren't being malicious in any way by not doing so. They just weren't sure how to broach the subject."

She shakes her head. "I've been fooling myself,

thinking I'm holding this family together. They don't really need me."

I grab her hand. What I really want to say is: You *have* been fooling yourself. You don't have to stay here. Come with me. Come be with me everywhere, all the time. But I don't say that. I say, "That's definitely not true. You're the heart of the family, it's clear. Men just aren't always very good at dealing with matters of the heart, that's all."

She's like a tight fist that's unfurling to reveal a lovely flower in the palm of its hand.

"Why *are* you so wonderful?"

"Will you come see me later?"

She shakes her head. "My dad...I should spend the night here. He gets sad..."

"I understand."

"I'll call you, though. Drive safe. Text me when you're home."

"Yes." I kiss her forehead. "Yes."

17

STELLA

*A*ll in all, the dinner could have been worse, but Evan Hunter could not have been better.

When we were washing dishes in the kitchen, Lauren—who is quickly growing on me—kept trying to get me to open up about my relationship with him. I never did, but she was pretty sweet about it.

"You should see how he looks at you." She smiled. There didn't appear to be an ounce of gossip or malice in her voice or expression, but for some reason, I just couldn't have that conversation with her. Not yet, anyway. "He's got it bad," she said.

I don't know if that's true, but I know how that feels, I thought to myself.

Now that he's left, I'm sad. My brothers are so noisy and rambunctious, but the house seems quiet and devoid of electricity without him. Besides Lauren, I've known him the shortest amount of time, and yet he seems to get me more than these beloved idiots I've chosen to devote my life to. I honestly don't know how to feel about that. Or maybe I'm feeling too much of it to understand it myself. I find my phone where it was charging in the kitchen and discover that there's already a text from him, asking me to call him as soon as I get it.

"Hi," he says before I even realize the call has been connected.

"Are you okay?"

"Yeah yeah, I just wanted to talk about something. Can you go up to your old room? Somewhere private?"

"Sure." I run upstairs. Is this where he tells me that he doesn't want to see me anymore?

"You there yet?"

"Almost. Where are you?"

"My car."

I go into my old room, which is still furnished, still has the remnants of me in it, mixed with overflow storage boxes from the gym office. I shut the door and sit on the edge of the bed. "Okay. What's up?"

"I just had a thought." He's smiling. I can hear it in his voice.

"Does it involve angles and positions?"

"Most of my thoughts about you involve those things. But before we get back to that again, I think you and I should go for that dinner at a restaurant."

"Really?"

"Really. I don't recall you mentioning a rule about not eating with me in public."

I kick off my shoes and sit cross-legged on the bed.

"Well no. It just seems like a bigger deal to do that with *you* than with any of the other guys I've…had flings with." I slap my forehead. I wish there were another way to say it.

"You still need to think of this as a temporary fling, don't you." He's definitely not smiling anymore.

"Well…is there any other kind?"

"I prefer to think of this as a never-ending fling."

"That's…" I lie back on the bed.

"Cheesy as fuck?"

"Romantic as hell."

"Come on. Let's have every kind of fun together while we can and then go out in a blaze of glory like Butch and Sundance." There's that smiley-voice again.

"I mean. Obviously you've sold me on having dinner with you if it means we'll both get shot to death at the end of it."

"Metaphorically speaking, of course."

"Well. Better pick a nice restaurant just in case it's the last meal we ever have."

"That's the spirit."

I roll over onto one side, press the phone up closer to my ear. I do love his voice in my ear. "You're not seriously considering this? You and me, I mean." I would not be able to have this conversation with him if I didn't have alcohol in my system.

"Aren't *you*?"

"I'm not a part of your world."

"Another person is always another world, my dear. Waiting to be discovered and explored."

"Is that a line from a play?"

"It's something I've learned from studying so many

plays and characters... You could very easily become my world."

"Please tell me *that's* a line."

"Depends. Did it work?"

I am quiet, but the truth is, it always works. Everything he says, everything he does, even when I didn't think it was working on me, it worked.

"I'm sorry, darling. I didn't mean to be flippant. Of course I'm seriously considering this. You're the one who's hesitant. I've been all in from the get-go."

Okay, now that's cheesy as fuck. "All in from the get-go?"

"Chuffed from the start. And if you must know, I already spoke to your dad about it, and I have his consent to publicly date you."

"You talked to my dad about this?" I sit up again.

"I know how important your family is to you."

"Yes."

"Yes. So I figured I should—"

"I mean yes. Let's go out to dinner. Let's take this seriously. Let's be you and me."

"Good. And another thing."

"Yes?"

"I want you to know that I saw your photograph on the website for your gym. When I was still in London. I wanted to meet you even before I got here. That's how chuffed I was."

Holy shit.

"Where are you?"

"I'm still in my car outside the house."

I hang up the phone, shove it into my back pocket, fly down the stairs, and run out the front door. I'm careful not to slip off the front porch or wipe out as I dash out past the parked cars. As soon as Evan sees me, he opens the car door, meets me at the edge of the driveway, collides with me, our lips smashing together. His hands are on my face, and I am grabbing at his coat, pulling him closer. The world is spinning and crashing down around me, but I feel so steady in his arms.

I never once fantasized about kissing a British movie star in a storm, but right now, the only thing falling harder than the rain…is me.

I don't even have a hangover when I wake up in my old bed, late on Black Friday morning. I can smell coffee and breakfast sausages from downstairs, and my cheeks are still sore from smiling so much. After my dad went to bed last night, I stayed up with Lauren in front of the fire, talking to her about Martin, and then had a late-night text conversation with Evan once I was by myself. It was the best Thanksgiving I've had in many years.

It's after nine, the gym doesn't open until ten all through the long weekend, and I don't have to be in until noon to teach a yoga class. My brothers are all already there this morning. I make a call to the deli to confirm that Mrs. Flauvich will be open for dinner tonight, because last year she took the day off to go to the outlet mall with her daughter. "Never again," she says. "I'll be open. You coming in?"

"That's the plan!" I don't tell her that I'll be making her dream come true by bringing Evan Hunter, in the off chance that she'll tell the whole town. But after thinking through my options while I stared up at the ceiling last night, that's where I want to go with him. She can finally move some of those crumpets.

I'm glad to see that my dad is in good spirits, despite a hangover, and on the phone with someone, because I want to keep girl-talking with Lauren. She is so cool and grounded, but she lived her whole life in Chicago before going to Western Washington to study kinesiology and nutrition. And she seems intent on moving here to be with my brother, even though they've only been together for a few months.

"Aren't you close to people back in Chicago?"

"Of course. My whole family and my girlfriends from high school and college. But we've been good at keeping in touch so far, and they want me to be happy. I'm happiest with Martin." She grins as she finishes swallowing her oatmeal. "Who are you happiest with?"

"Evan," I say quietly, feeling guilty.

"Why do you say it like that?"

"I don't know." I try to smile as I say it again. "Evan."

"Well, now you just look creepy," she says. "But oh my God. I mean, I feel lucky—don't get me wrong. But *you* are, quite literally, the luckiest woman I know. I can name ten friends off the top of my head who would sacrifice their left tit to date Evan Hunter and three who'd cut off their left ball. That's gross, I'm sorry, but come on. He's Evan Hunter."

Exactly.

"So you don't have any reservations at all about moving here because of Martin?"

"No. Why—should I? It seems kind of great here."

"It is. It really is. I'm glad you're coming to join us." I pat her hand. "Really glad."

"Yeah. I can cover for you whenever you need to fly off to London or LA or New York to be with Evan Hunter."

I drop my forehead to the table. "I don't think that will be necessary."

"Why not? You'd go, right?"

I shake my head.

"Are you kidding?"

I shake my head again.

"Stella…"

I lift my head to look at her.

She leans forward. "I know we just met and all, but Martin told me about your first boyfriend… You aren't still waiting for him to come back, are you?"

"God no! No!"

"Good."

"I mean, I was, for like a year. But no. It's not that. I just… I mean, me going to visit Evan somewhere is not even something we've discussed. It's not an issue. Why would it be?"

"Girl, please. He adores you."

"He's a world-famous actor."

"Who adores you."

"And lives in London."

"And as far as I can tell, you aren't chained to Port Gladstone."

I can't stop shaking my head. "It would never work."

"But it *is* working."

"I know! But we haven't even had our first public date yet."

"Yet."

I don't think I've ever been excited or nervous about a date before.

I've definitely never been so excited and nervous about dinner at the deli.

I just hope the crumpets don't suck.

18

EVAN

I've played a man in love so many times, but in real life I haven't told a woman I was in love with her since I was twenty-two. She was my first and last really serious girlfriend before I started devoting myself to my career. I consider myself a student of feelings and relationships. I know what lust is. I know what a dalliance is. I know what falling in love feels like, and I have no doubt that I've been falling in love with Stella since Day One. I'm just afraid that if I tell her this now, it'll scare her off. One day, hopefully, she'll realize that when I say "hello, darling" I mean so much more than that.

As if reading my mind (something she was thankfully never able to do while we were dating), Georgia sends me a text on my London mobile. Totally out of the blue. Not a peep since she'd called to let me know things were over between us, and now she writes: **Hey you! Just sayin' hey :) Hearing great things about our movie! Hope you're well... xx G**

That ellipsis is so offensive to me now. If you're asking a question, use a bloody question mark. If you want to know whether or not I'm pissed off at you, if I'm going to cause any trouble for you when it comes to doing publicity for our film, if I'm seeing anyone else and totally over you—just fucking ask the question.

That's what Stella would do. Or at least that's what she'd tell *me* to do.

So write and tell her you're in love with someone else, you twat.

Easy for you to say, Hugh. You won't have to endure weeks of press junkets with her in January.

Bollocks. You need to know that she's not completely over you. You need everyone to be in love with you. Fucking actors.

Yeah. Fucking actors.

It takes me thirty seconds to type out a message, and then I toss that phone into a drawer: **Hi. Great to hear. Really busy over here. Take care—see you next year.**

Less than a minute later, my temporary phone rings, and I reach for it, hoping it's Stella. But it's my publicist, Henrietta. This does not surprise me. Obviously Georgia reached out because her publicist asked her to. It's all about *Fallout*. Hen's assistant had sent me links to the new trailer that's out now, and it was very good. Seeing fragments of my scenes with Georgia reminded me of our chemistry on set, but that was all it had made me think of.

"Hi, this is Evan."

"Hi, Evan! Please hold for Henrietta!"

"Thanks, Sandra."

"How's my favorite client?" asks my whiskey-voiced old friend a few seconds later.

"Hello, Hen. I don't know. I'll be sure to ask Henry Cavill when I see him."

"Ohhh, he's my favorite client to lick. You're my favorite client to talk to, which is why it has been so difficult for me to put off ringing you. Listen, luv. I know you're trying to get away from all this, but the studio needs assurances that you'll be at the premiere of *Fallout* and that you'll do publicity with Georgia. They are quite literally up my arse about it now, and I have to give them a firm answer.

"Well, I'm sure you're thrilled to have an entire studio up your arse."

"Quite true."

"Of course I'll go to the premiere."

"Even if she's there with Braden?"

"For fuck's sake, when did my life become a CW show?"

"When you started dating the stars of CW shows, luv."

"Right. I deserved that. Although to be fair, Georgia had graduated from CW star to film star long before I met her. Don't act like you don't love all this."

"I certainly didn't mean to be acting that way—I adore it! How's it looking for you date-wise? It's early yet, but you still have time to knock up a supermodel. How are you getting on with this Jess girl? I hear she's a massive twat but she's really not a bad actress. Sounds right up your alley."

"Jess is nowhere near my alley, in fact."

"Don't tell me you're already dating someone else."

"You're my publicist, Hen. You're the last person I'd tell."

"*Gasp.* I've always been your friend first. This is strictly off the record. Now dish."

"Back to the *Fallout* issue. I'll do a few joint interviews and photo shoots with Georgia, for the big papers and magazines, but that's it. Nothing live except at the premiere. Nothing on air. Nonnegotiable."

"Oooh, I do love it when you get all bossy and growly."

"Good, because I'll be that way a lot more from now on."

"Please hold while I swap out my knickers. What's gotten into you?"

I'm quite sure she can hear me smiling through her headset. "More like who've I got into."

"Oh, you naughty boy! Tell me, tell me, tell me! Do I know her?"

"Definitely not, no. She's from Port Gladstone."

"From where?"

"Port Gladstone. Where I am. Right now. We've been seeing each other for a bit. I've already met her family. Had Thanksgiving dinner at her father's house yesterday, and she and I are actually going out together for the first time tonight."

Silence. The longest stretch of silence I've ever experienced with Henrietta—nearly five seconds.

"Fuck me running—are you telling me you're going on a date with a normal human girl for once?"

"There's nothing normal about her."

"An *abnormal* human girl?"

"She's quite something, Hen. I think you'd like her. Just please don't do anything stupid like send a photographer over—I want to enjoy this bit without having to deal with that rubbish."

"Please get over yourself, sweetie. There are no paparazzi in Bumfuck, Washington, and I hate to tell you—no one would send anyone there for you."

"It's only a two-and-a-half-hour drive from Seattle…"

"You are neither a royal nor a Kardashian. Unfortunately. Don't people get more excited about photographing whales and tall trees over there?"

"I suppose you're right. It's refreshing. Maybe I'll have a look into the real estate here."

"Oh Christ, Ev. You're not going to start singing right now, are you?"

"You should be so lucky. Anyhow, if and when it does get out that I'm seeing her and the whole thing starts up…"

"You can trust me to handle it with grace and panache."

I burst out laughing. Those are two words that have never been used to describe this woman's handling of anything, and she knows it. "Try not to cock it up is the most I can ask of you. Refer to her as my new friend and request privacy."

"I hope she's hot."

"She's completely stunning." I don't know why I feel defensive. It's completely true. "In a very natural sort of way. She's a yoga instructor, actually."

"Oh well—*Nama*-fucking-*ste* to you, dear boy. I've got to jump to the other line, but thank you for confirming the *Fallout* business and good luck with the non-actress fanny."

Strangely enough, I think I might need it.

When Stella told me we'd be dining at Delilah's Deli and Café on Main Street, I thought she was joking. She's not. I've passed by here several times and recall her saying it's her favorite place for lunch, but I've never paid much attention to it.

"So this is your location of choice for a last supper?" I ask as I hold the glass front door open.

"Did I not mention she has crumpets and marmalade and your favorite brand of tea?"

"Right. Say no more."

It's a cute spot, this. Not like a noisy family style New York deli or an Italian deli. It's a clean, modern space with wood-paneled and bright white tiled walls, marble countertops, and stainless steel shelves neatly stacked with high-end groceries. Ella Fitzgerald sings breezily from some hidden speakers. This is the kind of place you'd find tucked away round the corner from my flat in Notting Hill, really. I should have known Stella's favorite place would be this appealing to me.

There are only about ten tables in the dining area, a couple of families seated and eating, some singles at the window counter with their books and magazines. My Tom Ford slim-fit dress shirt may not have been the best choice for this outing, but I'm glad we're here. More than anything, I'm glad to be here with my date, who is holding my hand and pulling me toward the counter. A very cute plump lady in her late fifties is gaping at me with a massive salami in one hand, a baguette in the other.

"Holy schnitzel," she mumbles.

"Mrs. Flauvich, we're here for the crumpets and marmalade and English tea!"

Still clinging to the salami and baguette, Mrs. Flauvich stage whispers to Stella, "What's happening?"

"Delilah Flauvich, this is Evan Hunter."

"Very nice to meet you. I really like your café." I reach out to shake her hand as she points back and forth between Stella and me with the salami.

"You're here *together?* Stella baby—*what. Is. Happening?*" She puts down the salami and baguette, pulls off her plastic gloves, and fusses with her hair as she jogs around the counter to join us. She thrusts her phone into Stella's hand. "Take a picture of me quick, before I scare him off!"

Stella seems so happy to be introducing me to this woman. It's very sweet.

"I promise to stay for the crumpets," I tell Mrs. Flauvich as she wraps her arms around my waist.

"Let me give you a hug! I *love* you, you handsome, beautiful man! What is this? So many movie people have been coming in, but never you, and here you are! What's happening right now, Stella?"

"Stop moving your mouth so I can take a picture!"

Ten minutes later, after approximately twenty hugs and kisses, forty pictures, and one shameless ass grab (the lady grabbed mine, not the other way around), Mrs. Flauvich seems to finally comprehend that Stella and I are here together on a date. We are seated at a table in the center of the café, with my favorite Yorkshire Gold tea and a tray of biscuits while we wait for the crumpets and about ten other dishes that our hostess insisted we try, as well as one sandwich that Stella assures me will "knock my proper English socks off." I hold Stella's hand on the tabletop and can't stop smiling at her.

"You look especially beautiful tonight. Why is that?"

"Maybe it's the five pounds I gained yesterday."

"I think you're radiant because you're so happy to be with me."

"Or that. That might be it."

As one of the families is getting up to leave, the mother stops by our table and apologizes for bothering us but tells me she's a fan and glad to have me here in town. The locals here really are wonderfully polite and low-key. It's not like the restraint of my countrymen. It's more of a laid-back attitude and a respect for personal space. I like it. Once the family has passed by, Stella's smile slowly fades as she looks past me.

"Crap."

"What's wrong?"

"Nothing. It's Kwas."

I glance over my shoulder and see the fellow who was annoying Stella at the gym my first day there.

He's standing there staring. "Hey, guys! Hey —*Downton Abbey*! I *know* who you are now!"

"Good evening." I give him a nod.

"Hi there," Stella says as she reaches out to hold both of my hands across the table.

Mrs. Flauvich brings out our crumpets and butter and marmalade. It's a very weird starter, but I'm happy to indulge. Mrs. Flauvich kisses both Stella and me on the tops of our heads before retreating behind the counter and telling Kwas that he'll have to wait a minute to order.

"So these are crumpets?" Stella picks one up, inspecting it.

"They're griddle cakes," I explain. "A breakfast food. Delicious when warm and smothered with butter. Just the best. These are premade, but my mum and nan make them fresh with batter on a pan."

She takes a bite of buttered crumpet, chews, and makes a face. "Oh." She swallows, grimacing. "It's…spongy."

I take a big bite and wink at her. "Mmm. I love sinking my teeth into a nice, warm, spongy buttered crumpet."

She blushes. "Why does everything you say sound so dirty to me now?"

"It's because every thought you have about me now is so dirty."

She smirks and is about to say something witty and delightful, I expect, but her breath catches as her eyes dart over toward the counter. "Shit," she mutters, frowning.

I look over and see that The Kwas is standing over there with his camera out, filming us.

Stella is glaring at him. "That little turd. He isn't even hiding."

"Look at me, darling," I say calmly. She finally does as I tell her to. "Just keep smiling. Ignore him."

"But he's being an idiot."

"Yes, and it's important that you don't look upset in the pictures."

"Why? Oh my God—you don't think he's going to try to sell them to gossip sites or something?"

I continue to smile. "It's possible. He might be a very enterprising young man. You never know."

"No way. I'm gonna kill him." She scoots her chair back and starts to get up.

"Sit down, luv, right now." I use my stern school-teacher voice, and she seems to like it. She sits down immediately, her lips parting a tiny bit. I file that away for later. Out of the corner of my eye, I can see that the fuckwit is still holding his phone up and moving slowly to get different angles.

I lower my voice. "Just pretend you don't know he's there. If you yell and chase after him, that's the shot they'll use online and you'll look like a crazy person. I want to be the only one who sees you going crazy, when I look up at you from between your gorgeous legs." I raise my mug of Yorkshire Gold. "Cheers."

She clinks mugs with me. "Cheers. I'll drink to that." She laughs into her tea. "Well, at least I've already come clean to my family about you."

"Oh yes? What exactly did you tell them?"

"That we've been seeing each other. That we'd be going out tonight. That I'm rather fond of you."

I lick butter from my thumb. "I told my parents I'm fond of you too."

She appears quite shocked by that. "You did? Really?"

"When we Skyped yesterday. Calm down. They were just asking if I'd made any new friends here."

"Oh. Well, anyway. I still think Jason's too dumb to know what to do with pictures of famous people, but whatever. He'll probably just show his buddies at work."

"It's not so different, you know. Dating in a small town and dating a person of fame."

"Oh my God, just say *famous person*. It's like you do that just to bug me."

I grin at her.

"Oh. You *are* doing it just to bug me. Well done."

"As I was saying..."

"Yes, the paparazzi and everyone gossiping about us, I get it."

"Still, I would strongly encourage you to *not* Google my name for a while so you can avoid whatever may come of this online. I haven't Googled myself in years, and I'm so much happier for it."

"Yeah, but you pay other people to Google you."

"Indeed I do. But I also pay them to *not* tell me about it unless I ask them to or if there's something very important I should know about. So don't Google me. Promise? I'm here with you. That's all that matters."

She leans forward and takes my hand over the table again. "Tell me more about you between my legs. That's something very important that I'd like to know more about."

"Well, where to begin?" I say, as if she'd asked me about my favorite movies. "I like to begin by kissing your ankle and then slowly kissing up your bare leg as it rests upon my shoulder. And then grab you by the bum while I make my approach to your tight, wet, pink fanny and my tongue swirls around your perky little clit."

"Ohhh myyy!" says Mrs. Flauvich as she appears out of nowhere and places three plates of food on our table. "Holy schnitzel," she mutters as she scuttles off to the kitchen in back.

Stella covers her mouth with both hands, shaking with laughter.

"Yes, indeed. Speaking of pounded meat…" I continue.

19

EVAN

*I*t's the last night of our glorious long weekend together. Stella and I have enjoyed nights at my house, in front of the fire, in front of the telly, each with one hand holding a mug of hot toddy and one hand up the other's sweater. Now, I feel it's time for me to take things to another level.

I'm so used to reacting to my girlfriends' attempts to push the envelope of intimacy. So used to my girlfriends being the ones who ask for more than I'm able to give them. Here I am, plotting my moves with a woman who isn't asking for enough from me. Not nearly enough.

"You're leaving now? It's only eight o'clock."

"I haven't been spending enough time with my cat. I know that sounds like some lame excuse, like 'I have to wash my hair,' but I do have to spend time with my cat, and wash my hair, and do laundry."

I watch her pull on her coat and boots, and then I

go to my room to get something and call out, "Wait for me. I'm going to follow you in my car."

"Why?" She comes to my bedroom door.

"Because we're switching to night shoots starting this week and our schedules won't mesh very well for a bit. So you and I are going to your flat tonight because I get to sleep in tomorrow morning." I actually have her address because I've been having gifts delivered there, but I want to follow behind her anyway. To make sure she doesn't try to skip town so she can avoid having me in her home.

"Um. No."

"But I want to meet your Muffin Top."

"She doesn't like meeting people."

"She just hasn't met the right people yet. Also, I'm going to wash your hair and help with your laundry."

"That is not happening. Ever."

"It's happening."

"Okay, fine, but you're not spending the night."

"Right. But I'm bringing an overnight bag because I am spending the night."

She stands perfectly still, shaking her head and rolling her eyes at me, but there's a big smile waiting to be freed, I can see it. "Fine!" she says, blowing out a breath. "Fine." And there's that smile.

I'd never bothered to look it up before, but Stella's place is only a ten-minute drive from mine. This pleases me to no end, despite the fact that I'll only be at that house for less than a month more. As she pulls into a driveway and up past the main house, I park my car on the street, grab my bag, and get out quickly, eager to join her.

As I stroll up the drive, a middle-aged man in a sweat suit and coat comes out the side door of the main house, carrying a rubbish bag. He glances up as he drops it into a bin, squints at me through his glasses, and looks very confused indeed.

"Evening," I say, nodding at him and slowing my pace.

"Hi," he says. "Are you—is there a problem with the house?"

"The what?"

"The rental—I'm Whit. I'm the agent for the house you're staying at."

"Oh right, great, hi. I'm Evan." I shake his hand.

"Oh, I know who you are."

"No, the house is incredible, actually. I love it. No complaints."

"Okay good."

Stella gets out of her car and saunters over to join us. "Hey. He's just coming to meet Muffin Top," she says sheepishly.

Whit does an admirable job of not looking too bewildered. "Ah, well. You're in for a treat." He nods vigorously. "Have a good night."

Stella takes my hand, pulling me toward the smaller version of this house, near the back end of the property.

"Whit's a good friend. I figured he would have signed an NDA or something about the rental, so I didn't tell him I was seeing you. Because then it would have been hard for him to not say anything and blah blah blah."

"That's very considerate of you, but I honestly don't care about those NDAs. They're something my business managers and lawyers like to hand out because they think they're protecting me. From what, I'm not sure."

"You don't have stalkers?"

"Not exactly, no. I've been pretty lucky in that sense so far."

She curls her arm around mine and leans in against me as we walk. "I hope you stay lucky."

"I hope I *get* lucky tonight."

"I dunno. I've never had intimate relations with another person while my cat's around." She pulls a heavy ring of keys out from her coat pocket and opens the front door. "We'd have to be as still and quiet as possible." She waggles her marvelous eyebrows. "You up for the challenge?"

"Try me," I say, finding myself getting up for it already.

Stella switches on a light, illuminating a small but lovely kitchen and a lovely but large cat who's sitting in the middle of it. Just staring up at us, as if it has been waiting for her there for hours.

"Awww, hey baby," Stella says as she kneels down to kiss it. "This is my Muffin Top. This is a man. A nice man. So be nice to him."

The cat continues to sit there and stare up at me.

She is white with ginger markings, and she is not

quite the fattest cat I've ever seen, but her fluffy face is so cute I immediately want to hold it in my hands and kiss it. This is not my usual response to felines. Truth is, I usually respond by sneezing, but if Stella can overcome her indifference to English actors, I can overcome a mild allergy to cat hair.

"Hello, Muffin Top. What do you say?" I kneel down slowly and hold my hand out for her to sniff, which she does, cautiously, before nudging it, inviting me to pat her on the head. If only it had been this easy with her mummy.

"Wow," Stella says. "That is surprising."

I start to open my mouth, but before I get a word out she says, "Do *not* make a joke about having a way with pussies."

"Am I really that predictable?"

"Only where dirty jokes are concerned. I fear I've created a monster." She stands up, crossing her arms at her chest. "Well. This is it. You're in my home. Happy"

I give Muffin Top one last chin rub before standing up. "Deliriously so... Nervous?"

She scoffs. "I have no reason to be nervous, just because this is the first time a man I've been having regular intercourse with is inside my home." She states this very unconvincingly while fidgeting with the zipper of her coat. "I'm going to get my laundry. Shall I make you a cup of decaf tea? Are you hungry? I can make you a sandwich."

"Seriously, there's no need for you to be nervous, darling."

"I agree. I'm not nervous." She removes her coat,

gestures for me to give her mine, and hangs them both up near the door. "I'll make you a sandwich and a cup of decaf, and you can watch TV or something while I do my thing. I don't have a ton of groceries, since I've been spending so much time with you..." She pulls a bag of crisps from a cupboard, along with half a loaf of bread and a head of lettuce from the fridge. When she slams the fridge door shut, she frowns at me and says, "I'm making you a lettuce, mayo, and potato chip sandwich. You've probably never had potato chips in a sandwich before, have you?"

"You're saying you want to put potato chips—crisps —*inside* the sandwich?"

"Exactly. There are three things you will always find in a sandwich of my making, Sir Fancypants—potato chips, mayo, and awesomeness."

"Crisps? And mayonnaise. Together? Inside the sandwich? That is madness."

"It's a way of life, my friend." She slaps the countertop, shaking her head. "You know what—this will never work. We're too different."

"Right. Let's discuss this matter further in your bedroom, shall we?" As soon as she turns around to protest, I gather her up in my arms and carry her out of the kitchen. "Fuck the sandwich. Fuck laundry. Fuck washing your hair." I find my way to her bedroom and toss her onto the bed. Her expression is a delightful mix of indignance and excitement. I use my sternest schoolteacher voice while removing my shirt. "Take your fucking clothes off, Stella. Now."

"Fine. But you're not spending the night."

I spent the night.

Being in bed with this woman is fantastic, but waking up in her bed, once the sun finally reveals itself and I can see out the bedroom window... Christ. What a view. Different from the one at my rental house but just as lovely. Both of my charming bedmates are still sleeping, one with her back to me, and one has made herself comfortable on top of the puffy white comforter, curled up between my legs. I'd prefer it if Stella were the one between my legs, but Muffin Top is very warm and sweet.

However, that's not the view I'm referring to. The foot of Stella's bed is pushed up against the wall with the window, and with my head propped up on two down pillows, I can see out the picture window down to the shore, where a family of deer are currently frolicking about. Deer. Frolicking on the beach. What strange paradise is this?

This is her window to the world, and I completely understand why she is satisfied with this view alone. I suppose if I woke up to this every day, I wouldn't have much desire to go anywhere else either... It's just that I *have* to go other places. Always. And I like having her with me. I just don't know if I'll be able to have both.

She stirs, and the cat gets up, stretches, and climbs over me to snuggle with her. "Morning," she says to Muffin Top. "Oh hello," she says to me. "There's a man in our bed," she murmurs to the cat.

"It's a very nice bed," I say, turning my face away from the cat's bum.

"I'm glad you spent the night. Thanks for not snoring or kicking me or hogging the covers."

"I do still *sleep* like a proper Englishman."

She manages to move the cat to the side and sit up, looking out the window. "Oh, the deer!"

"Is that a regular occurrence?"

"Oh yes. Some would say we have a deer problem around here, but I love them. Don't see them as often this time of year, of course, but...yeah. Deer on the beach. Otters crossing the street. That's my town."

"I like it."

"Good. Can I ask you a favor?"

"Yes, but my jaw is still sore from the favor I did for you last night, so don't expect as high caliber a performance this morning."

"Actually, this one doesn't involve my vagina."

"Intriguing. But also boring. Do go on." I prop myself up on one arm.

"There are a few people I know who would really appreciate an autographed photo of you... Can I give you a list? I assume that's something your assistant does for you?"

"I'd be delighted to do it myself..." I pretend to write out, "'To Stella, my number one fan. Thanks for the shag, luv. Keep watching, darling.'"

"Well, to be honest, most of these women are approximately ninety years old. Including my friend Mona's grandma."

"Ahh! My hardcore granny fanbase. Love 'em to

bits."

"Evan…"

"Yes?"

"I'm a Hunterhoe too, you know?"

"What's that, darling? Is this an admission of admiration?"

She lowers her eyes, bites her lip, and nods. "I do. I admire you." When this darling bud opens, she is the most delicate flower.

"I admire you too." I kiss her on the forehead. "Give me the list. I always keep headshots with me when I travel."

She reaches for the notebook on her bedside table, tears out a piece of paper, and hands it to me. She's already written the list of eight names. It's the last name that gives me pause.

"You know someone named Ethel Beavers?"

She laughs. "I wish! I just wanted you to write the words 'Dear Ethel Beavers,' and then I was going to save that one for myself."

"You're a lunatic. I like waking up with you."

She tilts her head but says nothing as she lifts herself up out of bed. "I'll make breakfast. Or wait— you probably can't eat yet?"

"Alas, I cannot. I do have to get going, though. Supposed to meet the director for coffee later to discuss a few scenes."

"Okay." She pulls a cardigan on over her camisole and panties. The way she moves, even when she's getting dressed, just makes me want to undress her immediately. "You want coffee now?"

"Nah. I'm awake." Muffin Top hops to the floor with a thud, and I'm alone in this pillowy heaven and wishing I could stay here as long as I'd like.

She hugs me for a long time as I stand in front of the door. "So you'll be working at night and sleeping during the day?"

"Pretty much." I stroke her hair.

"Okay. I need to hang out with my dad this week anyway."

"Okay. But if you ever want to swing by my trailer to hang out with me, just let me know."

She looks up at me, resting her chin on my chest, smirking.

"Even for completely nonsexual hangout sessions. It would just be nice to see you."

"Okay. Well, maybe I can stop by for a bit after work."

I know I should be happy that we've come this far in the past week—dinner with her entire family, dinner out in public, me sleeping at her house—but I just can't wait to bring this up. "Also, if you'd like to come back to London with me when I'm done here, you're welcome to."

"What?" She seems genuinely shocked by this invitation.

"Well, you know, I'll have one week of shooting the film in London before the movie's completely wrapped. Then it's Christmas. I'm sure you'll want to spend it with your family, but I just wanted you to know you're welcome to come with me."

She's quiet for a terrifying few seconds. "In a month?"

"In less than a month."

"To London?"

"Yeah. And I'll probably spend Christmas in Cornwall with my family. You'd be welcome to join." Once I've brought it up, I can't stop. "I'll have a two-week break between Christmas and starting rehearsals for a play I'm doing in London, but I have to stay on the continent because I have meetings here and there. So if you can come visit me for a holiday, that's also an option... I'd also like you to come with me to the premiere of my next movie, in Los Angeles later in January, and to the wedding of a close friend of mine in February, in the English countryside."

She doesn't look too horrified, so I plow ahead.

"My work schedule is essentially full for the next two years. I usually get a couple of weeks or, if I'm really lucky, a month off in between projects. Also, I'm a goodwill ambassador for the UN, so I visit Africa once a year, and there are other international charity and publicity events like Comic-Con of course—but you don't need to know about all that now. My career is mapped out for the near future, and I'd like for my personal life to be a little less uncertain. That's not true —I want it to be a lot less uncertain. I want the certainty of you."

She's staring at me, wide-eyed. I hear her gulp. Her eyes get red-rimmed and wet again. She sniffs. "Um."

"You don't have to RSVP now. I just want you to know what I want, and I want you to think about it."

"Okay," she squeaks. "Thank you."

I kiss her on top of her head and open the door. "Thank you. See you soon."

I'm halfway home, about to turn off of Main Street, when I get a call from Henrietta's mobile number. If she's calling me from her own phone, then it must be important. Either that or she's pocket-dialing or drunk-dialing me. You never know with Hen.

"You'd better not be drunk," I say as I put her on speakerphone.

"I hope *you* are."

"Why?"

"It's not a really big deal or anything, just some pictures of you and your friend the yoga instructor in a café, all over the Internet."

Fuck. I'd forgotten about that incident. So Kwas isn't merely an idiot; he is also an asshole.

"I don't think I want to know."

"Well, if you like her, you might want to figure out how to placate her if she finds out."

"Shit. Is it bad? Fucking hell. Why are people such ghastly evil fuckwits? How could anyone write anything bad about her?" I pull over to the side of the road so that I don't accidentally hit the gas pedal and ram into some innocent local driver when all I want to do is mow down the Internet.

"No need to throw a wobbly. At least whoever sent

the video and photos out didn't know her name."

"Why d'you say that?"

"Because none of the blogs mention her name. She's 'unidentified natural-looking brunette woman.'"

"Interesting." Is he protecting her? Or trying to keep her to himself somehow? Fucking Kwas. What an enigma.

"Comment-wise, there are just some unfavorable superficial comparisons to the other girls you've dated, of course. And people assuming you just happened to share a table with her because there was nowhere else to sit. Or that you've been so gutted by Georgia that you're dating down because that way you could never be sad when you leave her. That sort of thing. People put a lot of thought into your inner life, really."

"Is that what you think, Hen?"

"Is *what* what I think, sweets?"

"That last thing. Because it's the opposite of true."

"I don't think anything, Mr. Hunter, you know that. I'm the fuckwit you pay to tell people what *you* want them to think. Oh, here's a funny thing that Sandra found—there's a Twitter account that's been trolling anyone who makes rude comments about your girl. Been very busy, this...MoaningMona. She basically Tweet replies to all critical people to fuck off because this is the best girl you've ever been with and you're clearly smitten."

I laugh. Mona. I'll have to sign a special eight-by-ten glossy for her as well as her gran.

"She's right, you clearly are smitten. I just wonder…"

"What? I've got to get ready for a meeting."

"Right, ho! Off you go, then!"

"No, finish that thought—you just wonder what?"

"You still want me to tell them she's your new friend the yoga instructor and to respect your privacy, all that? Not ready to use the term 'dating' or 'girl-friend' or 'new squeeze?'"

I mull it over for three seconds. "Yeah, for now that's all anyone needs to know."

"'Kay. I'm just wondering why you decided to take her out like that. If things are going so well. Are you testing her? To see how she handles things?"

After remembering to breathe, I'm finally able to respond with: "I had no idea anyone here would know to send pictures to bloggers. Doesn't anyone have anything better to do than try to analyze my inner life?"

"Good point. Toodles!"

I hang up and slowly pull out into the street again, but inside my head, thoughts are racing. How *will* Stella handle things? Is it fair to call it a test? That makes me sound like I'm playing games, and I'm not. And I'm not naïve, I knew this would happen eventually, but I didn't expect it to happen so soon. I just need to know if she's willing to put up with the crap she'll sometimes have to put up with if she's my girlfriend, because if she isn't, then I'm...

You are so fucking fuckity fuck fucked. You pathetic bastard.

That's right, Hugh.

I am so fucked.

20

STELLA

I don't know how it's possible to be so happy and sad and comforted and scared at the same time. I'm at work, smiling at members and delivery people, floating on a fluffy white cloud that's cushioned with every kind and sexy phrase and gesture that Evan has embraced me with. Meanwhile, the words: "premiere," "Los Angeles," "London," "Africa," and "wedding" thunder in the distance. I don't want to tell myself that I should be more excited by the idea of traveling to be with him. I just know that he should be with someone who is. Even if it isn't me. Even if it will crush me to not be with him. Even though I'm not one hundred percent certain that I'm still the person who doesn't want to leave this place.

I don't feel capable of eating when it's time for my lunch break, so I just head down to the beach for a walk to clear my head. To the spot my mother loved, the place where I first spotted a handsome stranger. The music of The National, whom I love, is too melancholy for me now. I switch to a nineties pop playlist, and suddenly I'm ready for whatever love has to offer.

Almost as soon as I take a seat on my favorite log, I get a text...

MONA: Are you okay???
ME: I'm better than I have been in years. I think. Why?
MONA: Nothing! Glad to hear it! Never mind!!!

A three question mark "Are you okay" plus a three exclamation point "Never mind" equals I'm giving her a call.

I can hear Portland street noise in the background when she answers with phony cheer, "Heeeeey, girl!"

"Mona. What?"

"Nothing! I'm so glad you're happy!"

My stomach clenches before my brain even remembers The Kwas incident at the deli the other night. "Oh shit. Are there pictures of us online?"

She pauses for a very telling half a second before saying, "Yup! But it's so not a big deal like—literally nothing compared to all the shit that's going on in the world right now."

"Oh God. I can't look. I promised him I wouldn't."

"No no no—it's seriously not bad! The pictures are so cute—really! You both look so in love and happy, and I love that you were at the deli! There are just so many idiots and assholes with Internet access, it's depressing."

"So are bloggers writing mean things about me or something?"

"No! No, they just post them and then people make stupid comments. Honestly, it's all so dumb, I shouldn't have brought it up. How was your Thanksgiving?"

"Tell me."

"Nope."

"Tell me the three worst things you've read."

"Ummm. Well, I'm in line at a food truck. I can't…" Her voice muffles, and I can tell she's putting in her order. "Hang on, Stel, I gotta get my money out."

All I can think about is that I should have gone up to Jason as soon as I saw him with his phone and given him a piece of my mind. And that I shouldn't have kissed him on Halloween. I refuse to regret going out to dinner with Evan.

"Hey," Mona says, thankfully putting a halt to my spinning thoughts. "So first of all, this is just what it's like whenever there are pictures of him with a new girl. I remember when he first started going out with Georgia March, all these die-hard Hunterhoes were like: 'she isn't good enough for him!' 'she's too young for him!' 'it's just a movie fling and will never last!' And now they're all: 'he's just rebounding from Georgia!' and 'she must be his assistant' or 'he'll be back with Georgia in no time.' One genius wrote that you're just a decoy so people don't find out Evan's actually dating his current co-star. Which doesn't even make sense. Oh, but my favorite was when someone commented that you look like Renee Zellweger at the beginning of *Bridget Jones*. So there. The worst anyone can say about you is that you look like a beautiful Oscar winner."

"Is there a picture of me making a face when I'm eating a crumpet?"

"What? No. You're frowning at whoever's taking the pictures in one of them."

"Kwas. It was Kwas."

"Are you fucking kidding me? What. A. Douchebag."

"Does it say who I am?"

"No, you're referred to as his 'unidentified female companion.'"

"Interesting."

"I can't believe Jason Kwasnicki even knows how to sell pictures to gossip sites."

"I know."

"I wonder how much money he made."

"Who knows... You know what? Who cares. It's just words in cyberspace."

"Exactly! All that matters is what's going on between the two of you... God, it was so weird suddenly seeing pictures of you and Evan Hunter in my Instagram and Twitter feeds, but also so great because you guys look so cute together. You honestly looked so happy and beautiful, and he looks like he's completely into you."

"Yeah. I think he actually is. How are *you?*"

"Oh. Awesome. Rob has decided that we're vegetarian, so now we ride the fart train to bed every night. It's sweet, but you know, enjoy your fling with a beautiful

British movie star while you can, because that's probably nice too!"

It's true what I said about not caring what people write about me on the Internet. I don't. What I care about is how it affects Evan. While I don't believe for a second that it would change how he feels about me, I do believe it would affect his career somehow if I were his girlfriend. He's worked too long and hard to become anything less than the brightest star. I make a promise to myself not to do anything to ruin what we have while he's here, but as I stare out at the storm clouds on the horizon, I know that it's only a matter of time before the fluffy white cloud I'm floating on tumbles back to earth and washes him away from this place. I do realize that's not how clouds work. But the point is, I'm just another Hunterhoe who's grateful knowing that he's alive out there in the world. Famous last words from a girl who didn't even give a hoot about him up until a few weeks ago.

Evan has completed filming of the fishing boat scene, and now he's invited me to join him and some of the cast and crew for a drink at McSmiley's "for a pint," because he remembered that it's my favorite pub.

It has been a week since I found out about the pictures online, and every day since, he has checked in with me to make sure I'm okay about it. Every time I have told him I am okay with it, and it will always be true until I get the sense that *he isn't* okay with it. Now I get to come face-to-face with the person that the collective brain of the Internet believes Evan Hunter *should* be with now.

I may be a tad overdressed for McSmiley's, in the same outfit I wore that first night I went to Evan's house, but he seems to appreciate it. I need my sexy sweater dress and my confidence boots now, and he seems to understand this as he removes my coat and slips his arm around my waist, telling me how hot I look while he leads me toward the back of the room where the cast and crew are hanging out.

I wave to my pal Finn the bartender and the regulars as we pass, trying not to dwell on the fact that the group of people we are joining in back look like the Photoshopped "after" versions of the locals in the front half of the bar. Even the camera operators and script supervisor and key grips (whatever they are) must exfoliate every inch of themselves and deep-condition their hair regularly. Evan keeps his hand on the small of my back while introducing me to every single person he knows here, including the film's director and one of the producers, but his arm is around my shoulder when he presents me to Jess the actress.

She must still be wearing her on-camera nomakeup makeup, because there's a hyper-real quality to her skin and the definition of her eyes, but surely anyone would consider her pretty. Her eyes don't quite match her sparkly white smile, though, and her limp cold handshake gives me a chill. "Hi! It's so nice to finally meet you," she says, looking back and forth between Evan and me. "I've heard so much about you. I love that sweater dress—I have one just like it. Is it Rag & Bone?"

"I don't remember… I think I got it at TJ Maxx."

She laughs, because obviously I'm joking (I'm not). "Well, it's so cute anyway. I'm stealing her from you, Evan! Sit next to me!" She scoots over on the long bench by the table and pats the space she has made.

Evan rubs my back and asks if he can order me something, but I shake my head and take a seat and give him a reassuring look before he allows himself to be dragged away by the director.

"So…" Jess says, her voice taking on a different tone now that Evan is not around, and it is even more fake. "You must be having so much fun."

"I can't complain," I say as I reach for an empty glass and the pitcher of beer nearby. Jess appears to be drinking sparkling water, and she waits for me to finish pouring myself a pint of local brew before continuing.

"You are so lucky you drink beer."

"You don't?"

"I mean you're so lucky you don't have to worry about being thin all the time."

"Yes. I do feel very lucky right now." I take a swig and raise my glass to Evan, who winks at me from ten feet away.

"This town is so cute. I'm not even kidding, I think it's the cutest town I've ever been in. You must be so happy here."

"I am. Almost all the time."

"Oh my God, I've totally seen your gym by the way —I was walking by and peeked in. It's so cute. Seriously. It's the cutest gym I've ever seen."

"Thanks."

"Seriously, you should be so proud of it—you're the manager, right?"

"Yes. I am proud of it."

"Oh good, because you totally should be. So that's all you do? Manage the gym?"

"I'm also a yoga instructor."

"Really? Wow, that's amazing." She scans me up and down, probably comparing me to the yoga instructors she's seen in LA and wondering if I ate one of them for dinner.

"Is it?"

"Oh, and let's just address the elephant in the room..." She leans in, lowering her voice, and I'm pretty sure the elephant she's talking about is me. "I hope you know that there has never been anything going on between Evan and me. I'm like, pathetically single, but he's such a gentleman and so professional." She pats me on the arm. "I know there were pictures of us online a while ago, but obviously it was just from when we were in character."

"Oh, I know," I say. "He told me."

"Oh." She seems disappointed for about two seconds and then shakes it off. "He's such a good actor. Do you act?"

"Do I act? Like do I want to be an actress? No. Never."

"Really?" She seems to find this even harder to

believe than the fact that I'm a yoga instructor. "Not even when you were younger?"

"Nope."

"Did you always want to work at a gym, then? And by the way, I'm totally interviewing you right now."

"For what?"

"For my character research. I'm playing a local, you know, small-town girl. I mean, I only have like four scenes left to shoot, but it would be so helpful if I could just get inside your head."

"Really? Because I keep trying to get out of it."

"Hah! Please, please, please, just a few questions. Like I guess the thing that I have trouble understanding is…why does she stay? I mean, my character. Like, she's born here and she has a job here, but this is the twenty-first century. Right?"

"Last time I checked."

"I mean, nobody's making her stay here. She's single. She doesn't have a kid. She doesn't have old parents to look after. She isn't poor. She could go anywhere. But she's here."

"What does your character do?" I glance over at Evan, hoping to be rescued, but he's clearly in the middle of some animated storytelling and has about eight people totally captivated.

"She's a waitress. That's how she meets Evan's character. But there's nothing in the script about her dreaming of being something else one day. She's just a waitress. Which is so fascinating to me."

"Uh-huh."

"But my theory is that she secretly wants to be

whisked away from her life here. Which is why fate brings her this British guy who's hiding out here. So she has this adventure thrust upon her. The world comes to her, and then she gets to go with him, to finally experience the world."

"Oh yeah? That makes sense. For your character."

"Because you know, it's my job to understand what my character wants. And it's a good script—oh my God, it's a great script—and I'm so lucky to have this part. But you know, the love interest roles are never fleshed-out in this kind of film. So it's my job to figure out *the want*."

My throat is constricting, and my stupid sweater dress is making me warm again. "Well, it sounds to me like you've got it all figured out, Jess," I say and smile at her in the shiniest most superficial fake-y way I can manage. When I scan the room, trying to find my exit strategy, I feel that fate has brought one to me in the form of hilarious irony.

"You know," I say to her conspiratorially, "if you *are* single, I think maybe the best way for you to understand why someone like *your character* would stick around a town like this is to get to know the awesome guys who live here. If you're interested, I could introduce you to the most eligible bachelor in Port Gladstone..."

She follows my gaze as I turn to make eye contact with Jason Kwasnicki. I don't know if he actually got paid for the photos, but he did clearly just get a professional haircut for the first time since prom, so Jess seems genuinely intrigued when she says that she would indeed like to meet this guy so she can do more character research. I look back at Evan while I pull Jess over to Kwas, and I can tell that he knows exactly what I'm doing and he approves of it.

I really do hope that Jess understands why a young woman would want to stay in a cute small town in the twenty-first century. For the benefit of Evan's film. And I really, seriously hope she doesn't get the STD that The Kwas was rumored to have last year...but I hear the actors guild has great health coverage.

Half an hour later, Evan and I are back at my place and taking each other's clothes off before we're inside. "I'll come visit you," I say as he's kissing my neck and pulling my sweater dress over my head.

"What?" His eyes are gleaming, and he seems so taken aback.

I continue to undo his belt as I repeat myself: "I'll come visit you. After Christmas. For a holiday. Let's spend New Year's together."

I squeal when he picks me up and carries me to my bedroom. Muffin Top has already learned that my squeals and moans don't mean that Evan's hurting me; it means she should leave the room. His shirtless upper body is strong and warm, and I never want to stop touching it. He places my feet on the floor, steps behind me, and pushes my hair to one side, kissing my neck as he pulls the bra straps down off my shoulders.

"This is excellent news," he says. I think the world-famous actor is standing behind me because he doesn't want me to see how happy he is. He brushes his hands down my bare arms before slowly dragging them up my stomach. "Will you come for two weeks?"

"I can't be away for that long."

He uncovers both breasts, peeling the lace front of my bra down and massaging with both hands.

"Oh shit," I whisper, squeezing my thighs together.

He bites my shoulder, reaches for my panties, applying pressure with his whole hand right where I need it. "One week."

"I can spend three full days in Europe. Two travel days."

I curl my arm back around his neck, bracing myself, when he starts to rub my clit lightly over the fabric. My other hand reaches behind for his hard cock, which is straining inside his trousers, but he pulls away from me.

"Three days is ridiculous."

I spin around. "Three perfect days together is what we'll have."

He pushes me onto the bed, presses himself down on top of me so there is no space between us. He takes my hands and pulls them up over my head, clinging to them as he stares down at me. He isn't happy anymore, but he isn't angry either. "Stella Starkey," he mutters. It's a statement, I suppose. He seems resigned to the idea of three full days with me in Europe already. Either that or he just wants to fuck me now and can't think about anything else. I close my eyes and feel his tongue teasing my nipple.

"Don't you want to know where I'll be taking you?"

I hear him unzip his pants. He pulls down my panties, and soon he will press himself inside me, and I would probably offer to be his sex slave for the rest of my life, so I will be very clear about this before that happens.

"I will meet you anywhere, Evan Hunter. For three days. And then I'm coming home."

He says nothing more as he enters, ramming into me without working up to it. I keep my legs together under him, so all he can feel is my tight warm wetness around him, hear me say his name over and over while I whimper and undulate and he groans and pumps away the frustration.

If it were this, only ever this, it would work and I would make every promise to him.

But even as we come together, his smooth, deep voice momentarily out of his control and reaching as high a pitch as mine, all I'm aware of is the end. Because knowing that there will be an ending is what keeps me together and gives this thing we have a shape that I can understand.

I will fly to the other side of the world to be with him one last time. I don't want to say good-bye to him here. I want Port Gladstone to be the place where we were together and happy. Even though there's a very good chance that I will be miserable here without him, for a while anyway. I want him to have good memories of this town, and for once in my life, I will make beautiful memories somewhere else.

21

EVAN

Two weeks. Two weeks since I've touched Stella Starkey's skin and hair and heard her voice in my ear without a filter between us. I have shown up on time for everything here in England—filming, interviews, dinner with my parents, Christmas with my family at my grandparents' house in Cornwall. I've been present in body and mind for every moment of it, but in my heart—each beat, each second that ticks away, is a countdown to the day that I will see her in person again.

Also, my throbbing lonely cock is just aching to be reintroduced to its favorite mouth and fanny.

I've had my driver drop me off at Heathrow Airport and have my bag with me, wearing my baseball hat and sunglasses. My assistant Wendy and I decided it would be best for me to meet Stella in the arrivals terminal, and then the VIP team will escort us to the exclusive lounge and private suite for check-in and to wait for our flight to Nice. I got Stella a first-class seat from SeaTac. It's a nine-and-a-half-hour flight—not deadly but made infinitely better by comfortable seating and ice cream sundaes.

It being December thirtieth, the airport is quite busy, and I'm glad of this because it means it's less likely that I'll be recognized as I stand here waiting for my lady love to walk through the sliding doors.

Would you like me to recite my soppy voiceover from the airport scenes in Love Actually *while you wait, dear?*

No need, Hugh. I'm all stocked up in the cheese department.

Before leaving Port Gladstone, when I entered my London mobile number on her cell phone, I recorded and set up a special ringtone of myself saying "hello darling." She said it makes her wet even before she's read a text or answered my call, and that was the idea. I also set her up with cat cameras and an app so she can monitor Muffin Top while she's away and her landlords look after her in the guesthouse. She decided that would be less stressful to the cat than moving her to her dad's.

As if I needed more proof that we're perfect for each other, Stella and I both gave each other copies of *Tender is the Night*. I had a first edition shipped from New York. It cost fifteen hundred dollars, and one day I'd like to get her an inscribed first edition, but a sixty-five-thousand-dollar gift would probably make her balk at this point. She found me an early printing, and in the accompanying card she wrote out a quote:

. . .

He looked at her and for a moment she lived in the bright blue world of his eyes, eagerly and confidently.

I have tried not to read into it too much. It's sweet and lovely, although the words "for a moment" make me nervous. But moments are all that anyone has, aren't they, and each moment I've spent with her so far has been a precious page that I've turned, delighting in the story and feeling relief when I find that there are more pages left to turn.

"Mr. Diver?" says a man's quiet deep voice behind me. I turn to find a suited gentleman with a photo ID tag. I'd forgotten that Wendy had arranged for someone from Heathrow VIP to meet me here. We'll be chauffeured to another terminal, which is great, but all I can think about now is how good it will feel to have Stella in my arms again.

"Hello," I say, shaking his hand.

"I am John, from Heathrow VIP. I'll be escorting you and your friend to the lounge. As you should know, her flight has landed and she should be clearing customs now. May I take your bag for you?"

"Sure, thanks." It's when I'm handing him my bag that I notice it. The darkly clad men across the terminal clocking me and heading my way. Shit. Despite the ingenuity of these special paid services, some people have figured out that they just have to keep tabs on the uniformed staff to catch sight of any celebrities as they're ushered in and out.

When Stella emerges from the international arrivals exit, I get to enjoy three beautiful seconds of her gorgeous unadulterated smile as our eyes meet. Even before I've reached her, the camera flashes begin their assault. When I hug her, I feel how tense her body is and say in her ear, "Just smile and don't look at them. This gentleman will lead us to a car right outside. They can't follow us to the lounge."

There are only three paparazzi, but with all the dizzying flashing of their massive cameras, it feels like there's an army of them surrounding us. Once they close in, people start rubbernecking and following them. There are some shrieks of my name. John takes Stella's suitcase and leads us toward the exit to the curb as I hold Stella's hand and wrap my arm around her. John is polite but firm in asking the photographers to stay back.

"Evan, is this your new girlfriend?"

"What's your name, luv?"

"Evan, is this your New Year's date?"

"Evan, are you still in touch with Georgia?"

"Evan, is this your rebound? Have you seen Georgia and Braden together in London?"

Does anyone still actually give a fuck about Georgia and me? Surely not. I maintain a polite smile, head up and looking past these little pricks.

It's quite a skill these men have developed—walking backwards while taking pictures and either trying to get a smile or a rise out of their subjects.

"OH MY GOD, IT'S EVAN HUNTER!!!!!!"

Christ. Where are the Beckhams when you need them? If I'd been by myself, I would have stopped to sign autographs for the fans, but I want to get Stella out of here as quickly as possible, and also it would be really great if I could kick this one guy in the bollocks. Just once.

Aww. You see? Love actually is all around.

Shut up, Hugh.

Considering how rattled she was for a good fifteen minutes at Heathrow, Stella has maintained a refined Grace Kelly-like composure ever since we arrived in the French Riviera. I swear, she looks like a glamorous nineteen-fifties movie star, as befits her name, but she repeatedly insists that she needs a long hot shower after spending twelve hours on planes today. I'm fine with that, as long as I can join her.

I instructed my assistant not to use Richard Diver as an alias here at the Hotel Belles Rives. She dropped my name to get us the cottage here in the Cap d'Antibes for New Year's but instructed them to make the reservation under the name Robert Parker (Robert LeRoy Parker being Butch Cassidy's real name). We will spend our treasured three days here, at the luxury hotel where F. Scott Fitzgerald wrote *Tender is the Night*.

While it's not a favorite novel for either of us, it was that first conversation with her, about this book, wherein I sensed deep down that I was completely, irrevocably, fucked for life. Even in the depths of winter, the cove with its view of nearby islands and mountains is the perfect place for us to take walks on the empty beach and jetty. The art deco elegance of the hotel is the perfect place for us to dine on room service while ringing in the New Year naked and planning the year ahead.

For me, getting this woman to reveal more of her inner self to me will be a prize equal to or possibly greater than spending uninterrupted hours upon hours reacquainting myself with every inch of her flesh.

"I'm glad you changed your alias," Stella says as we lie in each other's arms on the bed, still damp from our shower and breathless from the reunion sex. "You aren't like Dick Diver at all, not really. You aren't a fraud. You aren't so lost."

I raise her hand to my lips. "Not when I'm with you."

That line earns me an eye roll. "Stop acting."

"Stop managing."

She thinks about that for a second. "Okay."

All these little victories. My cup runneth over, but I want to know everything now. I drag my fingers down her arm. "Does your skin get tan in the summer?"

"A bit. If I forget to put on sunscreen. Yours does. I've seen you look all golden and sun-kissed in one of those movies of yours."

"I want to take you to Bermuda. In season. I want to see you run along a beach in a bikini."

"*Do* you now?"

"Yes. Are you hungry? Should we order food?"

She shakes her head. "I ate everything they offered me on the flight from Seattle, and we had that whole meal at Heathrow." She turns and looks out the window.

"I'm sorry that happened with the photographers."

She shakes her head again. "It's not your fault, I know."

"What they said about Georgia and Braden being in London... I have no idea what they were talking about."

She turns back to me, kisses my shoulder. "We don't have to talk about it. I just feel bad that you have to deal with that sort of thing all the time."

"Well, not *all* the time. It doesn't happen every time I'm at Heathrow. I usually don't even realize they're taking pictures of me from afar."

She rolls over on top of me, swirling her fingertip across my chest. "What's your flat like?"

"Come see it."

She winces, almost imperceptibly, but I catch it. "Do you have pictures?"

"I don't have pictures of my flat on my phone, no."

"Should we be going out to explore the hotel? It's so beautiful here."

"Tomorrow."

"Okay. You've never been here before, have you?"

"No. Not to this hotel. I've been to the Cannes Film Festival a couple of times."

"Oooh. Course you have. You're such a fancy actor."

"Yes," I say, propping myself up on my elbows to kiss her. "But I'm also just a boy, standing in front of a girl, asking her to love me... You probably don't get that joke, but it's a line from—"

"*Notting Hill.* Yes, I know."

"You've seen *Notting Hill?*" This girl really is full of surprises, but I think that this shocks me more than anything.

"Only very recently."

"Because of me?"

"I mean. Also because of hormones."

"I'm so sorry. Did you hate it?"

"Of course I did, it's terrible. It made me miss you so much. Hugh Grant reminded me so much of you."

"Oh piss off."

She cackles.

Christ, I'm so in love. I push strands of hair out of her face. I can imagine staying in bed with her here for three days straight, no problem. "Tell me something you've never told any of the blokes you've been with."

"Like what?"

"Like literally anything you don't usually tell the person you're shagging."

"Mmmm. I will, but you go first."

"Hmmm, let me think."

"Anything that you've never told one of the girls you've been with."

"Okay, but it will sound insane. And I'm not just saying this because of the *Notting Hill* thing."

"Okaaaayyy." She looks at me like she's expecting me to say I've dated Julia Roberts.

"I sometimes have the voice of Hugh Grant in my head."

She exhales, relieved. "Explain."

"Do I really need to? I mean, everyone has that voice in their head. It's the part of me that I struggle with, but I've cast him in the role. Like instead of a little devil on my shoulder whispering in my ear, it's Hugh Grant."

She laughs so hard. "That is so... Oh my God! That's so..."

"Incredibly alluring?"

"Deeply fucked up and totally awesome!"

"I knew you'd understand. Okay, you next."

"That is hilarious! Did he say anything about me?"

"Who—Head Hugh? Oh, he's always been very much in favor of shagging you."

"Are you friends with him? I mean in real life, outside of your head."

"Well, we all know each other from around, you know, but he's not a mate or anything. We've never worked together."

"Wow. And you think I'm a lunatic for putting potato chips in sandwiches."

"Well yes, that does make you completely mental in my book. Quit stalling. Tell me something."

"Okay, well..." She sits up, covering herself with the top sheet. "You know about my mom."

"The lovely painter."

"Yeah. The car crash was… I just want you to know why it's been so hard for me to…"

I sit up. She immediately starts crying. I've seen a hint of tears in her eyes so many times, but this is the first time she's really cried in front of me, and it feels as though my heart is being ripped from my chest. I cover her hand with mine.

"You don't have to tell me about this now if you don't want to."

"No." She sniffles and wipes her nose with the back of her hand. "I want to. I was planning to, while we're here. I want to." That hand covers her heart, and she continues. "It's so weird. I haven't cried in years, and then all of a sudden a month ago, it's like something got…dislodged or something."

I squeeze her leg. I know exactly what she means.

She sighs. "I was eighteen. After graduation. I took a year off to work at the gym before going to college, and the plan was to do some traveling with my boyfriend too. Cody. I'd been with him on and off since we were sixteen, but we were *really* together then. It was October. I was hanging out at his place, but he'd gotten drunk and we had a fight and I wanted to go home. I didn't have a car and didn't want him to drive me, so I called my dad to pick me up. He was in the middle of something, so my mom came to get me instead. It was pouring rain. Cody was living with his brother, about ten minutes from our house. But after half an hour, she still hadn't shown up…The guy who hit her lived two towns over. He wasn't drunk. He was texting and driving too fast. Someone saw him run the red light at the intersection, and… He died too. Supposedly it was instant for her. I try not to think about the details. I try not to picture it."

She's not crying anymore. I think it was getting to the part where she could tell me about it that was hard for her. I wait for a while before saying, "I'm so sorry, Stella."

"She was so wonderful, Evan. God, I wish you could have met her. It was always like the sun came out when she was around. She would have loved you."

"I wish I could have met her too."

"Anyway. Just like that. She was there and then she wasn't. I never got to say good-bye. I don't know if it would have been any easier if I had, but… Anyway. Cody felt so guilty about that night. So did I. So did my dad. But Cody, he was actually really great at getting me out of the house after that first month. I was just taking care of my dad and trying to keep the gym going. I never ended up going to college, and Cody and I never traveled together. But he was a really good boyfriend all of a sudden. For a few years. He stuck around and things got to be pretty fine, and then he started getting really restless. Five years ago, in the summer, he got a job on a fishing boat to Alaska, with his brother, making good money. He was going to spend the summer out there, based in Anchorage, and then come back. I heard from him less and less as the weeks went by, and once October had come around, he'd just completely ghosted me. I understood after a while that it was the guilt that kept him around before that, but he never said good-bye."

"Shit. What a dick."

She laughs. "Yeah. I mean. He just didn't know how to handle it. Whatever. My brothers were the ones who got me out of bed finally after weeks of depression, because my dad didn't want me going to work. He was trying to take care of me the way I did with him, but my brothers forced me to work out with them, and they blocked his number on my phone, blocked him on social media so I wouldn't obsess about him. And I didn't, eventually. I worried for a bit that he'd been injured or something, but Billy and Kevin know guys who were in touch with him. He was fine. I think for a while I still believed he'd come back. More than anything, I just wanted to talk to him about it. It's not like I was still in love with him. But it never happened."

After a beat, I say, "Now I'm feeling really bad about sharing my stupid Hugh Grant thing."

She puts her hand on my cheek. "I don't want you to feel bad about anything. You're so good. To me. *For* me."

I would do anything for this woman.

"I hated that I never got to say good-bye to my mom. I hated that Cody was too chicken shit to say good-bye to me. My best friend Mona moved to Portland last year, and we said we're just five hours away, we'll spend weekends together, we'll FaceTime. But... It's hard to stay in touch with people." She looks at me, her eyes brimming with tears again.

"It is. But I do. I've learned to. I had to."

"I've learned to say good-bye to people long before they're gone. I have to."

"I don't plan on ever saying good-bye to you, Stella. Not because I can't handle it, but because I don't want to."

She covers my face with wet kisses, and I know that we won't talk any more tonight. She's poured a lot of her heart out to me all at once, and I would do anything to keep her from hurting.

I would do anything for this woman...except say good-bye.

22

STELLA

*I*t's our last full day here at Hotel Belles Rives. At first I thought that "Belles Rives" meant beautiful dreams, but apparently it means Beautiful Shores or Beautiful Banks. Which also makes sense. But so far it *has* felt like a beautiful dream. It's not that I don't want to wake up and return to the beautiful shores that I call home. I just keep hoping that I'll return there a slightly different person. I really did want to wake up and find that the dream has transformed me into a person who can tell Evan, "Yes, I will go to the premiere with you. Of course I will come to the opening night of your performance in London. I would be honored to be your date to your friend Liam's wedding—I can come and go from my hometown any time at all, no problem!"

It's not that he keeps pressing me for a firm commitment, but it keeps coming up. After lunch in one of the hotel restaurants, we walked along the jetty, arm in arm, past all the empty sunbeds. The hotel's private beach isn't even open this time of year. I love beaches in winter, of course, but Evan said we should come back again in the summer to get the full Riviera experience, and I just made a weird noise in the back of my throat. I told him I was happy to get the full Evan Hunter experience in the cottage, and it almost filled the silence, along with the crashing waves, for a few minutes.

Once we got back to the hotel lobby, there were several guests lingering by the doors to the back terrace. Everyone here is very polite, and the staff seems very discreet, but apparently today is the day that people finally decided to start approaching the movie star while they have the chance.

I barely even noticed the way women looked me up and down and whispered to each other.

I was perfectly fine with it when the other guests would politely ask me to take pictures of them with him with their cameras, but once a crowd developed in the lobby and it became clear that he'd be signing autographs and taking pictures with them for a while, he insisted that I return to the cottage to wait for him. When Evan Hunter leans in and whispers in your ear with his fancy English accent, "Get your ass to the bedroom, darling," you get your ass to the bedroom.

I should just be here on the bed, naked and waiting for him.

I should just be happy to check on Muffin Top with my app, the system that this amazing, considerate man set up for me so that I wouldn't worry about my cat so much while I'm visiting him.

But my thumbs have a mind of their own, and they take advantage of the free Wi-Fi by opening up the Safari app and typing: *"Evan Hunter Heathrow"* into Google search. Just to see if I looked as tired and dehydrated as I felt when those pictures were taken. The top results, though, are images of Evan Hunter at Heathrow with several different girlfriends who are not me. They are all pretty young actresses, all shiny hair and dewy skin and camera ready. They're holding Evan's hand and smiling but careful not to look too excited to be captured by the evil paparazzi. Evan's face always has a neutral expression, and he's always handsome. And then there are the recent shots of Evan Hunter with me. The "unidentified, natural-looking brunette." Evan appears to be so protective of me, it makes my heart ache, but I look like I flew from Seattle to London clinging to the wing of the jet. I look like an extra in some Marvel movie and the dashing superhero is rushing me to safety in an epic earth's destruction sequence, right before he goes off to save his real love interest in the next scene.

I don't even read the comments. I don't usually care about how things look. If my yoga students knew I was fretting about this kind of thing, I would rightly have my certificate revoked. But I care about this. I care about Evan Hunter.

By the time Evan returns to the cottage, I am wearing the peach-colored lace Agent Provocateur lingerie that he had shipped to me back home. I had always planned to wear it on our last day here, with a sassy smirk and four-inch heels. Instead I am barefoot and frowning, leaning back on my hands at the edge of the bed, fully expecting him to take one look at me in this and ask if I'd feel more comfortable in my flannel pajamas. The answer would be "yes," obviously, and then he'd go back to the lobby to take his pick of the many glamorous women who wear this kind of lace under their clothes all the time and would gladly follow him all over the world, from bed to bed, always properly moisturized and depilated and plucky.

But the real Evan Hunter would never do that. The real Evan Hunter lowers his chin, drops his coat to the ground, and pulls off his shirt as he strides toward me, saying, "Fuck me, you're gorgeous." The real Evan Hunter wants the real Stella Starkey, but the real Stella Starkey doesn't know how to be herself anywhere other than Port Gladstone.

He pushes me down on my back, and his cold fingertips trace the scalloped edges of the deep V-shaped neckline, his lips planting kisses along the same path. For the first time in the brief history of this man's mouth on my body, instead of letting my body enjoy the unbearable pleasure of it, I let my mouth do the wrong kind of dirty work.

"So your fingers haven't cramped up from signing autographs?" I say in a much snarkier tone than I'd intended.

He sits back up immediately, as surprised as I am by my comment. "I was mostly chatting with people about my movies. Did it bother you that I asked you to come back to the room? I thought it would be easier for you than standing around waiting for me."

"Oh, it was. Much easier. Which is why I don't think I'd be a great date for you at your premiere."

He rubs his forehead. "Okay. You don't have to come to that if you don't want to."

"I mean. Any of it. I don't understand why you'd want me around for that stuff."

He winces, but then I can tell he's thinking things through, and while I'm prepared for an argument, he defeats me, as always, with his damn soothing voice and caring eyes.

"Those were just some of the events that I invited you to. You're also welcome to come visit me when I'm doing absolutely nothing at home, although I'm afraid I don't get to do that as much as I'd like to. You do understand that I don't live on the red carpet, right? It's part of the job, yes, but it's not the best part and it's not the worst. I usually take my mother to premieres or award shows when she's available, and she has a fairly good time. For me, the premieres are fun because it's a reunion for the cast and crew. Smiling for the flashing cameras and photographers who yell at you is bizarre, and constantly having to repeat yourself when you're chatting with reporters is just another form of acting. One does get used to it. What I don't think I can get used to is the idea of never seeing you again."

Damn you for being so fucking sweet. "I don't like the idea either."

He cups my face in his hands. "Then be with me."

"I can't just…"

He drops his hands from my face, stands up, and starts pacing around the room all of a sudden. "Yes. You can. But you don't think you can or you won't. Either way it's no good for me, and you seem to have this insane notion that it would be terrible for you."

Here we go... "I don't think it will be terrible for me. I just know it won't work out for you either."

"You don't know it, and I have to admit, I resent you for not trying."

"Trying what? To leave my life so I can try to fit into yours?"

"How are you leaving your life if you're joining mine?"

"You think I'll just drop everything to follow you around because I'm just the manager of a gym?"

He runs his hands through his hair and looks up at the ceiling. "Oh my God! It's felt like such a struggle, getting you to open up to me, when you somehow opened up something *in me* almost immediately. Don't you see? Because of you, I want something I've never wanted before—I want a partner. In life."

"You can't honestly believe that it's not going to get in the way at some point."

"What is?"

"Our totally different backgrounds. Our completely different lives."

"What exactly are they supposed to get in the way of?"

"Us. Staying together."

His eyes cloud over in a way that they never have

before with me. His jaw is clenched. This is it. I've been testing his limits, and this is it.

"What's getting in the way of us staying together, Stella, is you… Christ. I'm not going to beg you to be with me."

"I'm not asking you to!"

"I have to admit…I've grown weary of this."

"Of me?"

"Of wrestling with you." He stays where he is, but he fixes me with a gaze that is so full of anger and vulnerability, drawing me so close to him I can't breathe. "Fuck it. I love you, Stella, but I can't take much more of this. As I've said, I'm about to get very busy again. I'd prefer it if you were with me. I'd understand if you aren't for the most part, but I need to know if you're coming to visit me at any point, and I need to know if you're coming to the wedding in February. The wedding most of all. I don't want to be constantly wondering and worrying about whether or not you're my girlfriend. God, I can't believe I had to say that out loud, but there you have it. I love you. But you're really pissing me off."

I propel myself from the bed, run to him, and leap, wrapping my legs around his waist. He holds me up by my ass in this way that he's held me so many times now. "I love you, Evan."

I kiss him all over his face, sadly and furiously.

"I'm so in love with you. But I can't be your girlfriend. You know it wouldn't last. I don't know how to live that kind of life. I don't want to leave the life I have. I'm sorry. It's just too much. I don't want to hold you back. I'm not going to be able to go to all those big events with you, and you'd have to deal with all the questions and tabloid crap, or worse, you'd start turning down jobs and events to be with me instead. And then you'd resent me, all of your people would hate me, and it will just... You deserve better. You deserve the best of everything."

He drops me back onto the bed, like he's had it with me. I stand up and shove his chest. He grabs me, falls down to the bed with me, and kisses me so hard it's like he's trying to smother the life out of all those words I just said. I wrestle with his jeans to get them off, and he tears my lacy lingerie apart down the middle like it's tissue paper.

"I love you, Evan," I say, my voice cracking.

"I love you, Stella," he growls, full of hate. I'm not imagining that. I know he doesn't hate me, he hates the situation, just as I love him and hate these circum-stances.

"Fuck me like there's no tomorrow," I say through clenched teeth.

"There *is* no tomorrow, you twit." His voice is as hard as his tense body and his unforgiving touch.

He is so deep inside me, so relentless in the way that he penetrates me, but the orgasm that is generated by this storm of emotion is so slow and warm and sweep-ing, it seems to last forever, as if to prove to me that some things can. Even when this moment has passed, he *has* changed my molecules, and the all-encom-passing orgasm that is Evan Hunter will live in my cells for as long as I live.

I may not be his Juliet, but at least I'll get to live with these memories of him and the sounds he makes while he tells me over and over again that he loves me as he comes inside me, because we both know it will probably be the last time he does.

It's been so long since I've cared enough to have a fight with the person I'm having sex with that I'd forgotten how fights can bring you closer together. I'd forgotten how great sex can be when you're fighting. I'd almost forgotten that this was a fling between a small-town girl and the world-famous movie star who forgot who he was for a while when he was with her.

Which is why it's even harder for me to leave him, to do what I need to do.

It will hurt, but I've hurt before and I got through it. The only difference is that I'm choosing this. I'm hurting someone else in the process, even though I know it will only be temporary for him.

Beautiful dreams only last when they're captured on film, and now it's time for both of us to wake up.

23

EVAN

*W*hat I had wanted to say was, "I'm not going to make demands on you. I can't ask you to give up your life here to follow me around the world or to wait at home for me in London. I just want to be with you whenever possible, wherever possible. I want you to be mine because darling, I promise I am yours. I don't ever want to say good-bye to you."

But I couldn't. I was too angry. I could tell she had already made up her mind, right from the start, and the fact that all that time we'd spent together, including those precious hours and days in the South of France, hadn't changed things for her just pissed me right off.

And it hurt.

Oh, fuck, it hurts.

This feels worse than when I didn't get Loki.

This feels worse than anything ever has.

. . .

She left. She fucking left the hotel in the middle of the night like the thief of hearts that she is. Instead of flying back to London with me and then transferring to her connecting flight. She. Just. Left.

This way we don't have to say good-bye.

Says her tear-stained note. The one I couldn't bear to toss out and can't bear to read a second time.

I love you.
We went out in a blaze of glory.
I love you.
I'm sorry.
I love you.
I will always miss you.
I love you.
Please don't let this keep you from staying in touch with my brothers.
I love you.
I will always be sorry for leaving like this but I have to.
I love you.

As soon as I get back to my flat, I start trying to numb the dull pain in the back of my throat with Scotch.

So this is what it feels like to be rejected by the one you love, I moan to myself as I sprawl out on my sofa.

Really? This is what you're like when you're devastated over the loss of the woman who may be the love of your life? Quietly perturbed as you lay about alone in your living room? And you wonder why she can't imagine spending the rest of her life with you, you fucking bore.

Fuck you, Hugh.

The truth is, I'm demolished, wrecked, feel sick that she doesn't believe she can be with me, but I refuse to give up. It's not that I don't respect her decision. It's not that I can blame her for wanting stay in Port Gladstone. It's just that I will be so fucking pissed off if love doesn't really conquer all.

Hugh's right about one thing, though. I shouldn't be alone. I need to talk to someone, or I'll go mad. It's not too late, so I call Liam to ask if he's available to come round. He's happy to hear from me but can tell from my voice that he should bring another bottle of Scotch.

When I open the door to my townhouse, he takes one look at me and says, "Christ, you look like shit on a crumpet. I should have brought a bigger bottle." He holds an opened bottle of single malt, and I bring him in for a hug while taking the bottle from him.

"I've missed you, you wanker. Get in here."

He steps inside the foyer, notes the bag and coat that have been unceremoniously dropped onto the middle of the floor, the John Legend breakup song "All of Me" in the background, and nods once.

"Right, then. Before I forget—Cate wants me to thank your assistant for the engagement gift."

"Cruel! I ordered it myself."

"Did you? See, that's what I told her, but she didn't believe me."

"It was before I started filming, so I had time."

"Yeah. It's what I told her. So what's this, old chap? *Stellevan* on the rocks?"

"*Stellevan!*" I attempt to laugh, but what comes out is more of a pathetic choking death-moan that only ends when I bring the mouth of the bottle to my own mouth and chug that Scotch until my friend pulls it away from me.

"Let's get some food and a little sense in you. Shall we—to the kitchen?"

"I love you, Liam."

"Love you too, kid," he says in his flawless American accent. "You got any food in this palace of yours?"

"Wendy probably filled the fridge yesterday."

"Right. Off we go, then." He hangs his coat on the coat rack by the door and hangs up mine as well. He's been a married guy forever. Doesn't matter that they aren't technically married yet. He's been part of a couple for ages, and I want that now. I want it. "Evan?"

"What?"

"You're not moving."

"Oh. I thought I was."

When he finally gets me to the kitchen, he makes me an omelet and crumpets, extra butter.

"She left while you were sleeping?"

I nod as I bite into the buttered crumpet.

"That's cold."

"She was trying to make it easier on me."

"Well. Was it easier?"

"I don't know. How would I know?" I whine and push the plate away and lay the side of my face flat on the cold marble countertop. This is not a good look.

"Did you call her when you realized she'd gone?"

"No."

"Oh."

"What's that supposed to mean?" I sit up, almost fall off the stool, and then point my fork at him accusingly. "You think this is all my fault?"

"No, luv. I think nothing is your fault. I'm just trying to gather all the facts."

"The fact is, she doesn't want me. S'all there is to it," I slur. "On to the next one!"

"Right, well. Maybe not quite."

"I don't want another next one," I moan. "This omelet is really good."

"Well, if it matters at all, Cate thinks she's lovely."

I squint at him. "You have a Google alert for my name, don't you?"

"You don't know me!... Yeah. I do. It's the only way your friends know what you're up to."

"That's sad. For me. Not for you."

"Yeah. We saw the photos. She is lovely. She just looks uncomfortable with getting her picture taken, and who isn't at first?"

"Exactly! I tried to explain that to her. I think I did... I meant to. There was a lot that I meant to say to her, but we were just so busy fucking most of the time we were together."

"Well, that is a shame." He rolls his eyes.

"I don't mean for it to sound like that's all it was, either. It was so much more than that. So much more. More than everything... I just... Fuck, Liam. How do you manage it with a normal woman? I mean, I know your life is significantly more normal than mine. You hardly ever have to travel for work unless it's domestic, right?"

"Oh, I'm sure Cate would love it if I got out of her hair and the country more often than I do." He places his hands on the counter and leans in toward me. "You do realize you have a unique outlook on long-distance relationships because of your parents and your vagabond actor life? You grew up with two people who were very much a couple—right?"

"Absolutely."

"Even when they weren't in the same country. You just need to show Stella what that's like. And you need to reassure her that there's no reason for her to believe that it would be better for you to be with another actor. It may make more sense, conceptually, but that doesn't mean it's better. They still need to be reassured, these lovelies. Not in the same way as actresses need to be reassured about everything, thank fuck, but they do. As soon I got cast in that play opposite Keira Knightley, I came home to find Cate packing up her stuff because she was thinking: 'Right. That's it for me, then.' It wasn't easy for me to convince her that Keira's not my type, but she believed me eventually."

He turns and gives me a slow, melodramatic side-glance, and then we both burst into fits of laughter.

Keira's totally his type, but that's not the point. Cate's his person. She's The One.

"You'll sort this out," he says. "I have no doubt. You just need to pull that handsome head out of your ass and try to see things from her perspective. Not that you're as self-centered as they come, actor-wise. On a self-centeredness scale of one to ten, you're like a...*six?*"

I don't even ask if that means I'm more or less self-centered than the average actor, because we're going to spend the next half hour talking about him. I'm done moaning. My mate has said what I needed to hear. I won't even think about Stella the whole time we're chatting. I just hope she gets the chance to meet Liam and Cate one day soon.

When I wake up the next morning, my mouth is dry but my head is clear.

That's right, you fool. It's not you that she's rejecting. It's the life she thinks she'll have to give up if she's with you. For once in your life, be a man of action. Fuck words. Everything you say sounds like tits on toast to her—you need to show her what she means to you.

Thanks, Hugh. You're right.

I know exactly what I will do.

But I only just have time to put things in motion with my business manager before meetings with the director of my play, table readings, all this before the chaos of the *Fallout* press junkets and a photo shoot for Vanity Fair with Georgia.

Every time I start to write a text or email to Stella, I get interrupted. It's for the best, really, because nothing I want to say to her should be said in a message or, God forbid, a voice mail if she doesn't accept my call. I'm not going to start the conversation with her until I know I can finish it—or rather, until I know I can continue it for as long as necessary.

With my schedule, I never know. It might be in two days or two weeks, but I'll show her what she means to me. I'll show her that the real difference between her and every girl who came before her isn't her job or her dress size or where she lives; it's how I feel about her and what I'm willing to do to be with her.

We'll end each day in a blaze of glory together, even when my day begins hours and hours before hers.

Hang in there, darling.

This naughty seaman will become the admiral of your seasick heart yet.

24

STELLA

Two days after I've returned from Europe, Billy wakes me up dark and early by banging on the door to my guest house before coming inside and literally dragging me out of bed. Muffin Top nearly scratches both of our faces, she's so startled. Aside from the fact that I have a cat now, it's a lot like five years ago when he'd show up to take me jogging every morning once I'd realized Cody wasn't coming back. Except this time, he's partly making sure I'm still alive and partly making sure I know just what a stupid idiot asshole he thinks I am.

I do.

But I also believe that I'm doing what's best for Evan in the long run.

After an *actual* long run, on the treadmill at the gym, I feel slightly less terrible, and Billy looks at me as though he may actually be able to speak to me now.

"I love you and all, but you're an idiot," he says, bringing me a bottle of coconut water. "And an asshole."

"Roger that. Boy, jet lag is a real thing, huh?"

"You'd get used to it. Did you take melatonin? And vitamin C? And B-12?"

"No."

"Stupid. I bet Evan does. He got over the jet lag pretty fast. It can be done. Any goal can be accomplished if you set your mind to it."

Always the personal trainer. "Have you been in touch with him at all? The past couple of days?"

"Come do free weights with me."

"I need to shower."

"Come do weights with me. You need to build up your cowardly muscles."

"I'm not a coward." I follow him to the dumbbell racks. He hands me a pair of five pounders, grabs ten pounds for himself.

"Feet apart, tailbone straight down."

"I know how to stand."

"Oh yeah? Seems to me you know how to trip yourself up."

He begins the standing free weight routine we've been doing together for years, and we both glare at each other all through the dumbbell curls. "I'm really not in the mood for the tough love thing right now."

"Bend your knees more."

"You're not my trainer."

"You should be so lucky. You know, Mr. Hannam's

gonna win the holiday challenge thanks to me—*and* he's got the confidence to start dating again."

"He is? Who?"

"Greta from the knitting store."

"Shut up! That's so cute! Awww. Good for them."

"Yeah. Maybe when you're in your late sixties you'll be ready to date like a grown-up."

"Oh my God. *You* should talk!"

"No, I can talk because I know that if some awesome woman I got along great with came through town, I would do whatever I could to be with her. Guys don't behave the way Evan did with you unless they're serious about someone."

I pause my hammer curl reps to pout and wipe my tingling nose.

"Keep going."

I continue the routine and scowl at him, eyes stinging, biceps burning, brain screaming.

"If you're wondering how he is, maybe you should get in touch with him yourself."

"I just asked because I don't want your friendship to be affected."

"Very thoughtful of you. I'm not worried. He's a good guy. I'll give him a few days to cool down first."

"You think he's upset?"

"What the fuck do you think? You left without saying good-bye to him. He's the best guy you've ever known, and you ditched him in a hotel room."

"I didn't ditch him. I left early. I left a note."

"Why don't you want a great life, huh?"

"I have a great life."

"You have a good life. You have a nice life. You deserve a great life, Stella."

I know everything he's saying is true. I feel those words more than I feel the inflammation and the tiny tears in my muscle tissue. But every single Starkey is stubborn above all else. So what I say is, "For someone who claims to care about me, you're pretty eager to get rid of me."

"I do care about you *and* I want to get rid of you. They aren't mutually exclusive. We got along fine here when you were in Europe. Candace can handle whatever we can't."

"Nobody handles things the way *you* do around here, Stella," comes my dad's reassuring voice from the reception area. I was so busy hating my brother that I didn't hear the front door.

I exhale loudly and place my weights back on the rack, midroutine, heading for the ladies' change room to shower.

"Hey!" says Billy sharply.

"Go easy on her, Mickey!" My dad calls him Mickey, after the tough old trainer from the *Rocky* movies.

It is especially appropriate now, as Billy clearly doesn't seem to think I'm living up to my potential, just like Rocky in the first movie. This is tough to hear from the little brother who's supposed to idolize me and be forever grateful to me for making sure he was always properly fed and clothed and schooled after Mom died. But whatever. He thinks he's helping me by pushing me. I think I'm helping Evan by pulling away. The only two people I've seen who knew how to be with each other were my parents, and they didn't get to be together forever.

Everything sucks.

And the water pressure in the ladies' showers still sucks. Nobody remembered to call the plumber while I was gone, and that gives me a tiny pathetic crumb of satisfaction. It's barely enough to keep going, but it's something.

When I'm dried and dressed and back at the front desk, my dad stares at me while I check my phone and find zero messages from Evan. Good for him. I wouldn't text me either. I'm sure he's fine. I met him right after things ended with Georgia, and he was totally, totally fine.

"I better not be your excuse for staying here," my dad says, tough guy voice unwavering, but his eyes tell a different story.

"You're not an excuse, Dad. I chose this life. I love this life. I can't just leave because I met someone who doesn't live here."

"If your mom lived in London—if she lived on Jupiter—I would have gone there to be with her whenever I could."

"Yeah, but she lived here. Your lives just meshed together."

"Hah! You think it was easy for her to live with me, you're more deluded than I thought."

I put my arms around his neck and rest my head on his shoulder. "I'm not deluded."

"Everyone has to give up something to be with the ones they love, Stella."

"I know," I say. "I did."

He sighs. "He's not the one you're supposed to give up, dummy. Your mother's life wasn't supposed to end when it did. But it happened. I couldn't do anything to stop it. Your life was not supposed to end when hers did. It certainly wasn't supposed to end when that boy left for Alaska. And I've let it happen. All these years. It's beautiful here. But there's a whole world out there waiting for you and one man who'd give you the world if you'd just let him."

"He did give me the world. For as long as I could take it."

"You're allowed to want more, kid. Even if it scares you. Even if it feels like it's too much."

I manage to keep up appearances, like a stodgy old British lady, while I'm with people. Even when I get looks of pity. Even when I hear people on Main Street whispering about how I was dumped by Evan Hunter. I don't care about that. Let 'em talk.

When I'm alone at home, it's a different story. Snuggling with my Muffin Top and curling up with a good book by the fire at the end of the day just isn't as satisfying as it used to be. The quiet is so much quieter now. It's empty. I keep telling myself that this is just something I have to get through, but I'm afraid that "too much" has somehow become the only thing that's enough for me.

I'm afraid that while Port Gladstone will always be

my hometown, I might never feel at home again if I don't have Evan in my life.

Getting over Cody while living in the town we both grew up in wasn't easy, but trying to get over a celebrity who was here for less than two and a half months is damn near impossible when he has a movie coming out. When I'm buying groceries, there's a small side photo of Evan Hunter with Georgia March at the premiere of *Fallout* on the cover of a celebrity gossip magazine. They are both smiling, arms around each other's waists. The caption reads: ***Evangia back on, now that Georden is over? Georgia tweets pic of Evan: "I've missed this guy!"***

The checkout clerk and the lady behind me don't say anything when I flip the whole stack of those magazines around, back page facing out. They seem to totally understand. Maybe they'd understand if I took every copy outside and burned them in a metal trash bin too, but Kwas would probably take a picture of it and some gossip blog would caption it: *"Spurned Evan Hunter ex now homeless—only heat source is burned pics of Evangia!"*

Fuck celebrity gossip.

But good for Evan Hunter if he is back with Georgia. I have no reason not to believe it, since I haven't heard a peep from him in three weeks. They belong together.

When a teaser trailer for *Fallout* shows up in my Instagram feed, I can't look away. I turn the volume up and force myself to watch it. The movie's about the fallout of his affair with a politician's mistress.

Romance! Thrills! Dirty politics! They look so fucking good together, I almost want to see the damn movie. She really is a good actress.

The annoying thing is, I can't even be mad at him. Seeing him with her, whether he's just acting or posing for the cameras or not, does occasionally make me question every memory I have of him with me. But it doesn't make me like him any less. All I can think about is the good stuff. And it was all good stuff with Evan. I am still very much in love with him. It's a rare and wondrous form of absolute fucking torture.

Jason Kwasnicki—the man, the myth, the legend—comes to the gym to work out every day. He doesn't flirt with me at all or give me shit about anything. He's just trying to keep busy after being dumped by a starlet. He gives me empathetic looks, like we're somehow in the same boat, but we aren't.

He's trying to keep his head above water after a brief fling with a pretty actress who was doing research.

I'm drowning in an ocean of regret that I threw myself into.

I'm a sad, wanderlustful sailor who has held her own damn self captive.

Until I'm not.

25

STELLA

I know something's up because it's ten thirty and Mrs. Flauvich is jogging toward the gym at a faster pace than she's ever attempted on the treadmill. Her cherubic face is flushed and all smiles as she opens the door and waves at me with both arms, one hand clutching her iPad.

"I couldn't wait for you to come by the deli!" she yells. "Did you see? Did you see?"

"See what? No!" My stomach clenches because I expect she's going to tell me there are stories about the upcoming wedding of *Evangia*, but then I remember that Mrs. Flauvich knows about us and that she is kind.

She swipes at her iPad, impatiently waiting for the Wi-Fi to connect. She bounces up and down. "Did you change the password?"

"Oh yes—it's 'triceps123.'"

She makes an exasperated sound while typing with her index finger. Finally, she hands the iPad over to me and I see five paparazzi images of Evan walking on a

London sidewalk with a heavy coat open, revealing a white T-shirt that says: *I love you, Stella*.

My facial muscles are too confused to form a smile. "What? Is this real?"

"It's on all the gossip sites!"

I get a text from Mona that says *HOLY SHIT!!!!!!!!*, with a screen shot of similar pictures from her Twitter feed.

"Oh Stella—have you spoken to him?"

"No, not since we were in France. I don't know…"

"Oh, he's sending you a message! It's so cute! Call him now!"

"I don't…" I scan the gym for Billy, who is busy with training Mr. Hannam, but he looks over at me quizzically.

When my landlord Whit walks through the front door, I know for sure that something weird is happening, because Whit *never* comes to the gym. He is in a hurry, grinning and holding a small box. "Hey," he says, a little breathless. "I'm running late for a showing, but I had to drop this off to you, from a client." He winks and then looks over at Mrs. Flau-vich. "Hi, Mrs. F. This is confidential—oh you know what—fuck it. There's a key in the box. To a house that I have sold. We just closed escrow this morning." He gives me a look and says, "You know where to go. I gotta go. Bye. Later, Mrs. F!" He speed-walks out the door.

Mrs. Flauvich covers her mouth to muffle her squeal. "Do you think he's waiting for you at a house here?"

I don't know what to think. I look back for Billy, who is by my side in two seconds.

"What's going on?"

I open the box and show him the key, and Mrs. Flauvich shows him the online photos.

"Did you know about this?" I ask him.

He stares at the pictures. "I mean. He emailed me after the *Fallout* premiere to make it clear that he's not back with that actress." He raises his chin at me. "I figured you know what's best for everyone, so you'd figure all this out for yourself when you're ready."

I punch his bicep.

"I didn't know about the T-shirt or this key thing. Man, that guy is baller. I mean, if he fucks with you, he'll have the Starkey brothers to answer to, just like any other guy. But these fists are staying away from his pretty face. I wouldn't do that to the world."

He looks at me, and for one whole second he has the expression of little brother love and adoration that I used to see on a regular basis before he grew into a big tough guy. And then it's gone and he's throwing his hands up in the air. "Why are you still standing here? I'll cover the front desk—go!"

It's raining, and I am so excited and nervous that I overcompensate by driving under thirty miles an hour the whole way to the house that Evan rented while he was staying here. The key is still in the box, on the passenger seat. I have no idea what's going on, but I try not to get my hopes up too much that I will open up the front door and find Evan there, naked with his arms outstretched. To be honest, in my heart of hearts, that is what I've hoped to see every time I've opened a door since coming back to town.

My hand is trembling as I stick the key into the locks of the front door. I don't see anyone through the front windows, and there is no car in the driveway. When I finally get the door open and step inside, I say, "Hello," and there is no sound but for my own footsteps on the hard, shiny floor.

I can tell that Whit has been here. It smells like cleaning products and all of the furniture is gone—except for a small side table in front of the floor-to-ceiling windows at the back of the living room area. I spent so many nights here in this room but not enough days. Despite the rain, this view that he always wanted me to see really is breathtaking, no matter how familiar the landscape and seascape is to me.

On the small table is a fancy envelope with my name written on it.

Inside the envelope is a folded letter and another key.

The letter is handwritten. He must have had it delivered to Whit. Evan Hunter's handwriting is as long and strong and tidy and handsome as he is. As always, his words slay me and comfort me at the same time.

Hello Darling,
    I have always dreamed of buying a house by the sea.

I thought it would be in Cornwall, but it turns out it's not which town, country, or sea the house looks out to but who I'm looking out on it with.

No matter where I go in the world now, the tides will always bring me back to you, Stella Starkey.

I have absolutely no intention of ever getting over you.

Be the one that I look out at this beautiful view with.

Keep your guest house too, if that's what you want.

Muffin Top can have her pick of the guest rooms whenever you're here.

One key is to this house in Port Gladstone. One is to my home in London.

You already have the key to my heart.

I love you and I love you and I love you

Hello.

P.S. Stop laughing.

P.P.S. Please be naked whenever possible so I can enjoy that view too, thx

P.P.P.S. My assistant Wendy will be emailing you a plane ticket. Get your ass to London now, dammit. I need to say the thing I need to say to you in person and can't come to PG just now. Just do it.

I'm not laughing at all. I can barely read the postscripts because my eyes are filled with tears.

I pull out my phone. It may not be romantic that I immediately go into manager mode and call Candace to make sure she can cover for me at the gym and then I go into Cat Mom mode to make sure Whit and Brett can look after Muffin Top, but practicality is the thing that will get me on a plane and out of Port Gladstone. Love and romance was never the problem when it came to Evan Hunter.

When I get back to the gym, Wendy has emailed me a plane ticket from Seattle to London that leaves tomorrow afternoon, although she wrote that they will pay the fee if I need to change the flight. She has also arranged a car service to Evan's home in Notting Hill. My dad is there at the front desk, and I am already starting to get nervous about everything. He reads my face immediately and ushers me to the back office. I am burying myself in his chest before he has shut the office door.

"Hey now. Why aren't you happy and excited and at home packing your suitcase?"

"I don't want to leave for more than a couple of weeks at a time."

"Nobody's making you move away for good, kiddo. If this isn't the best of both worlds, then I don't know what is. We'll all be here when you get back. You are loved here. You are needed here. You'll be missed here. You are always welcome here. But if you don't go to London and to that wedding, or wherever he is, to be with him, I will carry you there myself."

I left Seattle early afternoon and arrived in London in the early morning. I was able to sleep on the plane courtesy of the melatonin that Billy got me and feel just drowsy enough to be functional without the nerves. It's a foggy day in London town, but so far from what I've seen, it is every bit as gorgeous and grand and thrilling as the man who has summoned me here.

The driver of this BMW informs me that we'll be arriving at my destination soon. I freaking love that destination. It's the right time to arrive. Finally.

Evan knows I'm coming because I sent him a picture that I had Billy take of me when he dropped me off at SeaTac. I'm wearing the *I'm a Hunterhoe* T-shirt that Mona sent me for Christmas, in return for the scented candles that I re-re-gifted to her. He doesn't have to be at rehearsals until the afternoon, and I plan to stay with him here until after his friend's wedding. Two whole weeks.

When the driver opens the door for me, in front of a white semidetached updated Victorian-era home with a gated small front garden, Evan Hunter opens the elegant black front door of the house, and I swear the sun starts shining just on us. He's wearing jeans and a sweater and slippers, and as always he is impossibly handsome and awake for this time of the morning. He jogs down the steps and short path to open the iron gate for me, hugging me so tight, not even letting go when he takes my suitcase from the driver and gives him a tip.

"Hello, darling," he says, kissing me on the cheek. "You're here."

"I'm so sorry I left you."

"I'm glad you're here now. There's so much I want to say to you. Come in." He closes and locks the front gate and leads me up the stairs by one hand while carrying my luggage in the other. As soon as we're inside, I'm covering him with kisses. "I'm sorry every-thing took so long. My publicist made me wait until after the *Fallout* premiere before wearing that T-shirt so the journalists would stay focused on the movie, and then it took a couple of days before anyone actually took pictures of me around town. Those fuckers are never there when you need them." He is removing my scarf and coat while I try to pull his sweater off over his head.

"You really never read the stuff that's written about you?"

"Not unless my publicist insists on it."

"Okay. I promise I won't either."

"I wish you never had."

I pull him down to the hardwood floor in the foyer and roll on top of him. "What about kids?"

He grins. "What about them?"

"You want kids?"

"As many as possible with you."

"Where would we have them?"

"Wherever you want. Wherever we are. Stella, I wanted to..."

"In a minute." I unzip his jeans. "In three minutes." I reach inside and take hold of him, this thing that I want, that is both too much and absolutely just right for me. "Put your big hard cock inside me first."

"As you wish."

Three minutes later, I roll off him, realizing that I didn't even wait to ask if there was anyone else in the house before ravaging him. "There's no one else here, is there?" I whisper as I cover my naked breasts.

Without missing a beat, he raises his arm and says, "Come on out, guys! Hope you got all of that on film! Should make a good lead-in clip for my next Jonathan Ross episode." He laughs.

I swat at him with my scarf. "Not funny." I finally look around, at the bright white high ceilings, crown molding, tasteful but enormous chandelier above us. I take in the huge light-filled space that extends up a flight of stairs and to a living room beside us, out to a huge terraced space in back. It's a beautifully designed sophisticated blend of traditional and modern styles. "Holy shit, this place is stunning. Just how rich are you?"

"A very un-English question indeed." He shakes his head. "I had a whole speech prepared, but as always, you've thrown me off my game."

"Serves you right for planning to use your game on me."

"Fair play. Get dressed so we can talk, and then I'll let you wreak havoc upon my genitals again."

I smile and bat my eyelashes innocently as I put my bra back on. "I'm listening."

He sits up and pulls his sweater back on, dragging his fingers through his hair and arranging himself directly in front of me on the floor. "Stella, I need to be very clear about what I want... I'm not asking you to follow me around the world and be by my side every day or to wait for me in my trailer on set. I know that this life I chose is difficult to share with another person, I know how different our lives are, but I want you to be a part of mine. I want to be a part of yours. I need you to know that I'm here for you. No matter where I am or where you are. As I've said, the next two years of my life are spoken for, career-wise. I won't have more than two or three weeks off at a time, but I will fly you to visit me whenever you want, I will come visit you in Port Gladstone whenever I can, and we can keep in touch in every way possible. One day, I hope, we can settle down somewhere and make little people who have beautiful eyebrows and know how to fish and do a pull-up and have funny accents. But for now, I just need you to come upstairs to my bedroom with me. Can you do that?"

"Yes, Evan Hunter. I will always do that."

His bedroom is spacious and masculine but warm and inviting, and it smells clean and sexy, and I know that I could live here for as long as he'd want me to. He leads me over to a sitting area near the bed. There is a small black jewelry box resting on top of the copy of *Tender is the Night* that I gave him, on a side table. He clears his throat and picks up the box, handing it to me. His blue eyes are sparkling, and his hand is steady.

I never once fantasized about a beautiful British movie star handing me a jewelry box in his bedroom, but I am so fucking happy to be here, and I take it and open it like my life depends on it.

"My nan gave me her engagement ring at Christmas so I wouldn't have to go shopping for one and attract attention. She wanted me to have it, after I told her about you. I guess that's why I was so...frustrated, when we were at the hotel."

I place my fingers over his lips. "You were perfect." I take the solitaire diamond ring out of the box and hold it up for him so he can put it on my ring finger. My hand is surprisingly steady. "The diamond is sort of shaped like a turnip," I muse. "It's so beautiful."

"I was thinking, since you didn't seem to know how to be my girlfriend, maybe it would make more sense for you to be my fiancée."

I nod, because strangely enough, that does make sense to me.

He slides the ring onto my finger. It is only a tiny bit too big, which is a good thing. There's no struggle at all in getting it on, and I'm not worried that it will fall off.

"I want to marry you. Say you'll marry me. It doesn't matter when. We can elope at the last minute or we can have two weddings, here and in Port Gladstone. A year or two from now. Just say yes to me for once, dammit. I'll always love everything you say to me, but right now just say yes."

"Yes, dammit," I say. "Darling. I love you so much. I love the whole world more because you're in it. Yes."

EPILOGUE – EVAN

Less Than One Year Later

How can one accurately describe such love and happiness? It's like trying to take a picture of a big beautiful full moon above the sparkling ocean. You just can't capture that kind of magnificence with anything you use every day, like words or a camera phone.

The world somehow feels a lot smaller when you're committed to one person, no matter how far apart you are in terms of miles or kilometers. It didn't take long for Stella to realize this. I knew she would eventually. I'm not going to say anything grandiose and soppy like "our adventure in love has spanned the globe," but it has. It has also been a much-needed oasis in the chaos of my work life. I'm also not going to wax poetic about Stella being my North Star when I feel lost at sea, but she really fucking is. I try to be that for her, whenever she needs it.

I'm feeling nostalgic because we're at a special

screening of *Cover-Up* at the Rose Theater in Port Gladstone. Stella already accompanied me to the LA and London premieres. The film has already opened to great success around the world, but this screening means the most to both of us.

Stella's whole family is here in the audience, including her grandparents and Martin's girlfriend Lauren, as well as Stella's friend Mona and Mona's fiancé. Kevin is still "going stag" as he says, but Billy has brought a date. She's the animal talent agent who now represents Chet. After his big dramatic barking scene in this movie, she insists on rebranding him as "the Tom Hardy of Labradoodles." She lives in Seattle and insists that she needs to stay there for her business, while Billy insists that he needs to stay in Port Gladstone for his. Stella has remained remarkably quiet and gracious in regard to this dilemma. I am certain that he will find a way to make it work if he wants to.

Joe Starkey may never get over losing the love of his life, and no one blames him, but at least Stella is trying to find him a suitable girlfriend now. She will. Once she sets her mind to something, she is a force to be reckoned with.

During the Q and A after the screening, my favorite natural-looking brunette is next in line at the microphone that's been set up in the center aisle of the theater.

"Hello, darling." I sit up on my stool in front of the screen and grin into my cordless mic. "Do you have a question for me?"

"Yes. Care to comment on the rumors around town that you are, in fact, currently a married man?"

"Yes, I would like to comment on that, in fact." This girl. Full of surprises. I was going to have Hen release a formal statement and pictures when we were ready, but apparently we're ready now. "Two days ago, I tied the knot with a local woman called Stella Starkey, who is now officially known as Stella Starkey-Hunter. We will be having another ceremony in Cornwall early next year. We met here, about a year ago, and had planned a long engagement, but then she went and got knocked up, so I decided to make an honest woman out of her... I suppose this is an appropriate time to announce it, since she won't be able to *cover up* her baby bump for much longer."

Stella groans and gives me a much-deserved eye roll, just as Mrs. Flauvich appears from out of nowhere and tackles her, giving my lovely wife a big hug.

Stella has continued helping to expand her family business, and now she's doing her part to expand the family.

"Also, I hope you don't mind, but you'll be seeing a lot more of me around Port Gladstone when I'm not working on location elsewhere."

The crowd cheers and applauds, louder than they did for the film. I take no offence. That's why I love this town and know that it will be the best place for our kids to grow up. I will happily make this my permanent home base. If we have a girl, her middle name will be Cora, after Stella's mother. If it's a boy, my wife is insisting that he be called Hugh. Probably not the best idea.

You'll be an excellent daddy, young lad. I remember back when I had only one little nipper's nappies to change. Enjoy it. Let's set up a play date when you're all in London.

Thanks, Hugh.

That *is* a good idea.

AUTHOR'S NOTES

Port Gladstone is a town that lives in my imagination (as far as I know), but it was inspired by the impossibly scenic town of Port Townsend in Washington. If you can't get yourself there for a visit, you can search #porttownsend on Instagram. It's a lovely little vacation for your eyeballs.

Regarding the title—for those who aren't as obsessed with English actors as I am (why aren't you, and also, good for you)—FYI, there is a hilarious and wonderful "Hello Darling" meme that has been dancing around the Internet for several years. It is the UK's answer to the Ryan Gosling "Hey Girl" meme. It's mostly a Tom Hiddleston thing, but sometimes they accompany Benedict Cumberbatch photos. It is always worth Googling "Hello Darling Tom Hiddleston". Always makes me feel all warm and happy, and I hope it does for you too!

ACKNOWLEDGMENTS

Many thanks to my UK consultant Jo, for putting up
with messages like: *Hi! **What do Brits call a baseball
cap?*** And ***Do Brit men use the term "balls?"***
and especially for responding with: ***Yes to balls.***

#yestoballs

Made in the USA
Middletown, DE
25 September 2024